TO HELL
AND GONE

TO HELL AND GONE

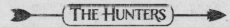

THE HUNTERS

CHARLES G. WEST

PINNACLE BOOKS
Kensington Publishing Corp.

www.kensingtonbooks.com

PINNACLE BOOKS are published by

Kensington Publishing Corp.
119 West 40th Street
New York, NY 10018

All Kensington titles, imprints, and distributed lines are available at special quantity discounts for bulk purchases for sales promotion, premiums, fund-raising, and educational or institutional use.

Special book excerpts or customized printings can also be created to fit specific needs. For details, write or phone the office of the Kensington Sales Manager: Kensington Publishing Corp., 119 West 40th Street, New York, NY 10018. Attn. Sales Department. Phone: 1-800-221-2647.

PINNACLE BOOKS and the Pinnacle logo Reg. U.S. Pat. & TM Off.

First Printing: August 2023
ISBN-13: 978-0-7860-5019-2
ISBN-13: 978-0-7860-5020-8 (eBook)

10 9 8 7 6 5 4 3 2 1

Printed in the United States of America

For Ronda

CHAPTER 1

"I reckon there ain't no use to try talking you out of it, no more," John Hunter said, making one final attempt to change his brother Duncan's mind about leaving. "We've always managed to get by so far, one way or another, ain't we?"

"I appreciate what you're saying, John, but you know, just like I know, this farm ain't big enough to support two families like yours and mine. We gave it a helluva try, but every winter after that has just gotten worse."

There was not much John could say to refute that. The winter of 1862–1863 was an unusually harsh one on animals and crops alike. But the cruelest blow it struck was taking the life of Louise Hunter, Duncan's frail wife, with a fatal bout of pneumonia. Twelve years ago, Duncan had brought Louise to live with John and Louise's sister, Mildred, on a ninety acre farm in northern Montana. Although not a sturdy woman, Louise gave Duncan three strong sons. "With three strong appetites," Duncan always said.

"There's a wagon train leavin' Fort Benton to take that new road the army built, that Mullan Road that goes to Walla Walla, Washington Territory. Me and the boys are gonna be on it."

"I swear, I just hate to see you go, Duncan. It ain't gonna be the same with you gone."

"I'm gonna miss you and Mildred, too," Duncan said, "but it'll make life a whole lot easier on you, and especially Mildred. I woulda gone a long time before this, but Louise didn't want to leave her sister. Mildred's got enough on her hands takin' care of her own young'uns. It wouldn't be fair to add my three to her chores." He gave his brother a big smile then and said, "Hell, my boys are raring to go. When we file a claim on a good piece of land out in Washington, you might wanna come out there, too."

"Maybe so," John said. "I don't know if Mildred is up to a trip like that or not. Right off hand, I'd say she ain't, seeing as how she comes from the same stock as Louise. Ain't you worried about Indians and things like that?"

"Not a whole bunch," Duncan replied. "They say there's not much danger if you've got a pretty good number of wagons in the train. They say the folks in the wagons usually have better weapons than the Indians attackin' 'em. Morgan ain't but ten, but he's already a pretty good shot with a rifle."

John just shook his head, still doubtful when he thought of his brother trying to drive his wagon and protect his three sons, Morgan, ten, Holt, seven, and Cody, five. "Duncan, for God's sake, be careful."

"You know I'll do my best," Duncan said. "I've spent dang-nigh every cent I've got, equipping my wagon for the trip, so I can't change my mind about goin'. We'll say goodbye tonight after supper 'cause we're pullin' outta here for Fort Benton in the mornin' before breakfast."

Mildred insisted on fixing one final big supper for them before a tearful goodbye and Godspeed, knowing in all likelihood, she would never see them again.

* * *

Arriving at Fort Benton, Duncan was to find only two other wagons waiting on the appointed date. He found the wagon master he had corresponded with at one of the wagons, a man named Luther Thomas. Duncan asked where the rest of the wagons were parked. There were supposed to be eighteen making up the train. Luther said all but Duncan and the other two wagons had joined a train that left a week earlier.

"I'm sorry about that," Luther said. "It sure caught me by surprise. You can talk to Mr. Frasier there in the other wagon. He's trying to make up his mind what he's gonna do. It's already after the first of May, so if you're gonna get through the mountains before the first snowfall, you gotta go now."

"What are you gonna do?" Duncan asked Luther.

"Me? Hell, I'm goin' to Walla Walla first thing in the mornin', even if I'm by myself. The army built that road, and I know it's in good shape 'cause I already took one party out there. There ain't been nothin' about no Injun problems reported back here to Fort Benton. So I'm goin'. How 'bout you, Mr. Hunter? I don't blame you one bit if you feel like it's too risky for you and your boys."

"I ain't got nothin' to go back to, so I'll go with you," Duncan answered.

"Good man." Luther said. "We're glad to have the company. We'll see what Frasier decides to do, now that he's got more company."

When they went to Frasier's wagon to get his decision, he said, "I'll see what my wife says," and went back into the wagon.

Luther looked at Duncan and cracked, "Wise man. Might as well get it from the boss."

Frasier returned with his wife.

"Howdy," she said and went straight to Duncan. "I wanted to welcome somebody as crazy as Robert and me." She looked around behind him before continuing. "I'm Rose Frasier. I wanted to meet your wife."

"I'm very sorry, ma'am. My wife has passed away. But I'm pleased to meet you. My name is Duncan Hunter. These towheads are Morgan, Holt, and Cody. Say howdy to Mrs. Frasier boys."

They all did in one polite "howdy."

"Outstanding young men," Rose said. "I know they'll be respectful around my two girls and friends with my two sons."

"My four are around here somewhere," Luther said. "Looks like we ain't gonna run short of young'uns on the trip. Why don't we all have supper together tonight, then everybody can get to know everybody else," he suggested. "And tomorrow we'll start day one of our trip."

And so the journey began.

Leaving Fort Benton, they started out west on the Mullan Road. Passing north of Great Falls, the road then dropped south to cross the continental divide west of Helena, following a path through Mullan Pass, driving for the Clark Fork River.

Tragedy struck the little three-wagon train just as darkness began to fall one evening. Coming out of the Mullan Pass, Frasier's right front wheel was struck by a small boulder that had come tumbling down the slope above the wagons. Unknown to them, the boulder had been set in motion by a large war party of Blackfoot Indians, and it smashed the spokes of the wheel, stopping the wagon.

Ahead of the doomed wagon, Duncan and Luther grabbed their rifles and tried to return fire, but they could not identify targets to shoot at. The Blackfoot snipers were too well hidden in the slopes above the pass. Frasier's fourteen-year-old son, Tim, started firing his rifle at anything he thought might be a target until a Blackfoot bullet slammed him in the chest. Luther's wife, Flo, called all the younger children to run and take cover in their wagon, which was the lead wagon and farthest away from the deadly ambush. Morgan Hunter, Duncan's ten-year-old, remained with his father to return fire, using his squirrel rifle.

"Duncan!" Luther yelled. "We've gotta get these wagons outta here!"

Duncan could see that. They had to move out of the deadly killing passage. But first, he had to jump down from his wagon to help Rose and Robert Frasier when he saw them running from their wagon. Morgan jumped down to help, too, only to provide better targets for the Blackfoot snipers. In a steady hail of rifle slugs, they retreated toward the wagon. From his wagon ahead of them, Luther could only watch as one of the families he was guiding ended their aspirations of starting a new life on the fertile plains of the far west right there in Mullan Pass.

"There," Spotted Pony said, pointing down a rocky ravine where they could see the glow of flames in the darkness of the mountains. "They have found something to attack." He and his Crow brothers had been avoiding the Blackfoot war party since first discovering their camp that afternoon. Judging by the sign left at their campsite, the war party was fairly large and surely outnumbered Spotted Pony and his five companions.

"That fire is too big to be a campfire," Walks Fast said. "Maybe they found a wagon on that white man road."

"Let's go see," Gray Wolf urged.

They made their way down from the top of the pass, descending carefully in the darkness to avoid creating any rockslides until reaching a flat ledge near the bottom. From there they saw that it was indeed a wagon burning.

"I smell meat," Gray Wolf said. "What are they cooking? I don't see anyone around."

"The horses," Spotted Pony said. "They are still tied to the wagon. There's no one here. The Blackfeet have gone."

They moved down off the ledge and looked around the burning wagon at the bodies lying there. All of them were mutilated and scalped. Suddenly, there was a rustling in a bank of low bushes, and all five of the Crow hunters were immediately alert to an attack, aiming their weapons at the spot where the leaves were shaking.

"Come out!" Spotted Pony ordered, but no one did. He moved carefully toward the bush, his rifle ready to shoot. With the barrel of the weapon, he pulled a heavy branch aside and immediately recoiled, surprised to see a wolf lying beneath the bushes. "Wolf!" he cried, alerting the others as he took a cautious step back to look all around him. For where there was one wolf, there were usually many. But there was no sign of any other wolves.

"Maybe he is wounded," Two Moons said. "Be careful."

Spotted Pony slowly pulled the branch aside again, his finger on the trigger of his rifle, ready to shoot if the wolf attacked. The wolf did not attack or run at once, as Spotted Pony expected, so he continued to hold the branch aside. The wolf continued to look at him but made no sign of aggression.

"Be careful," Two Moons cautioned again. "I think the wolf is crazy."

Since the wolf showed no signs of attacking, Spotted Pony continued to hold the branch aside while he reached down with his other hand and pulled some lower branches aside as well. He recoiled, startled, for he saw a small boy lying on the other side of the wolf, his body pressed tightly against the wolf's.

Seeing Spotted Pony suddenly recoil, the other Crows prepared to fire their weapons.

"Wait!" Spotted Pony exclaimed when a whimper and a slight movement of the hand told him that the boy was alive. Not until he reached into the bush to pull the boy out from under its branches did the wolf suddenly bolt away into the darkness. "This boy's been shot in the back," Spotted Pony told his companions. "He has not been scalped. He must have crawled up under the bush to hide when the Blackfeet shot the others."

Spotted Pony rolled the body over on its back and pressed his ear to the boy's chest. After a minute, he sat up and said, "He is not dead. His heart still beats."

"I think the wolf was keeping him alive until we could find him," Gray Wolf said. "It shook the bushes to get your attention, but it did not flee until you took the boy."

"I think you are right," Spotted Pony said. "I will take him back to our camp and see if he will live or die. I think that is what the wolf wanted me to do. Look around you. Everyone else is dead. There is a reason the wolf was sent to keep this boy safe."

"I think we missed a chance to have some fresh meat," Walks Fast complained. "You were so close to it, you could have killed it with your knife, instead of grabbing the boy."

"Maybe that is so," Spotted Pony said. "But I think the

wolf's spirit was keeping the boy alive. If we killed the wolf, then maybe we kill the boy."

"He looks pretty bad," Walks Fast said. "I think he's going to die, anyway, and we could have had fresh meat."

"That wolf had to be crazy. If it wasn't, it would have eaten the boy, instead of guarding him," Spotted Pony said. "If you had eaten the wolf you might have died."

Spotted Pony was right. The boy did not die, and he was given the name Crazy Wolf and raised by Spotted Pony to be a strong young Crow warrior.

CHAPTER 2

Sergeant Arthur Kelly walked over to the campfire to report the return of the Crow scouts to Lieutenant Preston Ainsworth. "Scouts are back, Lieutenant."

"Bring 'em on over here, Kelly," Ainsworth said. "Did they find that war party?"

"Yes, sir. I think they did." He signaled the scouts to come on over to the lieutenant's fire. Ainsworth was new in assignment to Fort Keogh, and consequently not familiar with the Crow scouts as yet. This, in fact, was his first scouting patrol. Aware of this, Sergeant Kelly told him the scouts were Crazy Wolf and Bloody Axe.

"Thank you, Sergeant," Ainsworth said. He watched them as they approached, one of them a head taller than his companion. The shorter of the two Indians seemed to hang back a little, so Ainsworth addressed the tall one. "Bloody Axe?"

"No, sir. I'm Crazy Wolf. You wanna talk to Bloody Axe?" He stopped and stepped aside for his companion.

Ainsworth shrugged indifferently. He didn't really care which of the scouts he talked to. He had just been guessing at the names, and in his mind's eye, he thought the tall one looked more apt to be Bloody Axe. "The sergeant tells me you found the Sioux war party."

Bloody Axe nodded rapidly. "We find Lakota. Better you talk Crazy Wolf."

"Oh?" Ainsworth replied and turned to look at the other scout again.

Crazy Wolf stepped forward. "We found the Lakota camp. As near as we could count, there are about seventeen of them. They're camped by a stream about four miles from here. Hard to tell how many of them have rifles, but we saw at least eight of them carrying them."

Ainsworth was surprised by the report. "Very well, Crazy Wolf. By the way, your English is very good."

"Thank you, sir, I try."

Ainsworth didn't say anything more for a few moments while he studied the young man standing before him. His clothes were similar to those Bloody Axe was wearing and his hair was worn in two long braids, but he was different. Then he realized his tanned face was not that of an Indian. "You're not Crow, are you?"

Crazy Wolf smiled. "Well, I am and I ain't. I was born in a white family, but I was raised as a Crow since I was five years old. So I forgot what it's like to be white. My Crow father, Spotted Pony, taught me everything I needed to know to live in this world."

Ainsworth was fascinated by his story. "But your English," he said. "If you have been a Crow since the age of five, I would think you would have forgotten English."

"Well, I reckon part of that is because when Spotted Pony found me, I made a promise to myself to never forget my mother and father and my two brothers, and that I wasn't an Injun. I didn't know there were good Indians and bad Indians, just like white folks. But most of the reason is because of a Jesuit priest at Fort Laramie when our village wintered there two years in a row. He even taught me to read and write a little bit. I think he spent so much extra time with me because he realized I was born a white child."

"You mention a mother and father and two brothers. What happened to them?"

"My mother got sick and died. My father and brothers were killed by Blackfoot warriors. I was left for dead with a bullet in my back, but I hid till Spotted Pony found me and took me home with him. And now, I'm scouting for the US Army with my brother, Bloody Axe." He could have told the lieutenant that he and Bloody Axe were the same as brothers, for it was Bloody Axe's father who'd carried Crazy Wolf away from that field of massacre when he was five and took him in as a son. It was an act of compassion that could have caused a jealous rivalry between the two young boys, instead of the close friendship that resulted.

"Him talk good white man talk," Bloody Axe offered, a wide grin on his face.

"Yes, he does, and you're not bad, yourself," the lieutenant said. Back to Crazy Wolf, he asked. "Do you remember your name when you were five?"

"Yes, I do. My name is Cody Hunter. My father was Duncan Hunter, my brothers were Morgan and Holt. I'll catch up with them when it's my time to go."

"Well, I hope it's not on this patrol," Ainsworth said. "That's quite a story." He took a look at his pocket watch and said, "We still need to wait about thirty minutes and then we're gonna move on that Sioux war party. You think your horses will be rested enough?"

"Yes, sir. They'll be all right. Like I said, it's not but four miles to their camp, so they ain't worked very hard up to now."

"There's probably a couple cups of coffee left in that pot on the fire there," Kelly said, pointing to one of two pots sitting in the edge of the fire. "If you want a cup, help yourself."

"Thank you, Sergeant," Crazy Wolf said. "Bloody Axe and I appreciate it." He turned to relay the message to Bloody Axe in the Crow language, and they went to get their cups out of their saddlebags.

When they left, Sergeant Kelly said, "I reckon I shoulda told you about Crazy Wolf really being a white man, but I didn't know whether you already knew it or not. Him and Bloody Axe used to scout for Lieutenant Ira McCall, D Troop of the Second Cavalry, when they were temporarily assigned here. When the whole Second Regiment was sent to Fort Ellis, Lieutenant McCall wanted to take Crazy Wolf and Bloody Axe with him. But they had been signed up here at Fort Keogh and the colonel said he couldn't approve their transfer. Between you and me, sir, that's what he said, but the real reason was because Crazy Wolf and Bloody Axe are the two best scouts in the whole regiment. And Colonel Miles wanted to keep 'em right here."

"Well, that's good to know, Sergeant," Ainsworth said. "I'm glad you told me."

When the horses were rested, Lieutenant Ainsworth gave the order to mount up. The fifteen-man patrol moved out to attack the Sioux war party that had raided a Crow camp two nights before, killing several and wounding several more. There had been an increase in the number of such attacks upon Crow camps within their reservation ever since Custer's devastating defeat at the Little Bighorn. The Sioux victory over Custer was a stinging defeat for the Crows as well as the US Army because the battle was fought on Crow territory against a combined force of Lakota Sioux, Northern Cheyenne, and Arapaho. After the battle the combined Indian forces scattered. But the Sioux continued their attacks on Crow villages in the Crow reservation. It was time for the US to finally come down hard on the Sioux, and the man they relied on to end the Sioux aggression was Colonel Nelson A. Miles. Operating out of Fort Keogh on the Yellowstone River, Miles conducted raids on the scattered bands of Sioux warriors, either capturing them or causing them to flee to Canada.

After they had ridden about three miles farther south, Crazy Wolf rode back to confer with Lieutenant Ainsworth. In English, Crazy Wolf said, "You see that ridge yonder? There's a healthy stream on the other side of it. You can see the tree line running up to it. The Sioux are camped by that stream on the other side of the ridge. If they've got somebody on top of that ridge as a lookout, they'll see us comin' so you might wanna wait till dark to go any farther. When we found them earlier, they were just makin' camp to rest their horses, I suppose. They didn't seem too worried about anybody botherin' them. They didn't send a lookout up on that ridge the whole time Bloody Axe and I were watchin' 'em." Noticing Ainsworth looked confused, Crazy Wolf added, "If you wanna take a risk that they didn't post a lookout on top of that ridge, we can ride right up to their camp, then catch 'em in a crossfire from both ends of the ridge. Oughta make quick work of 'em, if there ain't no lookout."

Ainsworth thought it over for a minute. The chance of making quick work of it was very important to him at that particular point. When they had left on patrol, they had rations for fifteen days. Already out fourteen days chasing that band, and still two full days away from the fort, he said, "Let's see if we can move on them now."

He turned to Sergeant Kelly. "Sergeant, tell the men to rig for silence. We'll divide the patrol in half. You take half and find a position at the east end of that ridge. I'll take the other half and take the west. Hold your position until I order them to throw down their arms and surrender, then at the first sign of resistance, open fire. You understand? I'll give 'em a chance to surrender, but I'm not going to wait long for their decision."

"Yes, sir," Kelly said. "I'll take one of the scouts with me."

"Right," Ainsworth said. "I'll take Crazy Wolf with me."

Continuing their advance upon the ridge at a slow walk, all eyes scanned the top of the ridge for any sign of a lookout, or an ambush. Crazy Wolf wasn't overly worried about either. Scouting the camp earlier, he'd seen no signs of caution and believed the Sioux had no idea they were being tracked.

Ainsworth reminded Sergeant Kelly he would demand a surrender before opening fire, and possibly that would drive the Sioux warriors back toward him and his men. "If you hold your fire for a brief time, you should be able to take a toll on the warriors if they choose to fight."

Kelly understood what the lieutenant was planning and conveyed it to his men.

"Let's try not to shoot each other," Ainsworth said in conclusion.

When they reached the base of the ridge, they split up and rode to opposite ends of it and dismounted. One man was left to guard the horses. At the western end of the ridge, Ainsworth designated Private Cary Fitzgerald as the horse guard, since he was the youngest and least experienced trooper in his company.

Crazy Wolf led Ainsworth and six troopers cautiously around the end of the ridge and down into the trees beside the stream where they stopped to look the situation over. The ridge was approximately one hundred yards in length, but the Sioux campfire looked to be closer to the western end. Kneeling in the trees by the stream, they could see the Indians, apparently at their leisure.

"They haven't got any idea," Ainsworth whispered. He looked around at his men. "Everybody ready?" He received all affirmative nods. He stepped out from behind the tree he planned to use for cover and yelled to a startled camp of Sioux. "Throw down your weapons! You are to be taken back to your reservation."

A cry of surprise went up from the startled warriors and they sprang up from their blankets to grab their weapons. Ainsworth ducked back behind his tree as the first shots came his way. His men didn't wait for an order to fire but cut down on the exposed Indians, killing three in the first volley. As Ainsworth had predicted, the other warriors backed up rapidly toward the opposite end of the ridge, only to engage the fire from Sergeant Kelly's men and suffer more casualties. Ainsworth's men advanced to new positions, pinning the Sioux down on the creekbank as they returned fire at targets they were still having trouble clearly defining. As their casualties gradually increased, and their already meager supply of ammunition steadily decreased, it became clear they had little chance of surviving. The survivors raised their voices in cries of surrender, all except one.

Black Dog, the leader of the Sioux war party, dropped into a gully that ran down from the top of the ridge. Only a few feet deep, it nevertheless offered him enough protection to crawl up it without being seen. Reaching the top of the ridge, he raised his head high enough to see out of the gully.

Sure no one had seen his escape, he slid his body out of the gully, onto the top of the ridge, and rolled a few feet over the other side. Then he looked back down at his Sioux brothers with their hands held up over their heads. He knew the soldiers must have left their horses at the base of the ridge. He ran along the length of the ridge, weaving his way through the shoulder-high bushes that covered the slope, until he saw the horses.

Young Private Cary Fitzgerald held his rifle tightly in his hands as he heard the gunfire from the other side of the ridge. He knew why the lieutenant had picked him to take care of the horses, but he was just as glad not to be shot at by a bloodthirsty Indian. He had never killed a man, Indian or soldier, and he wondered if he could if the time came. Suddenly, he realized the shooting had stopped. What if the Sioux had won the battle? Would they come looking for the horses right away? How would he know who won until somebody came for the horses? He realized how hard he was squeezing his rifle, and released his desperate grip from the stock and wiped the sweat from his palm.

He turned toward the ridge and froze, his eyes locked on those of the savage, Black Dog, several feet above him. His war axe was drawn back in his hand prepared to strike. Cary's whole body recoiled from the shock of the rifle shot behind him that slammed the fierce warrior in the chest, sitting him down to drop the war axe on the ground beside him.

"Are you all right, soldier?"

Cary turned around to find the scout, Crazy Wolf, ejecting the spent cartridge from the Henry rifle he carried. He reached down and picked up the brass cartridge, a practice he had learned since working for the army. "I figured it'd be a good idea to make sure none of those Sioux back there slipped over the ridge and got to the horses." Realizing the blood had not yet returned to the startled young man's brain, he thought to ease his pride. "I hope you ain't mad 'cause I jumped your shot. I saw that you were gettin' ready to shoot, but I was already aimin' at him, so I went ahead and shot."

Finding his voice again, Cary swallowed hard and took a step back from the fierce-looking body that had rolled down at his boots. "No, I-I ain't mad," he stammered. "Don't make no difference which one of us killed him."

"That's a fact," Crazy Wolf said. "I thought you'd feel that way about it. We might as well take the horses around to the other side where the rest of the men are gettin' the prisoners ready to ride. Gimme a hand, and we'll throw this ugly devil on one of the horses and take him back with the other dead Sioux."

They put their rifles aside and picked up Black Dog and laid him across the saddle on one of the horses.

Recovered from his recent fright, and grateful Crazy Wolf had chosen not to ridicule his inability to act, Cary studied the Crow scout. He was inspired to comment, "You know, you don't talk like an Indian a-tall."

Crazy Wolf laughed. "Just when I'm talking to the likes of you—soldiers and such. I do when I'm talkin' to Indians."

The eight surviving warriors of the raiding party were stripped of all weapons, placed on their horses, with their hands tied behind them. Under guard at all times, including the night when they tried to sleep, the horses were led to Fort Keogh, a journey of two days.

They made it back to the fort in time for the five o'clock mess call, and after turning the Sioux prisoners over to the stockade sergeant, the mess hall is where they headed.

Crazy Wolf and Bloody Axe ate with the other Indian scouts in a special section of the enlisted men's mess hall.

Beans, beef, and bread was simple fare, but it was especially good, since there had been nothing to eat but a couple of strips of jerky for all of the day before. They washed it down with the mess hall's version of fresh coffee. Talking with some of the other scouts at the table, Crazy Wolf paid no attention to B Company first sergeant when he came into the mess hall and stood scanning the scout section until he spotted the man he was looking for.

He walked directly over to Crazy Wolf and Bloody Axe. "Crazy Wolf," he began. "I'm Johnny Douglas, first sergeant of B Company. Captain Boyd, my company commander, would like to have a word with you if you don't mind."

Surprised, Crazy Wolf looked past Sergeant Douglas, expecting to see Captain Boyd behind him somewhere. He knew who Captain Boyd was, but he had never scouted for him before.

"Right now?"

"When you finish eatin' your supper," Sergeant Douglas said. "He's in the officers' mess right now, and when he's done eatin', he's goin' back to the orderly room. He'd like you to come there. You know where the B Company orderly room is, don't you?"

"Yep, I know where it is. What's he wanna talk about?"

"I'll let him tell you. He's hopin' you'll do him a favor," Douglas replied. "After you finish eatin'. B Company orderly room, right?" he repeated and waited for Crazy Wolf's answer.

"Right."

"What you think?" Bloody Axe asked when Douglas walked away. "Maybe he's going to give you Freeman's job. Make you chief of the scouts."

"I don't think so," Crazy Wolf answered in the Crow tongue. "He said the captain just wants a favor." He grinned at Bloody Axe and joked, "Anyway, I don't want Cliff Freeman's job, and have to deal with crazy people like you."

When they had finished their supper, Bloody Axe said he would see him at the camp the Crow scouts had made by the river, and Crazy Wolf walked across the parade ground to the long building that housed the different company headquarters. He went in the door with COMPANY B painted above it.

Company Clerk, Private George Cousins, looked up from his desk, surprised to be confronted by a wild Indian. Thinking the man must be lost, Cousins said, "This is B Company. What are you trying to find?"

"I found it. I am Crazy Wolf. Sergeant Douglas said your captain wants to see me."

"He does? Well, he didn't say anything to me about it. What was it about?"

"The sergeant didn't say. Just said he wants to see me."

The captain hadn't said anything about wanting to see one of the Crow scouts, and Cousins was not inclined to have him surprised by a wild Indian when he got back from supper. He was about to tell Crazy Wolf the captain was gone for the evening when the door opened and Captain Boyd walked in.

"Crazy Wolf, right?" Boyd asked.

The scout nodded.

"Thanks for dropping by," Boyd continued. "Cliff Freeman tells me you're actually a white man."

That remark caused Cousins to raise his eyebrows in shock.

"It's true I was born to a white woman," Crazy Wolf

said, "but I was raised by the Crows since I was five. I reckon I feel more Crow than white."

"Come on into my office and I'll tell you why I asked you to come talk to me," Boyd said. "You come highly recommended by Lieutenant Ainsworth. As you know Ainsworth is fairly new to this post, as am I. He thinks you are head and shoulders above every other scout in the regiment, and we've got some pretty good scouts."

"I appreciate that, but I don't know why he would think that," Crazy Wolf replied honestly. "Everything I know, I was taught by my Crow brothers."

"Ainsworth said it was you that found that Sioux war party he brought in tonight," Boyd said.

"It was Bloody Axe and me. We both tracked that war party."

"Ainsworth said it was you," Boyd insisted. "But never mind that. I want you to go with a patrol tomorrow, a patrol that is very important to me personally. It's not against a Sioux war party. In fact, I don't expect contact with any Indians. This is an escort assignment. You see, I was posted at Fort Abraham Lincoln for several years before I was transferred to this post. I was attached to the Seventh Cavalry, but they were moved out of Fort Lincoln after Custer's tragic defeat. I've been a widower for seventeen years." He paused to ask, "Do you know what a widower is?"

"It means your wife died. Like my mother did."

"That's right," Boyd continued. "My wife died giving birth to our only child, a daughter we named Amy. My daughter is seventeen now. She is the only family I have, and I am the only family she has. She's never known her mother. She was raised by nursemaids and the US Army. When I was transferred from Fort Lincoln, there were no quarters here for family, so I have had to wait until they were built before I could send for her. Now, thanks to Colonel Miles, I have my private quarters, so my daughter can come live with me."

Crazy Wolf began to understand what the job was. "You want me to go get her?"

"No," Boyd said. "I've already sent a detail of six troopers and a wagon driver to escort her safely back here with all her belongings and our furniture. It's about one-hundred-and-seventy-five miles from here to Fort Lincoln. I had Corporal Tyree wire me from Lincoln the day they arrived and again on the day they departed to return here. I can pretty well guess about how much longer it will take them to arrive. Because of the recent increase in the number of Sioux raiding parties, I'm sending a couple more cavalry men to meet them about halfway back, and I think it would be helpful if they took a scout along. I want you to be that scout. Do you have any problems with that?"

"Nope. You're payin' my wages. Whatever way you wanna use me is all right with me, as long as it ain't scrubbin' out the latrines."

Boyd chuckled. "I'll keep that in mind. And I should have said so in the beginning, but Lieutenant Ainsworth is fine with my wanting to steal you for this personal job. In fact he recommended you."

"About how far do you figure we'll ride before we meet your escort party?"

"As I said, I instructed Corporal Tyree to wire me to let me know the day he left Fort Lincoln. According to my calculations, if you leave in the morning, you can ride two good days and meet them about halfway. The two men you'll be riding with already know about this and they've drawn rations for all three of you. They'll be here in front of the orderly room ready to go right after breakfast tomorrow morning. Eat a good breakfast before you start." Boyd watched Crazy Wolf for his reactions, then asked, "You have any questions or concerns?"

"No, sir. I think I pretty much understand how concerned you are to get your daughter here safely. I'll do what I can to help." Although he didn't express it, Crazy Wolf was somewhat puzzled the captain wanted him specifically. From what he'd just heard of the mission, there didn't seem any need for scouting, and would be no tracking involved, since the escort party was supposedly taking the common wagon road from Fort Lincoln. He also wondered why Boyd chose to send two men and a scout to meet the escort party. If he had concern for his daughter's safety, why not send a fifteen-man patrol? But Crazy Wolf had learned long ago soldiers often did things that didn't make sense to him so he didn't ask any questions.

Reading some skepticism in the scout's expression, the captain explained. "You wonder why I'm sending only the three of you. Right? It's not so much in the form of reinforcements with just two men and a scout. Actually, it's because of the recent increase in reports of Sioux raiding parties up that way. I'm counting on you three to pick up any signs of potential trouble between here and that escort party so the escort could be warned in advance."

Crazy Wolf nodded. "I reckon that makes sense. Like I said, you're payin' my wages, so I would do what you told me to, even if it didn't make sense to me. I will be ready to ride first thing in the morning."

CHAPTER 3

Crazy Wolf was waiting in front of the B Company orderly room when Corporal Ben Walker and Private Fred Castle rode up to join him. Castle was leading a packhorse loaded with a coffeepot and a frying pan, and food enough to feed the three of them on the short ride to meet the escort, plus enough for the slower ride back.

"Crazy Wolf?" Corporal Walker asked when they pulled up before him.

"That's right. Are we ready to go?"

"Waitin' on you," Walker said.

"Right." Crazy Wolf climbed up on the dun gelding he had named Storm because of the horse's fierce stride in full gallop. He had never ridden with either man but was aware of the corporal's intense scrutiny of him as he settled into the saddle. *Probably wondering why the captain is sending a scout,* he thought.

"I don't have any idea why Captain Boyd is sendin' a scout with us," Walker remarked, as if on cue. "We sure as hell don't need one. We're gonna ride straight up the road that leads to Fort Lincoln and meet a six-man escort with a wagon, turn around and ride straight back down the same road. What the hell do we need a scout for? Did he tell you?"

"Nope. All he said was he thought it would be a good idea to send a scout along with you. Since he's a captain, I didn't question him on it."

"Well, there shouldn't be any problem, as long as you remember I'm in charge of this little trip to welcome the captain's daughter," Walker said.

"I'll try not to cause you any problems, and maybe we'll have a nice little ride up and back."

"That sounds like a good duty call to me," Private Castle offered. "It beats goin' on patrol."

Walker didn't comment further, but he cast a wary eye in Crazy Wolf's direction before he led off toward the road to Fort Lincoln. Wondering why the corporal seemed to resent his presence, Crazy Wolf thought maybe Walker just didn't like Indians.

They traveled up the road that followed the Yellowstone River for a distance of about eighteen miles before Walker called for a halt to rest their horses and eat some dinner. Crazy Wolf took care of his horse, then started collecting some wood for a fire, and soon had one going.

"I've got the coffee and the pot," Castle said. "I hope you've got a cup."

"I do," Crazy Wolf replied. "Want me to help you slice that bacon?"

"I'd appreciate it," Castle answered, so the two of them fixed the dinner.

Walker didn't volunteer to do any of the preparation of the food.

As they sat down by the fire to eat it, Crazy Wolf was aware of the corporal's close scrutiny of him again.

Finally, Walker said what he was thinking. "I never

could figure out what would make a man decide to turn Injun."

It was a statement and not a question, but since it was obviously aimed at him, Crazy Wolf chose to give him an answer. "I suppose that's a man's own business, and if that's what his conscience tells him is right, then that's what he should do. In my case, I didn't have a choice. I was five years old with a Blackfoot's bullet in my back. My father and my two brothers were all killed. A Crow warrior saved my life, and the Crow people became my people. As I got older, I found out that we Crows are an honorable people. I am proud to be a Crow."

"That's quite a story," Fred Castle commented. "I reckon you oughta be proud to be a Crow. That was a mighty bad thing about your pappy and your brothers, your white ones, especially for a five-year-old young'un."

Walker did not comment. His mind was too entrenched in the idea that all Indians were the same, just different brands of blood-thirsty savages. And all Indians were the enemy of the US Army. To his thinking, all the army's Crow scouts were warriors who had turned their backs on their own people. And the only thing worse than an Indian was a white man who chose to turn Indian. "I'm gonna catch a few minutes of shut-eye before we're ready to ride again," he announced and laid back on his saddle.

"Don't worry, Corporal, Crazy Wolf and I'll clean this up," Castle said with a wink for the scout. "We'll leave it just like we found it."

Soon, they moved on up the road, heading northeast toward Dakota Territory with Crazy Wolf occasionally leaving the well-traveled road to check on stray hoof-prints. Satisfied there was recent evidence of some unshod ponies close to the road, he reported his findings to Walker. The corporal warned him he might be seeing his own hoofprints, since his horse wasn't shod, either, but Crazy Wolf was convinced the Sioux were still doing some scouting up that way. Captain Boyd's concern was justified.

As they traveled farther up the road, in fact, the signs of lurking Sioux scouts increased. These increased signs of enemy activity were what Boyd wanted the escort to know about and be ready for an attack.

Close to noon on their third day out from the fort, Crazy Wolf pointed to a thin column of smoke wafting up from the trees down near the edge of the river, some distance ahead.

"All right, *scout*, go check it out," Walker said sarcastically, emphasizing the word *scout*.

Giving Storm a little tap with his heels, the big dun gelding broke into a lope immediately and Crazy Wolf left his two companions behind. They maintained a slow walk as they watched him disappear into the trees close to the riverbank.

"Boyd sent him along. Might as well make him useful," Walker grumbled to Castle.

As he came closer to the smoke he had seen from the road, Crazy Wolf slowed his horse and carefully made his way along the riverbank until he decided it best to dismount and go on foot. At a point where he could see a small clearing near the water, he was stunned to see the smoke was from the charred remains of a wagon. He dropped immediately to one knee and strained to see any sign of living beings, red or white. There was no sign of anyone. It must have happened that morning, or more likely, the night before.

He hurried back to get on his horse and race back to the road to alert Walker and Castle. They knew he was bringing bad news when they saw him strike the road at a gallop.

"What is it!" Walker demanded before he came to a stop before them.

"Wiped out!" Crazy Wolf exclaimed. "It's the escort party! They got hit hard!" He wheeled his horse and they followed him as he galloped back to the scene of the massacre. He led them back to the clearing by the river where they saw the bodies scalped and mutilated and the contents of the wagon strewn all about the clearing. They accounted for all the bodies of the escort, including that of the wagon driver. But there was no body of a young woman.

"They carried the captain's daughter off with 'em," Castle stated what all three were thinking.

While he and Walker talked about getting the tragic news back to the captain as quickly as possible, Crazy Wolf began scouting the area to read any message the tracks might tell him. Of the many hoofprints in the clearing around the ashes of the fire, his interest was mainly in those that were not shod. He would also seek to find an exit trail with shod and unshod prints combined, for the warriors would be driving six cavalry horses, plus two that had pulled the wagon. When he was sure he found the way they had left the massacre, Crazy Wolf studied the mixture of hoofprints carefully, trying to separate the shod from the unshod in an effort to make a reasonable guess of the size of the war party. He decided there were seven or eight in the party, maybe nine. Based on their careless departure with no apparent care to hide their trail, he also decided they'd struck before daylight. He went to advise Walker and Castle, who were still sorting through the wreckage.

"I have learned all this place can tell me. We must not

waste any more time here while their trail is still fresh. If we hurry, maybe we can catch them before they kill her."

"Whoa!" Corporal Walker stopped him. "We've got bodies to bury here first. It's too late to do anything for that girl. You bein' an Injun oughta know she's dead by now."

"These men are already dead," Crazy Wolf insisted. "We can come back and bury them."

"Damn it! I give the orders on this job," Walker demanded. "To hell with them damn Injuns. It's too late to catch 'em now."

"Bury them if you have to, but I must hurry before their trail grows old. The men who lived in these bodies are gone. They don't care if you bury them or not. The girl may still be alive. She would want me to come at once. If there's any chance I can help her, I have to try. You two have a sad story to take back to the captain. Tell him I will do my best to find his daughter." Crazy Wolf walked over and grabbed Storm's reins, then jumped onto his back. He turned the dun away from the camp and started up the bank.

"I'll be damned." Walker growled and pulled his pistol out of his holster, but Castle was quick enough to grab his arm to prevent him from aiming at Crazy Wolf riding away.

"Corporal Walker!" Castle shouted. "He's right! There might be a chance for that poor girl."

Walker wrenched his arm free of Castle's hand, but Crazy Wolf was out of pistol range by then. Out of sheer frustration, he fired a shot in that direction, anyway. "The lazy bastard is just gittin' outta diggin' the graves. Those Sioux are long gone, and that little gal is most likely already dead. Even if she ain't, she ain't no good to anybody no more." He holstered his pistol and looked at Castle. "You ever grab my arm like that again and I'll shoot you."

"We gonna bury these fellers now?" Castle asked.

"No, the buzzards will take care of 'em," Walker said. "We ain't got no real shovels, anyway. We'll go back to the fort and tell 'em what happened. We'll tell 'em we buried the seven soldiers. Ain't nobody gonna find them bodies."

Finding the trail easy to follow from the start, Crazy Wolf had first surmised the reason was because the warriors were riding in the dark. He was still convinced of that, but it also occurred to him the Sioux were not concerned about being followed. They had lucked upon the party of soldiers obviously taking the girl somewhere, most likely to the fort at Tongue River. Thinking they were not attached to a larger force of soldiers and knowing they were not close enough to the fort, the Sioux wouldn't worry about a patrol coming after them until long after the soldiers and the girl were even missed. In addition, they were trying to drive the captured horses.

He followed them up from the river, and realized they'd driven their stolen horses back toward Miles City, causing him to wonder why he had not noticed the sudden number of hoofprints on the road before. His question was answered when the hoofprints turned off the road again to follow a winding stream to the north.

He would have expected the Sioux war party to go in the opposite direction, if they were going back to the reservation. The fact that they chose to follow this wild stream, cutting its way through some rugged, almost treeless country, told him they had no plans to keep the girl very long. The fact that they didn't kill her at the river caused him to worry about what they planned for her. He hoped his effort to overtake them was not in vain. Knowing there was a good chance she had already met her fate, he wondered if there was a large camp up the winding stream, or if the warriors were just looking for temporary cover while they enjoyed the spoils of their raid.

He continued following the obvious tracks left by the horses until the stream broke out of the rocky walls that confined it and cut across a small grassy plot before it entered a narrow canyon. He stopped. Before riding out across the grassy expanse he took a good look at the rugged foothills beyond, sparsely covered with tall pine trees. The Sioux war party might not be concerned about anyone following them, but anyone riding across that open meadow would be an easy target. He looked up at the sun. Hours of daylight were left. A lookout at any of a dozen spots on the face of the foothills before him would have an easy shot at anyone passing across that open grass plot. It didn't make sense the Sioux had just decided to follow that little stream to see where it led, which gave him a feeling there was a camp in those hills on the other side of the canyon..

He cleared his thoughts and decided he was just being overly cautious, for the war party he was following had passed that way many hours before. He nudged Storm with his heels, then immediately pulled back hard with his reins when he suddenly spotted a thin stream of smoke drifting on a sudden breeze across the brow of the hill beyond the canyon. "Maybe I better pay more attention to my gut feelings, boy," he confided to Storm. "We need to see whose camp that is, but we best not go in the front door."

He turned his horse around and went back along the stream until he felt sure he could not be seen leaving it by anyone who might be watching on that hill. Then he rode out of the cover of the trees by the stream and took a wide circle around to the west of the line of hills. Reaching a point he thought was even with the back of the hill where he figured the lookout would be, if there was one, he rode toward it. Stopping as close as he thought safe on his horse, he dismounted and went the rest of the way on foot. Armed with his Henry rifle and wearing an Army model handgun, high on his left side with the handle forward—in what was called the cavalry grip—he made his way up the hill.

On all fours when he reached the very top of the hill, he crawled up behind a large rock where he could see what he had guessed at before—a camp at the bottom of the hill. From the look of it, one that had been used many times. Where the stream came into the tiny valley, it formed a small pond that drained out to form the stream he had followed to the hills. From his position at the top of the hill, he couldn't tell if the pond was made by man or formed by nature, but it served to water the small herd of horses the Indians had acquired. The captured cavalry horses were easy to distinguish since the Sioux had not bothered to take the saddles off. A short distance from the pond, he counted six warriors lounging around a fire, obviously making small talk and enjoying some of the food supplies they had taken from the wagon. He could also see there was no lookout on the first hill he had been cautious about approaching. Obviously, they were not concerned about anyone following them.

Seeing no sign of the woman caused him a deep feeling of regret, for he could well imagine what her final hours had been like. But then another warrior appeared. He came from a small clump of pines about thirty yards from the fire. Some of the warriors sitting around the fire called out to him, joking. Crazy Wolf could not understand what they were saying, but he could guess. If what he suspected was true, the girl was in the clump of trees, and he might be too late. Still, he had to check to make sure.

He reasoned that, if she was dead, they would not hide her body so close in their camp but would more likely drag it well away somewhere to rot. No, he thought, they were not finished with her. The use of the clump of trees was for their privacy, not hers. He would have preferred to wait until darkness before attempting to see if she was in that clump of trees, but that would not be for a few hours yet. Too much could happen in a few hours' time. He was pretty fast when it came to rapid fire with his Henry rifle, but he was not willing to have a shootout with seven Sioux warriors face-to-face. He had to create a diversion to reduce the number of warriors in the camp, and he only knew of one way.

He backed away from the top of the hill, hurried down to his horse, then used the cover of the hills to circle around to the east of the camp. Figuring he was directly opposite the hill he had just left, he looked for the best place for his diversion. He picked a spot at the bottom of a gully grown up in sagebrush, most of it dead, far enough away from the trees. He had no desire to start a forest fire and was confident the gully would contain the fire, and the sagebrush would make a nice volume of brown smoke. He hurried up into the few trees on the side of the hill and collected enough dead limbs to get a good fire going. With his flint and steel, and a generous wad of dried sagebrush, he kindled his fire, and stayed with it until the pine limbs were burning strongly. Satisfied it would do the job he intended, he climbed on Storm and circled back to the west side of the camp and the hill from which he had first seen the camp. He took his horse farther up the hill, so it would be closer at hand when the time came to act, climbed up to his position behind the rock, and waited to see if his distraction would do what he hoped.

Although it seemed a long time, it was actually only a

few minutes before he saw the first plume of brown smoke rise above the top of the hill opposite the one he was on. He watched the group of warriors anxiously, but there was no response. *What's wrong with you?* he thought, even though he had to allow for the fact that he would see it before they did, since he was at the top of the hill.

Finally, it was discovered, and his main concern became whether they would all go to investigate the source of the fire or send just one man.

"Look," Lame Fox suddenly blurted and pointed toward the hill to the east. "Smoke!"

The others looked in the direction he indicated, at first only curious. As they continued to stare at it, however, it increased in density and volume.

"Something is wrong," Walking Bird declared, concerned now. "We'd best go and find out what is on fire."

The others didn't wait to make any decisions. They were already running for their horses.

"What about the woman?" Lame Fox asked. "Should someone stay?"

"She can't go anywhere," Walking Bird answered. "But maybe you should stay here to make sure she doesn't free herself."

"That would be wise," Lame Fox said. "It is best that one of us stay and watch the camp and the horses. Be careful. It might be an army patrol."

Crazy Wolf watched as they rode away between the hills east of their camp. And when the last man rode out of his sight, he went straight for the little clump of trees where the woman was tied to a tree.

Sitting on the ground with her feet under her, her hands tied together, and tied to a small tree, she heard the now familiar rustle of the pine limbs that signaled another visit from one of her captors. Almost overcome by the

overpowering feeling of dread, she was not aware of the
faint sound of whining coming involuntarily from deep in
her throat. When he pushed through the branches, she
almost sobbed when she saw Lame Fox. He was excep-
tionally brutal. She knew his name but didn't know what
it meant because she didn't speak the Lakota language.
He stood over her, glaring down at her with the evil smile
of the conqueror. She dropped her chin to her breast, but
he ordered her to look up at him.

Knowing it would only be worse if she didn't do as he
said, she looked up and gasped in alarm when she saw his
head suddenly jerked back and the one swift slash of the
knife across his throat. Lame Fox struggled briefly against
the powerful hand holding him up by his hair while the
blood flowed from the severed arteries in his neck. When
he dropped to the ground, she saw that he had been killed
by another Indian, but not one of those who captured her.
He wiped the blood from his knife on Lame Fox's shirt
and she cringed, horrified, as he approached her.

"Amy Boyd?" he asked softly as he cut the rope tying
her to the tree.

She couldn't speak, but she nodded her head rapidly as
he untied her hands.

"My name is Crazy Wolf. I'm a Crow scout. Can you
ride?"

"Yes!" she answered, finding her voice again when she
realized he had come to save her. She was not a great rider,
but her answer would have been the same had he asked if
she could fly. She tried to cover herself as best she could
with what remained of her torn blouse.

"Come," he said, extending his hand to help her up.
"We don't have much time before his friends return."

She took his hand, and he pulled her up to her feet.
When she looked as if she might falter, he picked her up

and carried her to the pond where the cavalry horses were drinking, still with saddles on. He made a quick choice and put her up in the saddle.

"Can you hold on?"

She nodded rapidly again and took hold of the saddle with both hands.

"I'll adjust the stirrups after we get away from here." He took the horse's reins and led it back to his horse, climbed on board, and led her away from the camp.

On the other side of the hill, east of the camp, the six Sioux warriors made their way cautiously toward the smoldering column of smoke coming up out of a deep gully in the valley floor. With no sign of anyone around the gully, they approached close enough to look into it.

"It's nothing but dead sagebrush," Broken Foot said.

Walking Bird peered down at the burning sagebrush, wondering what caused it to catch fire. He squinted in an effort to see through the dark smoke. "This fire did not start by itself," he suddenly declared. "Look! There are limbs stacked to make a fire. We must get back. Someone is trying to steal the army horses. Lame Fox may be in trouble."

"There have been no gunshots," Broken Foot said. "He may be with the woman again and not know the horses are being stolen."

Since the hill was too steep to ride over, they jumped on their horses and circled back around the hills. Finally back, they found the horses were still there, minus one. And there was no sign of Lame Fox.

"See if he is in the thicket," Broken Foot exclaimed.

Two of the warriors ran to the pine thicket and reported the discovery of the body and the woman gone.

"Lame Fox is dead!" one of the warriors yelled. "His throat has been cut, but his scalp has not been taken!"

"It must be one of the soldiers we did not see," Broken Foot said.

Crazy Wolf would have preferred for them to know that Lame Fox was killed by a Crow warrior. And he would have taken the scalp had it not been in the presence of an already severely traumatized young girl.

"It must be only one man, and that was the reason he made the fire to draw us away from here!"

"We must catch him before he gets too far away," Walking Bird declared. "He has the woman and he will be slowed down by her."

"What about Lame Fox?" Broken Foot asked.

"We will come back and bury him properly," Walking Bird said. "It is important we avenge his death. I agree with Broken Foot. It is one man who has done this. And we must catch him and gut him."

So resolved, they wrapped Lame Fox in his blanket and left him in the pine thicket. Then the six Sioux warriors jumped back on their horses and went after Crazy Wolf and Amy.

Now, the Sioux warriors had the easy trail of following two galloping horses.

CHAPTER 4

Amy held on to the saddle with all the strength she could muster, gripping with her hands and pressing with her knees, determined not to fall off the horse. She didn't care where he was taking her as long as it was away from the nightmare she had been cast into. The path was the same the Sioux had taken into their camp, following the stream. Crazy Wolf deemed it the most direct line back to the road. Knowing for sure the pack of Sioux warriors would definitely come after them, he hoped to get a sizeable lead on the Indians.

When they reached the road to Fort Keogh, however, he stopped to adjust Amy's stirrups and attempted to give her some encouragement while he quickly adjusted them. "This will make it a lot easier for you to hold on," he told her as he put her foot in the stirrup. "I want to push the horses for a good way down this road to get as much lead as we can on that party of Sioux . . . because they will come after us. We can't stay on this road all the way to Fort Keogh. It's seventy-five miles from here, and they would catch us before we got there."

He didn't tell her the main reason he didn't choose to

race the Sioux to the fort was because of the condition he had found her in. She was barely hanging on after having obviously suffered a great deal of physical abuse. He was also concerned about her ability to cope mentally with what she had experienced at the hands of her captors, and wondered if a race for life would be the final weight to collapse her mind.

"We will leave this road after we push the horses for a while," he continued. "I will take you to your father at the post, but you must get some rest first. And I must find some food for you to regain your strength. All I have is some jerky and hardtack, so I will have to hunt. But I want you in a safe place first. Do you understand?"

She said she did, but couldn't really grasp what he was trying to explain. Feeling too tired to care, she did sense his good intentions and was grateful, but was too sick in her mind to understand his reasons for whatever he did.

Realizing all that, he got back on his horse and started down the road at an easy lope, leading her horse behind him. After about two miles, they came to a stream crossing the road. He eased the horses back to a walk when he entered the stream, but instead of going across, he turned and walked the horses in the middle of it, following it all the way to the river. At the river, he rode the horses out of the stream, dismounted on the riverbank, and walked back to Amy.

Gently, he asked, "How are you doin'?"

"Better since I can put my feet in the stirrups," she said. "Do you think they are coming after us?"

"I'm pretty sure they are," he answered honestly, since he was encouraged to see she seemed to be handling the situation a little better than before. "You're doin' fine so far. Can I put you to a tougher test?"

Thinking she had little choice, she answered, "I suppose so, I don't think anything can be much worse than what has already happened to me."

"For a number of reasons, I think we'll be better off on the other side of the river. Can you swim?"

She looked disappointed to hear the question, but answered yes.

He continued. "The river's too deep for the horses to wade across, so we'll have to swim 'em across. If you just hang on to the saddle, the horse will take you across. You're gonna take a bath, but I'll build a fire to warm you up after we get across. Do you think you can do it?"

"I don't see that I have a choice," she said with a smile until she felt the pain from a split in her lip.

"I promise you things will be better on the other side of the river. I will get some help for you on the Crow reservation. But first, we have to go swimming." He removed his deerskin rifle scabbard from his saddle, took a handful of cartridges from his cartridge belt and dropped them into the scabbard with his rifle. He stuffed a dry cloth from his saddlebag in with them as well. Then he handed her the reins for the horse she was riding. "It'll be better if I don't try to hold on to your reins while we're crossin'. They'll most likely get separated in the water because of the current. If you just hang on he'll come out on his own, and I'll be there to get you. Can you do that?"

She nodded, and he climbed back on his horse and led them into the water. Her horse remained standing at the bank for a few seconds until she gave it a kick with her heels, and then the horse followed the dun into the water.

With no reluctance, Storm entered the deeper water and headed straight across, and when he reached a point where he could no longer wade, he began to swim. Crazy Wolf held his rifle scabbard up with one hand until the dun gelding could wade again, and they proceeded to come out on the other bank. As he had expected, Amy's horse had drifted a little apart from Storm's trail but came out of the river a dozen yards or so downstream.

Seeing she was soaked he rode over to meet her on the bank. "Good work. You should feel better to have washed all of that Sioux offa you. Think you can ride that horse now? Or do you want me to take the reins and lead you again?"

"I can ride," she said, feeling a small bit of pride for her accomplishment.

"I thought you could. We ain't gonna ride far, though. Just far enough to pick a good spot for our fire."

He first selected a little rise in the bank that gave him a good view of the point where the stream joined the river. He guessed it was about fifty yards from the middle of the river. Then he walked back from there and picked a place to build a fire. He settled on a spot about twenty yards back from his lookout point at the top of the rise and proceeded to build his fire, much to the puzzlement of Amy.

She could not understand why they were not running as fast as they could. Finally she summoned the courage to ask, "Why are we waiting for them to find us?"

"We're lettin' our horses rest," he answered. "Plus, we need to let those Sioux know this is Crow country on this side of the river, and it will cost them to enter it. I'll take some of those limbs and make you a prop so you can dry your shirt by the fire."

"I can't take my blouse off," she said at once. "They left me with nothing under it."

"Oh," he responded and thought for a few moments. "I'll take my shirt off. It's wet, too, but it'll give you cover while your shirt is dryin'. It looks like it'll cover you all the way down over your fanny." He immediately unbuckled his pistol belt and pulled his buckskin shirt off and handed it to her. "We're lucky it ain't winter, ain't we? Don't worry about your privacy. I'm goin' to take my rifle and my pistol up there on that rise, and I'll be watchin' the river the whole time." He picked up his saddle scabbard and started to go but stopped when he remembered. "I'll take some of those limbs and fix a prop for you "

"I can do that," she said. "You go on up there and watch the river."

"Yes, ma'am," he said, happy to see a little show of resilience from her. "If you're hungry, there's some jerky and hardtack in my saddlebags. I'm sorry I don't have anything more to offer you, but I hope I can come up with something after we take care of the Sioux party."

He left her to dry her flimsy blouse while he settled himself on the rise overlooking the river. He took his rifle out and was satisfied to see that it was dry, as was the extra ammunition. Laying it aside, he pulled his Colt .45 out of the wet holster and began drying the pistol with the dry cloth he had stuffed in the scabbard. One of his first jobs when he got back to the fort would be to take his pistol apart and give it a thorough cleaning.

The time ticked away slowly as the sun hovered down closer and closer to the distant hills in the west. Figuring the war party would have just about caught up with them, he began to wonder if they had missed his exit from the main road when he rode in the creek to the river. Even better if they did miss his exit from the road. Maybe he'd lost them for good.

But he was not to escape that easily, for they appeared at the mouth of the creek at the next moment. He counted them. All six were there, as well as the horses they had taken from the soldiers, five with saddles still on them and two without saddles. He surmised that to be the reason they were late catching up to Amy and him.

They came crashing out of the little stream to the bank of the river with the extra horses around them like runaway cattle and quickly found the tracks he and Amy had left on the bank where they had entered the water. While the extra horses gathered at the water's edge, the warriors held a brief discussion, then the one who appeared to do most of the talking entered the water and started across. The others did not hesitate and followed, spreading out to either side of him. The extra horses started across as well.

It was what Crazy Wolf had waited for as he knelt on one knee beside the only large tree on the knoll he had chosen for his execution platform. He leveled the front sight of the Henry rifle on the chest of the warrior in the lead. It would have been an easy shot, but he wanted to make sure the warriors behind the leader reached the deep water, too, so it wouldn't be easy for them to turn around and go back. He waited until the leader's horse lost its footing and started swimming.

Moving his sight to settle on what he could see of the warrior's neck and shoulders, he squeezed the trigger. There was no hesitation then. He cranked another cartridge into the chamber as fast as he could and fired at the next closest warrior, then shifted his aim to strike the warrior to that man's right. Ejecting another spent shell, he shifted back to the left to aim at the fourth target. Up to that point, the confused warriors didn't know what was happening. The extra horses they were herding caused additional confusion.

When it dawned on them they were being picked off

from the opposite bank, it was too late for target number four. He caught Crazy Wolf's fourth round in his forehead just as he started to duck under the water. Aware of the ambush they had been led into, the two surviving warriors rolled off their horses and ducked under the water. It had become a deadly game as Crazy Wolf watched the surface of the river and waited for one of them to come up for air.

One head suddenly broke the surface. The scout turned quickly and fired but was not quick enough, and the head disappeared again. While he stared at that spot, the other warrior broke the surface, took a big gulp of air, and submerged again as Crazy Wolf's bullet streaked through the water right above his head. It was enough to encourage Broken Foot to turn around and swim underwater, back the way he had come. A dozen yards away, the other surviving warrior was doing the same thing.

Coming to that same conclusion, Crazy Wolf aimed his rifle toward the opposite side of the river and scanned back and forth, waiting for the first man to reach the shallow water and come up on his feet. At that range, it would be a more difficult shot because of the Henry's limited accuracy range. From where he knelt, he estimated the distance to the opposite bank of the river to be almost two-hundred yards, maybe more. However, he would have a bigger target when each man reached water so shallow that he had to get on his feet and wade out of the water.

Finally, he saw one of the warriors crawling on his hands and knees in the shallow water. Crazy Wolf waited for him to get to his feet and run out of the water, but he could not move very quickly in the shallow water. The first shot missed. Judging by the warrior's flinch to his right, the scout aimed a hair more to the right and knocked him down with a round in the center of his back. Left with still one target to avenge the deaths of seven soldiers and the brutal molestation of Amy Boyd, Crazy Wolf waited to deliver the same justice to the last one. It came in much the same manner as the previous warrior. When the water became too shallow to swim, he scrambled up on his feet and tried to run as a bullet struck the water beside him, followed by the fatal one in his back a few seconds later.

Remaining there for a while longer, Crazy Wolf watched the opposite bank of the river for any signs of life from the Sioux warriors, but there were none, and not a single horse had been hit by an errant shot. The ambush had been more successful than he had thought possible. His hopes had been to reduce the number of his pursuers in what he had anticipated to be a longer chase.

He quickly changed his plans. Instead of putting Amy back on her horse and fleeing into the darkness descending over the hills, they would camp right where they were for the night. They would dry out their clothing and his bedding. It struck him then that he had other work to do as he watched the small herd of horses coming out of the river and advancing up the bank. Not only were they Sioux horses but also five cavalry horses, still saddled, and two horses that had pulled the wagon carrying Amy and her possessions.

Unfortunately, Amy had nothing, not even enough rags to cover her body. He must do something about that. He could not take her to her father in the condition she was presently in.

While he thought about how he would take care of all the horses, he suddenly had a feeling he was being watched. It was so strong a feeling that he suddenly turned to look back toward the fire, thinking it must be her. But it was not her. He could see her sitting on the ground on the other side of the fire, her arms hugging her legs tightly up against her breast.

Sure all his shooting was traumatizing her no end, he stepped out away from the trunk of the big tree he had knelt behind and looked up to discover the eyes he thought he had felt and the big raccoon who had no doubt also been disturbed by all his shooting. *One more problem solved*, he thought as he slowly picked up the pistol he had just dried, reloaded, and took aim. The pistol fired as he expected, showing no damage from the dunking in the river. It seemed almost too much to ask for, killing all the war party, and then having supper drop from the tree.

The first thing he had to do, however, was to tell Amy the Sioux warriors she feared were no longer a threat. Seeing him walking back down the rise, she got to her bare feet. Her shoes were parked next to the fire, his buckskin shirt hanging on her like a heavy robe. The distress he saw in her eyes told him she was prepared to hear bad news— that they must run.

He told her right away that all was well. They were no longer being chased.

"You think they went back?" she asked, thinking his shooting must have discouraged them.

"Well, no." He hesitated a moment. "They didn't go back. They just ain't gonna chase us no more."

"How do you know they won't—?" She then understood. "Did you kill all of them?"

"Yes, ma'am, they're all dead. They came to kill us," he added, in case she thought him a savage as well.

"I prayed you would. Thank you, Lord, and thank you,

Crazy Wolf." She sank down on her knees as if a crushing weight had been lifted from her.

"Are you hungry enough to eat a raccoon?" he asked her.

"I'm hungry enough to eat anything," she answered. "I've never eaten a raccoon, but I'm ready to try it."

"It's not bad eatin'. Usually a little tough, but it's got a good flavor, especially when you're as hungry as we are right now. I'll skin him and butcher him and we'll cook him, but first, I wanna take the saddles off those horses."

The cavalry mounts had been carrying their saddles ever since the Sioux war party ambushed the escort detail.

"I'll untie our horses now and let 'em go down to the river to drink. I expect all the other horses will most likely gather together, and I'm hopin' I can keep 'em headed in the same direction we're goin' when we leave here in the mornin'. That's somethin' I'll talk over with you later. Right now, I'll go get the horses taken care of and your supper ready to roast."

"I can help," Amy volunteered, realizing how much stronger she felt just from knowing her life was no longer in danger. "What do you want me to do?"

"There ain't much you can do till I get the raccoon ready for the fire. Those five cavalry horses have all got bedrolls rolled up behind the saddle. When I take them off, you could open up those blankets and hang 'em in the trees to dry off. And while you're at it, you might wanna pick out a couple to make your bed tonight." He hesitated, then said. "I mean, if you ain't particular about who mighta been sleepin' in it for a good while before you."

She looked up at him as if to see if he was serious. "I don't suppose I have to be particular about anything like that anymore after what they did to me." She looked away from him when a tear began to form.

"Listen to me, miss. You have no need to bow your head. You fought for your honor. The cuts and bruises I see tell me you battled bravely. Every enemy who wronged you has been sent to hell where they belong. Since they are dead, it's the same as if it never happened to you. No living man on this earth has defiled you. That is a truth you can hold on to. You need to hold your head up high. You have no shame to apologize for . . . to anyone."

She smiled at him, grateful for rescuing her and saving her life. She knew she would have been killed as soon as her captors were finished. She was also grateful for his efforts to boost her self-esteem. "Thank you, Crazy Wolf." Then she asked, "What is your real name? I know you were not always a Crow."

"I feel like I have always been a Crow. I have been ever since I was five years old. My birth name is Cody Hunter. I will tell you about it later. Right now, I have to prepare a raccoon for you to cook."

By the time a heavy dark fell over the river, their camp was surrounded by blankets, as well as one coonskin, drying in the branches of the trees. Although he'd left the head of the raccoon attached in the event it might become a headpiece for some young brave, that was questionable—due to a bullet hole in the fur. The meat of the animal was very well received by both parties.

While they ate, he presented her with a plan that might appeal to her sense of dignity. "I took us across the river here because this is part of the Crow reservation. About twelve or fifteen miles from here is the village of Wounded Owl. I think that we might find some clothes for you in that village, so you wouldn't have to go to your father wearing my shirt."

Since her blouse was practically in shreds, she was

receptive to that suggestion at once. She'd been anticipating the reunion wearing nothing but a blanket wrapped around her. "I would like that very much, but I have no money to buy any clothes."

"You don't need any money. We have plenty to trade with—horses, saddles, blankets. If you feel like goin' for another swim, there's also some rifles at the bottom of that river, courtesy of the Sioux Indians. But I think we've got plenty to outfit you up in style without diving for rifles. Wounded Owl's people can trade for many things at the trading post with one good horse."

"But don't you want to keep the horses?"

"I don't want the horses. I'll just turn the cavalry horses over to the army, since they are the army's property. We can make better use of the other horses. We will use them to buy you some new clothes. That is, of course, if you are not against wearing deerskin."

"You are a generous man, Cody Hunter," she said. "I'm so lucky they sent you to find me."

He laughed. "It's easy to be generous with the enemy's property." He saw no reason to tell her he hadn't been sent to find her, and in fact, was actually shot at when he decided to go after her on his own. He was pretty sure Corporal Walker would submit a scathing report on his disobedience as soon as he and Private Castle returned to the fort.

Maybe he should take Amy straight to her father as quick as their horses would take them. But he hoped to return the captain's daughter to him looking less like the tortured wretch he had discovered in the Sioux camp. He watched her carefully to see her genuine reaction. "It's up to you, however. It might take us a day or more longer to get to the fort, if we go by Wounded Owl's village. If you'd rather go straight to the fort, that's all right with me."

"Let's go by the Crow village," she said. "I don't want my father to see me like this."

"Fine, then that's what we'll do." He had been pretty sure she would prefer that. "You want some more of this meat?"

"One more little piece," she said. "It's surprising how good something like this tastes when you're hungry enough to eat a coon. Then I'm gonna see if any of those blankets have dried a little more. This one I'm wrapped in is still kinda wet."

By the time they decided to turn in for the night, they had enough mostly dry blankets to make two beds. He knew he would have no trouble sleeping but was concerned about her.

In the morning, he found that he had worried needlessly, for in her state of exhaustion she slept like a rock, especially since her mind told her she was safe in her rescuer's arms.

By the time she awakened, he had already saddled all of the horses and was in the process of rolling up the dry blankets.

"Good morning," she called out to him.

"Good mornin'," he returned. "I'm real sorry I don't have a hot cup of coffee for you this mornin'."

She laughed. "I'm sorry you don't, too."

"It'll take about a two-hour ride or more to Wounded Owl's village, and I'm sure we'll get something to eat there. If we don't, I'll shoot one of our horses and we'll butcher him. They may not have any coffee, though. At least, I'll be very surprised if they do."

"I'll be grateful for anything they've got," she said.

"There used to be a lot of deer in this part of the reservation, but they've pretty-much hunted 'em all out." He said it kind of apologetically.

She said, "Don't worry about feeding me. I'm fine. I'm sure when you left Fort Keogh, you didn't know you were going to need to feed me."

"Actually, I also didn't know I was gonna have to worry about feedin' myself."

CHAPTER 5

Wounded Owl came out of his tipi when some of the young men called for him. "What is it, Crooked Arrow?" the old chief asked.

"Someone comes!" Crooked Arrow said. "Two riders, driving horses."

"I think one of them is a woman," Wind Runner said.

Soon others in the village became aware of the visitors and gathered around Wounded Owl.

"It's Crazy Wolf!" Wind Runner declared. "And a white woman!"

They stood watching the army scout as he drew near, then rode his horse toward the leaders to turn the small horse herd away from the tipis and let them graze on what grass they could find. The spectators, some waving to him, stood wondering at the five horses with saddles but no riders, and the obvious Indian ponies, some with Sioux markings on them. Everyone was anxious to hear the explanation.

"Crazy Wolf!" Wounded Owl exclaimed, anxious to hear the story that brought the young warrior to his village. "Welcome. Who is this you bring with you?"

"This is Captain Boyd's daughter. He is the commanding

officer of B Company at the new fort where the Tongue meets the Yellowstone. She was on her way to the fort from Fort Abraham Lincoln in Dakota Territory when the soldiers escorting her were ambushed by Sioux warriors. They killed all the soldiers and captured her."

"Come." Wounded Owl was eager to hear how he came by the horses, but ever mindful of his manners, he said, "You must be tired and hungry." He looked at Amy wrapped in a blanket, then turned to address his wife. "Bright Water, take the woman inside and give her food and water."

Amy looked at once to Crazy Wolf and he nodded yes. She took the hand Bright Water offered and was led into the tipi, followed by two younger women.

"Tell me how you came to have the woman and the horses," Wounded Owl said when the women had gone inside.

Sure that Wounded Owl might have some concern he could expect a Sioux war party to be tracking the stolen horses, especially those with Sioux markings, Crazy Wolf first told him no one was tracking the horses, then he told him why. After he'd completed the story, he then told Wounded Owl why he had come to his village instead of going straight back to the fort.

"I see. The woman was badly mistreated, and her clothes were destroyed. That is why she has wrapped herself in a blanket."

"I hoped that some of the younger women in your village might be making some new clothes or have some they would be willing to trade for a good horse," Crazy Wolf said. "A good horse will buy many things at the trading post on the river."

"You would trade one of the horses you captured?" Wounded Owl asked, thinking a woman's skirt wasn't worth a horse.

"I would trade more than one horse, if I could get your women to dress the woman up to return to her father."

"I will tell Bright Water," Wounded Owl said.

"I will tell Red Basket," Wind Runner said. "She is making a new dress now." He was thinking about the possibility of trading for one of the horses. It was a thought that caught on with many of the younger husbands, just as Crazy Wolf had hoped.

In the short time Amy was being pampered by Bright Water and the two younger women, a contest was underway in an effort to win the chance to clothe the poor white girl. When Amy was brought out of Bright Water's tipi, she was met by a group of the other women of the village who immediately greeted her cordially.

One of them, a young woman like her, stepped forward and took her hand. "Come," Red Basket said and motioned for her to follow. Uncertain again, Amy looked to Crazy Wolf standing with the men who had gathered to watch. He nodded again to assure her, so she let Red Basket lead her toward one of the other tipis.

Wind Runner grinned at him. "They are the same size." Then he looked at Wounded Owl and repeated it, confident his wife would offer her new dress.

The two young women were inside the tipi for some time before Amy reappeared. She was dressed in a fringed deerskin dress that extended from her chin to her feet, like those the Crow women wore. Her dress was splendidly decorated with a pattern of bone shaped to resemble elk teeth. On her feet, she wore soft deerskin moccasins, also decorated with the same designs. Behind her, Red Basket, proud and smiling broadly, followed.

Carrying her shoes and shredded blouse, Amy walked back to the group in front of Bright Water's tipi. Crazy Wolf saw the tears of gratitude that threatened to fill her eyes, and knew she was trying to control them before she spoke, so he spoke for her.

"You look like a little Crow princess. How do you like your outfit?"

She still couldn't speak, so just nodded vigorously.

"Well, I guess we can get started back to the fort then. We can get back by dinnertime tomorrow if we leave pretty soon."

"What say you, Crazy Wolf?" Wind Runner asked. "Is new dress, moccasins, and leggings worth a horse?"

"No," Crazy Wolf answered, still looking at Amy's face. "It's worth five horses!" He smiled when he saw the look of joyous surprise in Wind Runner's face. "Take your pick of the horses without saddles or shoes. After you pick your five horses, that will leave two Sioux horses. I will give those to Bright Water for her hospitality."

That brought a smile to the old chief's face. "You are very generous, Crazy Wolf."

"The others belong to the army, so I will take them to the fort with us. You and your village have done much to help this woman. It is well worth the horses I give. The woman was hurt bad inside her head as well as her body. Your kindness to her has done much good to restore her spirit."

Watching him as he spoke to Wounded Owl, Amy nodded her head in agreement, even though he spoke in the Crow tongue. She knew not a word of Crow but somehow understood what he was saying.

As Wind Runner and a couple of the other men led the seven Indian ponies away from the army mounts and tied them so they would not follow when Crazy Wolf and Amy left, she put her shoes in her saddlebag, then spread her tattered blouse across the saddle and waited for him to give her a boost up.

"I don't think there's enough of that blouse to mend," he said. "Don't you want to just throw it away?"

"No, no," she quickly said. "I need it." When he looked puzzled, she confided, "I don't have any undergarments."

"Oh," he replied. "I guess that is kinda rough."

"It's not gonna be easy riding with this long skirt either. I'm gonna have to hike it up to get my leg over the saddle. You have to turn around toward the horse's rump when you boost me up."

"It'll be easier this way," he said and picked her up in his arms. "Now, hike your skirt up to your knees and spread your legs and I'll set you right down in the saddle."

She did as he said, and he lifted her up and dropped her in the saddle. "I declare. You really are wearin' leggings, too."

She was cheered and applauded by the village watching.

"I'm sitting on my skirt. It gives me a little cushion." She wiggled around to get a little more comfortable. "When it's time to stop, I think you might have to get me down the same way you got me up."

They waved goodbye and set out toward the river again, driving the army horses and following a trail from the village that led to Fort Keogh. They traveled a little over twenty miles before they reached the Powder River at a point about another twenty miles from the fort. Amy was immediately concerned with crossing so soon in her new dress and leggings, but he told her at that time of year he didn't expect to find the river deep enough to make the horses swim. The trail had evidently been struck during times when the river was high. It took a couple of turns that enabled them to cross where there was an island in the middle of the river.

"We'll stop here for the night, since it's already startin'

to get dark. We can go on across to the other side, though, so you won't have to cross it in the mornin'. All right?"

She agreed.

"You could get your feet wet, but if you take your feet outta the stirrups and cross your legs in front of you on your horse's neck, you oughta stay dry. Can you do that without fallin' off the horse?"

"I don't know. I think so." She pulled one leg up and stuck it out on the horse's neck then very carefully lifted her other leg up and crossed her ankles. She sat that way for a few minutes then said, "I guess I can do that."

"Are you ready to go ahead and cross now?" he asked, thinking she still looked a little reluctant, but had said she was ready.

Although she remained upright she still didn't look very stable.

"You go ahead, and I'll come right behind you. If you feel like you're gonna tip over, drop your feet 'cause it'd be better to get your feet wet, instead of your whole body."

She started across to the little island, watching the water as it came up higher and higher on her horse's legs. As it rose no higher than the horse's belly before the horse climbed out on the island, she appeared to be solid in her saddle and continued on into the second part of the water with Crazy Wolf still right behind her.

The seven other horses had stopped to drink then went on across, and were passing on each side of the two riders. That seemed to make Amy a bit nervous as she tried to concentrate on keeping steady with her feet out in front of her. The second part of the river was a little deeper and the water kept rising on her horse's legs and up to its belly. When it rose over the stirrups, she began to waver.

Crazy Wolf pulled up beside her, reached over to take

her arm, and they continued on across with him holding her steady until they reached the other side.

She dropped her feet back in the stirrups as her horse climbed up the bank. "I just got my new moccasins a little bit wet when I put my feet back in the stirrups," she told him, genuinely excited. "I feel like I just crossed the ocean on a raft."

"You did just fine. Ready to get down?"

She put her arms up to give him room and he reached up and pulled her off the horse.

Something suddenly occurred to her. "But the fort's on the other side of the Yellowstone, not the side we're on now, isn't it?" He said that it was, so she asked, "We can't wade across the Yellowstone, can we?"

"Nope," he answered and let her fret about that for a few moments before continuing. "But there's a fellow operatin' a ferryboat across the Yellowstone right there, just before you get to the Tongue. At least he was there when I left the other day." He grinned when she gave him an accusing look. "Let's pick a good spot to build our fire, and I'll get it going. We can eat some of that pemmican Bright Water gave us to keep from starvin' to death. After I take all the saddles off our horse herd, I'll take a little walk down the river to see if maybe I can find something else to eat."

"Maybe you'll see another raccoon," Amy said. "That would be nice." She paused then said, "I never thought I'd hear myself say that."

He laughed and left to take the saddles off the horses.

After he pulled his saddle off Storm, he took it back to the fire where he planned to sleep and dropped it on the ground, then moved his rifle scabbard and bow out of the way of his bedroll. Seeing the bow caused him to think the area looked like good rabbit hunting country.

Of course, rabbits were *everywhere*, but some spots were more prime for hunting than others. *Like this place*, he thought. It was close to water with plenty of thick brush and bushes, places for rabbits to hide.

He carried the bow for small game but seldom hunted with it unless he was starving. *Like now*, he told himself. "I think I'll go rabbit huntin'," he declared aloud then strung the bow, took his quiver of arrows, and announced to Amy that he was going rabbit hunting. "Will you be all right here by yourself for a little while?" he asked her. "I won't be very far away. I can leave my rifle with you if you like, but if you yell, I should be close enough to hear you. Can you shoot a lever action rifle?"

"I think so," she said.

He showed her how to cock it and fire it. "You have to crank the empty shell out after every shot."

"I think I can do that. Good luck with your bow."

He started walking upstream and soon disappeared from her sight. She picked up a piece of the deer pemmican Bright Water had given them. "I'll eat this before I starve to death," she mumbled to herself, "but I sure hope he kills a rabbit. God, I wish I had a cup of coffee."

Walking quietly along with an arrow notched on his bowstring Crazy Wolf checked every likely-looking thicket he came to, shaking a branch here, stomping the ground there, rattling the brush, making any kind of disturbance he could to frighten a rabbit out of its hiding place. He had no luck until he stepped on a dead limb that cracked under his weight causing two rabbits to dart from the thicket. He picked one and let his arrow fly. The rabbit tumbled back legs over front, with the arrow protruding out of both sides of his body. Turning at once to see where the other rabbit had gone, he was quick enough to see the direction but that was all. Moving to the dying rabbit to put it out of its misery, he grabbed it then held it up to admire it. The sizable doe would make a nice meal for two people, but he would like to make it a feast and decided to look a little longer for the buck.

Amy put more wood on the fire, then turned to look in the direction Crazy Wolf had gone. No sign of the tall warrior and already the darkness was beginning to filter through the trees along the river. He had said he wouldn't be gone long, and she was sure it hadn't been as long as it seemed.

Then, as silently as the approaching darkness, he appeared, his bow in one hand, the other holding a rawhide string with two rabbits hanging from it. "You looked kinda hungry," he joked, "so I got one rabbit apiece for us."

"It's a good thing you did," she replied. "I feel like I could eat both of them."

"Then I'd better get down to the river and skin 'em, and get 'em ready to cook." He dropped his bow beside his saddle and moved down to the edge of the water.

If I go on a trip again sometime, she told herself, *I'll have to remember to take an Indian with me.* "If you skin them, I can butcher them and clean their entrails out," she called after him, genuinely looking forward to eating some fresh rabbit meat. "And you can cut a couple of green limbs to hold them over the fire."

They roasted both rabbits over the fire, but since one proved enough to take the edge off their hunger, they saved the other one for breakfast the next morning.

The night passed peacefully, and when Crazy Wolf woke up with the first light of morning, he made an effort to revive the fire as quietly as possible. It was good that she seemed in deep slumber. Sure she needed the rest, and with only about twenty miles to go, he was in no particular hurry to get started. He didn't notice when her eyes flickered open, for she continued to lay still.

Seeing him moving so carefully in an obvious effort not to disturb her, she thought about what a kind and gentle man he was. Then she remembered her first introduction to him when he pulled Lame Fox up by his hair and slashed his throat open.

A not so gentle touch, she thought. At that point, she had been terrified, thinking she had been captured by a savage more brutal than the one he killed. But when he took her away from the Sioux camp, he was respectful of her feelings and gave her his shirt to cover herself. He was the same man, however, who knelt on the rise by the river and methodically shot each Sioux warrior helplessly swimming in the middle of the river. It occurred to her that she did not really know either Cody Hunter or Crazy Wolf well enough to decide which was the dominant being. One thing she was certain of was that she had nothing to fear from him.

After consuming the other rabbit, they set out on the final leg of their journey together. And as Amy realized she was almost there she began to think again about her fate at the hands of the Sioux war party and how that had engraved a new image of herself in her mind. She wished she could stay away from the fort for a while longer, maybe in Wounded Owl's village, at least until the cuts and bruises on her face and body healed. The two women in Bright Water's tipi had tried to treat the worst of her wounds with some kind of grease. It had helped, but not enough to hide her shame. She hadn't liked the feel of it on her face, so had washed it off in the river before she retired to her blanket.

When their campfire was out, and Crazy Wolf had saddled all the horses, he placed Amy in the saddle as he had done before. When he stepped up on Storm and they set out on the final leg of their journey together, she found herself wishing she could stay with him a little longer. He knew what she had been subjected to at the hands of the Sioux warriors, yet seemed not to brand her for it.

Sensing the woman's reluctance to face her father and the people at the fort, Crazy Wolf made no effort to increase the pace of the horses.

At Amy's request, they stopped, supposedly to rest the horses, when they came to a little creek about halfway there.

"Do you want me to go rabbit huntin' again?" he asked in jest.

"No," she answered and chuckled. "I just suddenly felt tired. I guess I'm a little emotional right now about seeing my father."

"I think I understand how you must feel, but you should remember you are a brave woman. You survived your attackers. If you have any concerns about me, put them out of your mind. I have no reason to tell anyone what happened to you. As far as I am concerned, you escaped before anything serious had a chance to happen. I am your friend. I will not betray your trust."

"Yes, you are my friend. Only a friend would do for me what you have done. And I am your friend." She wanted to hug his neck but was afraid it might spook him. "Just put me back on my horse, friend. I'm ready to face my father, even if we have to swim across the Yellowstone again."

He laughed and picked her up and placed her in the saddle.

Much to Amy's relief, the ferry was still in operation across the river. Operated by Clarence Duggan and his son, Daniel, Clarence was quick to assure her the barge could carry her, Crazy Wolf, and all their horses safely across. "We've ferried a whole cavalry patrol across more than once," he said.

Unable to get the price lower than a dollar-seventy-five, Crazy Wolf had no choice but to pay it. As Amy was not willing to swim across, he figured it was money well spent. Once across they still had a few miles to go before finally reaching the fort, so he drove his herd of seven army horses right through the center of the fledgling town.

They made quite an entrance at the fort when the five riderless horses, all with cavalry saddles, loped onto the parade ground, followed by two without saddles, a Crow scout, and what appeared at first glance to be a Crow woman.

Crazy Wolf dismounted and lifted Amy off her horse. "We'll be headin' for that door yonder." He pointed at Company B's building. "That's where your daddy oughta be, if he ain't gone to the mess hall. I'll be along in a minute," he said as a soldier he recognized ran toward them. But she waited for him to go with her.

"Crazy Wolf! What the hell?" Sergeant Lionel Green demanded. "Where'd them horses come from? And you know better'n to bring that Injun squaw in here!"

"This ain't an Indian woman. This is Captain Boyd's daughter."

"Beggin' your pardon, ma'am," Green blubbered awkwardly. "I didn't go to— I didn't take a good look at you. I mean I'm mighty glad to see you're safe and sound. When we heard you was took by the Sioux . . ." Completely flustered, he couldn't complete a thought.

Then he remembered. "Captain Boyd's in the mess hall. I'll go tell him you're here. Do you wanna go wait in his quarters? Oh, that's right, though, you probably ain't got no key to his quarters."

"She'll wait for him in the B Company orderly room," Crazy Wolf said.

"Good idea," the sergeant said. "I'll go tell him that. What about those horses?"

"The six horses with the saddles are the horses Miss Boyd's escorts were ridin' when they were attacked. All six were killed. The other two were pullin' a wagon. I brought 'em back because they're the army's property. I expect Corporal Walker and Private Castle musta reported all that when they came back."

"Well, Walker did," Green replied. "He reported the whole story. I'm sure Captain Boyd wants to talk to you. Why don't you go wait outside his orderly room."

"Yeah, I'll do that. I'll bet Miss Boyd would appreciate it if you were to tell the captain to bring her something to eat from the officer's mess."

"Yes, ma'am," Green said to Amy. "I'll suggest that to your father."

"Thank you, Sergeant. I would appreciate that very much."

"I'll send word to the stable to come get them horses," he said to Crazy Wolf before he turned to leave them.

Detecting a bit of irritation in his tone, the scout replied, "'Preciate it, Sergeant. I'da drove 'em down to the stable, but I thought it best to deliver Miss Boyd to her father."

"Of course," Green replied as he walked away.

"I don't believe the sergeant wants to be bothered

with those horses," Crazy Wolf commented to Amy. "He shoulda seen all the trouble we had gettin' 'em this far, shouldn't he?"

She chuckled, thinking about it.

"Well," he said then, "let's go wait for your father, Miss Boyd."

"You can drop the *miss*," she countered. "You know I'm always *Amy* to you."

"All right, Amy. You can call me Mr. Hunter," he joked.

"Like hell, I will," she came back in kind. "I'll call you Crazy Wolf."

He was glad to see her mood lighten up a little before she had to meet her father. He had worried her tragic experience with the Sioux captors would remain a weight on her for the rest of her life. He also knew that would depend a great deal on her father's attitude toward her. It might not be the best reunion for her father to see her in a deerskin dress and moccasins, but Crazy Wolf felt certain it would be better than to have seen her in the few tattered garments the war party had left her.

Private Richard Bryant, seated at the company clerk's desk, removed his feet from the corner of the desk when he heard someone outside the door. Seconds later, he was astonished to see what he thought was an Indian couple enter the orderly room. "Can I help you folks?"

"We're waitin' to see the captain when he gets back from eatin' dinner. Crazy Wolf didn't recall ever having seen the soldier before. "The lady might be more comfortable sittin' in the chair in the captain's office. I can just wait here on this bench."

"I don't know if it'd be all right for her to go in the captain's office," Bryant said. "The company clerk oughta be back any minute now. I'm just settin' here while he goes to eat. It ought not be long now."

Crazy Wolf was about to inform him who Amy was when the door opened, much to Bryant's relief, and Private George Cousins walked in.

CHAPTER 6

"Crazy Wolf!" Cousins blurted when he saw who was standing just inside. "You came back!" He stood there holding the door open, looking genuinely surprised, and ignoring the frantic silent little signals Bryant was sending.

"Did you think I wouldn't?"

"I'm just surprised you did," Cousins answered, dumbfounded when he closed the door and discovered Amy standing over near the window. Only then did he see the reason for Bryant's apparent finger spasms of a few seconds before. Her costume gave Cousins pause at first glance, but after staring wide-eyed for a moment, he asked, "Are you Amy Boyd?"

"Yes, I am," she replied.

"Holy mackerel!" He exhaled, flabbergasted. "Your father's eatin' dinner at the officers' mess. I'll go tell him you're here. No, wait! Bryant, you go tell him."

"No need to do that," Crazy Wolf offered. "Sergeant Green knows we're here. He went to tell Captain Boyd we're waitin' for him here."

"Good," Cousins replied. "That's good." He was trying to think what Captain Boyd would want him to do. "You might be more comfortable sitting in that chair in the captain's office, ma'am."

Amy thanked him and went into her father's office.

Cousins looked back at Bryant. "Well, what are you hanging around for? I'm back now. You're relieved."

"Oh . . . right," Bryant replied, disappointed. He had hoped to stay long enough to see what happened when the captain returned. He walked out the door to see Captain Boyd coming from the officers' mess, walking at a rapid pace and carrying a tray covered with a cloth. Bryant saluted him when he passed, and Boyd returned it with a nod of his head since his hands were full.

Boyd kicked the orderly room door with his foot and yelled, "Cousins! Open the door!"

Standing near the door, Crazy Wolf opened it for him, and Boyd charged into the room.

"Crazy Wolf! Where's my daughter?"

He pointed toward his office.

"Don't go anywhere," Boyd said as he passed by him. "I want to talk to you." He went into his office and stopped abruptly, astonished, when Amy stepped forward to meet him. He placed the tray on his desk, then turned to embrace her. "Thank God you're safe. When we got Corporal Walker's report about the escort detail I sent to get you, and Crazy Wolf's desertion, I ordered a fifteen-man patrol to search for you. How did you end up with Crazy Wolf? I can't believe he had the gall to come back to this post."

"Papa," Amy replied. "What are you saying? The only reason I am alive today is because Crazy Wolf came to rescue me from the savages who killed the soldiers bringing me here. He found the Sioux camp where they had taken me and took me away from there. When they came after us, he killed them, all of them, then brought me here."

Her statement caused her father to pause and reconsider

the information he had been given by Corporal Walker. "I'm going to have to get all the facts on this business. But why are you dressed up like an Indian?"

She looked at her father for a long moment, amazed that he suspected Crazy Wolf of anything dishonest or evil. Then she answered his question. "Because Cody, or Crazy Wolf as you call him, didn't want you to see me like he found me. And since there were no dress shops between here and the Sioux camp where he found me, we had to settle for a Crow village for my new dress. I had hoped that you would approve of my choice."

He paused a moment to look at her. She could see by the hurt in his eyes that he was looking at the cuts and bruises on her face.

"Of course, I approve of your choice," he said. "I think you make a perfect little Indian princess. Welcome home, darling. I thought I would never see you again. I'll take you to see our new home, complete with a kitchen and two bedrooms. But for now, I brought you some food. Sit down and eat it before it gets any colder."

"I am hungry," she admitted. "I had half of a rabbit for breakfast." She laughed. "Crazy Wolf shot it with a bow and arrow."

Her father frowned. "I'm going to talk to him now. I received a report from Corporal Walker that reflected poorly on Crazy Wolf. He said when they were going to bury the bodies of the men in your escort, Crazy Wolf refused to help, and said he had better things to do. Then he rode off and left them to honor the dead."

"That was before I knew him, so I don't know what happened at the place where they ambushed us. But I don't believe Crazy Wolf would have done what the corporal said. I know he is an honorable man."

"Eat your dinner, and I'll go hear his version of what

happened at the site of that ambush," her father told her. He turned and walked back into the orderly room.

"Cousins was tellin' me you got a full report from Corporal Walker on that little detail you sent the three of us on," Crazy Wolf said.

"Yes, I did," Boyd replied. "And I have to tell you it was not a very good one when it came to your performance. He said you refused to help bury the bodies of the soldiers who died trying to protect my daughter. Is that true?"

"Yes, that's true. It sounds pretty bad when you say it like that, but there was more to it than that."

"Well, I'd like to hear your version of the incident because right now the army is considering relieving you of your duties as a scout for the US Army . . . here and at every other post in the country."

Truly astonished, Crazy Wolf had anticipated nothing short of a celebration for the return of the captain's daughter. He was willing to bet Walker and Castle never even buried the seven soldiers that were massacred. "To paint a better picture, I'd wanna point out the fact that Walker and I don't care much for each other to begin with. I stuck in his craw for some reason.

"Now back to that scene at the massacre. It was my opinion those men were dead, and there wasn't anything we could do to bring 'em back to life. But your daughter was alive, and she was being carried off by a band of Sioux warriors. I said we had to track 'em while their trail was relatively fresh. Walker said no, there wasn't any use. Your daughter was good as dead. But I knew I could track that war party, and as long as there was a chance, that's what we had to do. That's when he told me he was in charge, and we would forget the Sioux war party, bury our soldiers, and come back here. I wasn't ready to give up on your daughter, so I went without them. And to tell you the truth, I'm mighty glad I did, especially after I found out what a fine young lady she is. I didn't go back to see if Walker and Castle really buried anybody or not. I thought it was more important to get your daughter somewhere safe."

"Amy just told me there were seven warriors in that party of Sioux," Boyd said.

"That's right. There were seven of 'em."

"She said you killed all of them."

"That's right. I had to kill one of 'em to free her, but the other six came after us." Crazy Wolf went on to tell him how he set up a target range in the middle of the Yellowstone River. Then he completed the story up to their arrival at the fort.

"That's one helluva story," Boyd said. "And I believe it. But I'll tell you the truth, if I didn't have Amy to confirm it, I'm not sure I could, especially that part about luring them into the middle of the river. Whether it's true or not, I do want to express my deepest thanks for saving my daughter's life and bringing her safely to me." He offered his hand and Crazy Wolf accepted it. "I expect I'll reopen the investigation of Corporal Walker's charges against you in the morning. You aren't planning to go anywhere are you?"

Crazy Wolf said that he wasn't, and that he would be at the Crow camp on the river with the rest of the Crow scouts. "If that's all you need from me right now, I'll go give my horse some attention."

"I imagine Amy might like to say so long, if you want to stick your head into my office," Boyd suggested.

"Yes, sir. Thank you. I surely hope she likes it here at Fort Keogh." Crazy Wolf walked over to the door and looked in. "I'll be leavin' now. I hope everything works out

the way you want it here. Let me know if you get a cravin'
for raccoon. They know how to get in touch with me."

Amy got up from the desk where she was enjoying a
plate of beef stew and a cup of cold coffee and hurried
around to give him a big hug. "Thank you, thank you,
thank you for coming to get me."

"You're welcome. Just call me anytime you get on the
wrong path. Now, finish up that plate. You're startin' to
look a little skinny."

He left the Company B orderly room and stepped up on
Storm's back, then turned the big dun toward the road that
led to the army stables. He was allowed some privileges at
the stables since he was a scout and he thought to take advantage of one of them. Storm had worked pretty hard for
quite a few days, and he was due some grain.

Crazy Wolf always got along well with Sergeant Roy
Grissom, who usually gave him free rein with the horse
feed.

"I was wonderin' when you'd show up," the sergeant
said, seeing the scout pull up to the horse trough. "I had a
couple of the boys round up them horses you turned loose
on the parade ground."

"I didn't turn 'em loose. Those horses came to the fort
on their own. I was just followin' 'em. Storm worked
pretty hard on this trip. I oughta give him a portion of
grain."

Grissom chuckled. "I'll bet," he scoffed. Then he got
serious for a moment. "It ain't a very good sight to see
them empty saddles comin' home, though."

"I reckon not," Crazy Wolf said solemnly.

Grissom remained serious. "Do you know what Ben
Walker reported about you when him and Castle got back
to the fort?"

"Yes, I just found out from Captain Boyd a little while ago."

Grissom told him, anyway. "He said you refused to help 'em bury the bodies of the soldiers that was killed, and you deserted the detail. I told him that don't sound like you a-tall. Lionel Green came in here to tell me about the horses runnin' loose. He said you brought Captain Boyd's daughter with you. Said she was dressed up like an Injun."

"I reckon that's what Walker calls *desertion* when I left to track the Sioux war party that ran off with Boyd's daughter, instead of helping him and Castle dig some graves."

"I knew it had to be somethin' like that. I never believed that lyin' snake for a second."

"'Preciate you sayin' that, Sergeant," Crazy Wolf said.

Grissom suddenly frowned. "Speak of the devil." He was looking toward the front of the stable. "Here, help yourself." He handed over the grain bucket. "I'll go see what he wants."

With his back turned toward the front, Crazy Wolf couldn't see who the sergeant referred to, but from Grissom's tone, he could pretty well guess. With no particular desire to talk to Walker, he took the bucket and went into the barn to get his horse some grain.

He was not going to be able to avoid Walker, however, for the corporal had seen him going to the stable. Walker went over to the watering trough where Storm was. "Well, there he is," he announced as Crazy Wolf came to his horse. "The big hero. Brought the captain's daughter back, didja? She musta figured out a way to escape, or they left her beside the trail somewhere after they were done with her. She musta stumbled over you on her way back here."

Feeling nothing but disgust for the man, Crazy Wolf had no intention of discussing the chain of events that had brought Amy and him safely to the fort. "Walker, I don't choose to discuss the captain's daughter with you in the stable. I don't think the captain would appreciate it, and I'm damn sure the lady wouldn't appreciate it. I understand you made an official report on my misconduct. I've given my report on the matter to Captain Boyd. I'm satisfied to let the soldiers handle the issue." He walked on past him and started feeding his horse.

"He talks mighty damn fancy for a man that's turned Injun, don't he, Grissom? He even turned the captain's daughter into a little squaw. I reckon she decided she liked it after them Sioux bucks got done with her."

"All right, Walker, you've gone too far now," Crazy Wolf said. "That poor lady has gone through hell and made it back, and she's too fine a lady to be discussed in the stables by outhouse slime like you. Keep your mouth shut about her 'cause the next insult about her that comes outta your mouth is gonna get shoved down your throat."

"You heard him threaten me, Grissom, didn't you? Mr. Crazy Wolf, a damn Crow scout, threatenin' a corporal in the US Army. Who the hell does he think he is? You better get smart before you go makin' any threats. I'll have you throwed outta the scouts. Then see if your little squaw likes livin' on the reservation with you and the rest of the Crows when she's raisin' that little Sioux bastard she's already carryin' in her belly."

It was too much to tolerate. Crazy Wolf launched his body like a battering ram, full speed, into Walker's midsection, driving him off his feet to land hard on his back after flying several feet in the air. The hapless man landed solidly, knocking the wind out of his lungs, with the fierce Crazy Wolf on top of him, his skinning knife in his hand, the point of which was pressed under Walker's chin.

In shock and knowing he was going to die when he felt

a trickle of blood run down his neck from the tip of the knife under his chin, he tried to scream. But with no wind in his lungs, the only sound he could make sounded like a squeal from a small child.

"Crazy Wolf! Crazy Wolf!" Sergeant Grissom shouted. "Don't kill him, man! They'll hang you! Let him up!"

The scout paused but continued to hold the knife at Walker's throat.

"Let him go," Grissom pleaded. "He ain't worth a hangin'."

Crazy Wolf sat there for a few moments more before pulling his knife away from Walker's throat. He wiped the little bit of blood off the tip of the blade, using Walker's shirt for the purpose. "If I had meant to kill him, he would already be dead. This is only a warning. Next time, I will finish it." He returned the knife to the sheath on his belt and got up off the quivering man.

Walker rolled over to his hands and knees, still trying to fill his lungs with air. He knew he had seen his death only moments away.

"Was there somethin' you wanted here at the stable?" Grissom asked him.

Walker struggled to his feet and tried to talk. After a few tries, he was able to make a rasping sound. "You made a big mistake, Injun," he managed, trying to regain a little bravado.

"I know. I should have killed you. You can thank Sergeant Grissom for that." Standing there, poised to make a sudden move if necessary, Crazy Wolf watched Walker for any sign of retaliation. His rifle, which was his weapon of preference, was in the saddle scabbard on his horse. But he was comfortable with the Colt handgun he wore on his left side, the handle facing forward for an easy cross-draw with his right hand.

"Another time, things might turn out different," Walker suddenly said, turned, and walked away.

"Damn, Crazy Wolf," Grissom declared as they watched him depart, "you've got yourself an enemy right there. That's for dang sure. And I ain't talkin' about callin' you out in the street. A shot in the back is more likely his style. You'd best watch yourself, boy, even when you're on the post."

"I intend to. Right now, I'm thinkin' I'd like to find something to eat. It's too late to get anything at the mess hall." He chuckled. "Captain Boyd brought a big tray of food to his daughter, but he didn't bring any for me."

"You can get you some coffee and ham biscuits at the canteen," Grissom suggested. "That oughta hold you till supper."

"That sure would, but I can't go there."

"Hell, if you're broke, I'll lend you some money."

"I've got some money. I can't go there because they don't serve Indians."

Grissom fixed an impatient look upon him. "Hell, Crazy Wolf, you're not a real Injun. Most ever'body on the post knows you're a white man. What is your name? I knew it once, but I can't recollect it."

"Crazy Wolf," he replied, laughing.

"Damn it, you know what I mean. Your white name, the name your real parents gave you."

"Cody Hunter."

"Cody Hunter," Grissom repeated. "Why, that's a fine name. I'd use that name if I was you. It fits you better'n Crazy Wolf. How'd you pick a name like that, anyway?"

"I didn't pick it. My Crow father gave me that name." Crazy Wolf went on to tell Grissom about the massacre of his family and how Spotted Pony had found a wolf guarding him. "They said the wolf had to be crazy to stay there until the Crow hunting party came. So that's the Crow name he picked for me."

"That's a helluva story, Crazy Wolf. I'll go to the canteen and buy you some coffee and ham biscuits. I might get a couple for myself. Come to think about it, I'll just buy the ham biscuits and we'll just build a pot of coffee here."

"That sure suits my taste. But I've got some money. I'll pay for the ham biscuits, since you're supplyin' the coffee and goin' to get the biscuits."

So that's what they did. Grissom rode Storm to the canteen, since it was already saddled, and Crazy Wolf set the coffeepot up to boil on Grissom's little iron stove. They enjoyed an uninterrupted repast in the fresh air by the corral. The two of them had always gotten along well together, but after their afternoon coffee, they became real friends.

After the coffee and biscuits were done, Crazy Wolf headed to the Crow scout camp down by the river. He knew his brother was probably anxious to know what had happened to prevent him from returning with Corporal Walker and Private Castle. That thought brought up doubts again and he decided to seek out Private Castle and ask him about the burial of the seven soldiers. He had an idea he might get the truth from him. Castle didn't seem to be cut from the same bolt of cloth that had produced Ben Walker.

"Crazy Wolf!" Bloody Axe called out when he saw his brother ride into the Crow camp by the river.

His greeting caused the others gathered in the center of the camp to turn and look at him. They knew Crazy Wolf had not returned with Corporal Walker and Private Castle, and were at once eager to hear the reason.

Cliff Freeman was also in the gathering, which reminded Crazy Wolf he should have let Freeman know he was back and available for assignment again. *Good,* he thought. *Now he can see it for himself.* Stepping down from his horse, Crazy Wolf returned the greetings from his fellow scouts.

Cliff Freeman, chief of the Crow scouts, stepped forward to meet him. "Funny thing, you ride in here right after I just got done telling them you didn't come back from that last job. Maybe you'd better bring me up to date on what's goin' on with you."

"I tell him you be back," Bloody Axe interrupted. "They say you deserted."

Crazy Wolf looked at Bloody Axe and smiled, then he responded to Freeman's request. "Corporal Walker didn't waste any time making his report, did he?" Once again, Crazy Wolf went through the sequence of events that led up to his eventual return to the fort and Amy Boyd's reunion with her father. "Captain Boyd told me there would be another meeting on Walker's report, since he now knows all the facts of the matter. And I reckon I'm ready to go on patrol again."

Freeman hesitated, then said, "I can't send you on patrol again until I get new orders. The orders I just got said you were prohibited from accompanying any troop activity, pending your final discharge from the scouts." He looked at Crazy Wolf in helpless dismay. "I believe what you just told me, but I'll have to get new orders before I can assign you to a new job." He shook his head and exhaled a deep breath. "Lieutenant Ainsworth is takin' a patrol out tomorrow morning for about fifteen days he expects. He asked for you and Bloody Axe. I'm givin' him Red Moon, instead of you."

Crazy Wolf didn't reply at once, then he nodded slowly. "Red Moon is a good scout, maybe better than me. Have I been fired from the scouts?"

"It doesn't say that on my orders," Freeman replied. "It just said don't send you out right now."

Crazy Wolf calmly nodded his understanding of the orders, based on the report submitted by Corporal Walker.

Bloody Axe, however, was not indifferent about his brother's suspension. "Everybody knows Crazy Wolf is not deserter. I need to be here for hearing. Send someone in my place."

"Lieutenant Ainsworth asked for you," Freeman said.

"You say Lieutenant ask for Crazy Wolf and me," Bloody Axe insisted. "You not send him what he ask for, anyway."

"You've been hired by the army to scout," Freeman patiently reminded him. "You're paid to go where we send you."

"Send other scout. Don't pay me." Bloody Axe did not want to be gone for two weeks without knowing what was going to happen to Crazy Wolf.

Freeman was not surprised by the Crow warrior's fierce loyalty to a man he considered his brother, so he didn't make a big deal of his refusal. "All right. I'll send Turns His Horse in your place, and you can stay here and see how the hearing goes."

"When they say you deserted and were not coming back," Bloody Axe said, "I told them you would come back. But if you didn't come back tonight, I was going to go look for you in the morning. I have been thinking. Maybe it is time to quit this scouting business, you and me, and go to the high mountains like we talk about before. Maybe on the way we could go to Red Lodge to visit Spotted Pony. He may not be here many more moons."

"I don't know, Bloody Axe," Crazy Wolf said, also speaking the Crow tongue. "Maybe you are right. Sometimes I have thought this way, too. You are right, we should go to visit Spotted Pony. We will talk about this later, after they have the hearing to clear my name."

CHAPTER 7

On the chance that he might see Private Fred Castle, Crazy Wolf decided to ride back into the fort before the bugler sounded evening Mess Call. He didn't own a watch, so he could only guess the time of day. But he knew after the twelve-noon dinnertime, the bugler blew a Drill Call, and that kept the men busy at whatever the drill was until the bugle told them drill time was over. That was called Recall. About half an hour later the bugler blew Stable Call. If he was lucky, he might catch sight of Castle between Recall and Stable Call on his way to take care of his horse. He had a very slim chance but couldn't think of anything better.

Close to time for Recall, he rode over to the back corner of the corral and dropped Storm's reins to the ground and waited.

About fifteen minutes later he suddenly heard the bugle for Recall. That meant it was four o'clock, and the next call would be Stable Call at four-thirty. It wasn't long before the men started showing up at the stable, anticipating Stable Call.

He focused his attention on them but saw no sign of Castle until after the bugle sounded Stable Call, and he almost missed him then. Castle hurried into the stables with two other soldiers, laughing about something that must have happened during drill time. Crazy Wolf hurried toward the stable door and followed after them. As soon as they were inside, the three men split up to go to their individual stalls.

"Private Castle," the scout called when he caught up with him.

Castle turned around, then recoiled in surprise when he saw who it was. "Hey! Crazy Wolf," he exclaimed. "When did you get back?"

"This mornin'. One of those horses yours?" He nodded toward the two horses in the stall, thinking to start with a little small talk.

"Nah, my horse is in the pasture with the rest of the nags. This is just the stall I'm responsible for. What happened to you after you went after them Sioux? Did you ever catch 'em?"

"Yep. I caught 'em."

"No," Castle responded. "Did you really? Was the woman with 'em?"

"Yep, she was with 'em. I brought her here this mornin'. She's with her father now."

"Well, I'll swear, that's really fine news to hear." He unconsciously looked around as if not wanting anyone to hear before saying, "Wait till ol' Walker hears about that. He said you was full of it. Said there weren't no way in hell you'd catch up with them Sioux, much less save that poor woman."

"I was lucky, I reckon," Crazy Wolf said. "I did feel kinda guilty, though. Me off trackin' those Sioux while you and Walker were back there diggin' all those graves."

"Shoot," Castle scoffed. "Are you serious? We never touched a shovel. You know he ain't gonna dig no holes, and he didn't wanna wait around for me to dig 'em. He said the most important thing was to get back here as soon as possible to give Captain Boyd the bad news."

"What did you do with those seven bodies?"

"We didn't do nothin' with 'em. Just left 'em to feed the buzzards," Castle said, looking kind of sheepish at that point. "He said it was best if we don't talk about it. But I expect it's all right to tell you about it 'cause you were on that mission with us."

"That's right. Matter of fact, I think it's all right to talk about it to anybody now, since the captain's daughter is here all safe and sound. That was the whole purpose of that mission. Right?"

"That's right," Castle agreed. "Did you have any trouble trackin' those Sioux? How many of them was there?"

"There were seven of them. And there was really no trouble trackin' them because there were the eight extra cavalry horses they were drivin' with 'em. I doubt they were worried about anybody comin' after 'em, anyway. The important thing was to get to them before they killed Amy Boyd."

"How'd you snatch her?" Castle wanted to know the whole story. "Did you slip into the camp that night and steal her?"

"Something like that," Crazy Wolf replied.

Castle asked next if he killed any of the Sioux. He kept pumping for details until Crazy Wolf finally gave up and told him the whole story. It seemed to give Castle a great deal of satisfaction.

"Is that woman gonna be all right?" he asked, seeming genuinely concerned. "You know, a lotta women that gets captured by the Injuns go crazy in the head."

"I think this one is gonna be all right. She's young and strong."

"I hope so, for the captain's sake," Castle said. "I think she's all the family he's got." He looked around him then at the work going on in the other stalls. "I'd best get to work on this stall, or I'll be back here tonight finishin' up."

"Maybe I can give you a hand," Crazy Wolf offered.

"No, thank ya, anyway," Castle replied. "Ain't enough room for both of us to work with two horses in here. Besides, it ain't gonna take much."

Crazy Wolf left the stable, thinking to look left and right before stepping out in the open, remembering Bloody Axe's warning to watch his back. His brother was concerned after hearing about the tussle he had with Walker at the stable.

Now Crazy Wolf's priority was to clear his name on the scouts roster. Since Mess Call had not been sounded yet, he hoped to catch Boyd in his office before he left for supper. Maybe he had not gone to his quarters yet. Grinning, he wondered if Amy had found anything in her new home to cook for her father.

He was in luck. The captain was still in.

"I'm glad you stopped in, Crazy Wolf," Boyd said in greeting. "I was just getting ready to run over to my quarters to have supper with Amy. Then I have to be back at six to stand Retreat. I wanted to tell you we're holding a court tomorrow afternoon to review those charges against you. I want you at the headquarters building at one o'clock. We'll be meeting in Major Grambling's office, right next to Colonel Miles' office. All right?"

"Yes, sir. I'll be there. And sir, I talked to Private Castle today. He said they did not take the time to bury those six men you sent to get Miss Boyd. They just left them lay where they found 'em."

That captured Boyd's attention right away. "You think he'd be willing to testify to that in a court hearing?"

"I think he might," Crazy Wolf answered.

"I might summon him in the morning. I want you back working for the army."

"There's one more thing I think you need to know in case it comes up tomorrow. I ran into Corporal Walker in the stable earlier today. He made trouble. I shut him up. Nobody got hurt."

Boyd considered that for a moment. Since the scout wasn't forthcoming with any details, he asked, "Was anybody else there when it happened?"

"Sergeant Grissom was there."

"All right, then, I'll see you tomorrow in Major Grambling's office."

"Yes, sir. I'll be there." Crazy Wolf walked out of the orderly room just as the bugler blew Mess Call, so he headed in that direction.

Without knowing if he had lost his eating privileges when he had been pulled off the scouting roster, he waited outside the mess hall until Bloody Axe and some of the other Crow scouts showed up. He hadn't thought to ask Captain Boyd when he was at his office. Gambling on the possibility the cooks in the mess hall didn't know and probably didn't care, he walked through the line with Bloody Axe and the others, and no one on the serving line paid him any attention. His presence did not go undetected, however.

Bloody Axe nudged him while they were eating and asked, "Is that Corporal Walker?"

Crazy Wolf looked toward the larger section of the mess hall where the enlisted men ate. "Yes, that's Walker."

The corporal was standing near the end of the chow line, holding his plate and cup. Evidently on his way to a table, he was staring in their direction, obviously upset to see Crazy Wolf there.

"He doesn't look like he enjoys seeing me eat. Maybe he's already found out about the hearing tomorrow."

Walker turned around and went back to the head of the chow line where the mess sergeant was standing.

"Uh-oh. Maybe I'd better eat fast. I might be leaving soon."

They watched as Walker talked to the mess sergeant, but the sergeant didn't seem aware of anything having to do with Crazy Wolf. They talked for a few minutes more, then Walker took his supper to the table and sat down. He still looked irritated, and the mess sergeant busied himself with a check on the kettles and pots on the serving line.

After an uneventful night in the Crow camp, Crazy Wolf ate breakfast the next morning with Bloody Axe and the others, again with no questions from the mess sergeant. Then Turns His Horse and Red Moon left on a fifteen-day patrol with Lieutenant Ainsworth.

Left with nothing to do until one o'clock, Crazy Wolf spent the morning in the Crow camp, cleaning his rifle and handgun, with special emphasis on the Colt six-gun that had taken a thorough bath in the Yellowstone River. He went back on the post when he heard the twelve o'clock Mess Call, took his time eating, then reported to Major Grambling's office a few minutes before one.

Private Castle and Sergeant Grissom were already seated in a row of half a dozen chairs facing the major's desk. An empty chair stood on each side of the desk and one empty chair had been placed apart from all the others off to the side. Crazy Wolf was pleased to see Castle there but was surprised to see Grissom.

He walked over and sat down beside him. "I didn't expect to see you here, Sergeant. What are you doin' here?"

"I'm a witness to when you almost killed that poor defenseless corporal," Grissom japed and gave him a big grin.

A few minutes before the hour, Captain Boyd came in and promptly told Crazy Wolf he was supposed to sit in the chair on the end of the row. Crazy Wolf moved to the designated chair, and Boyd sat down beside Grissom.

At precisely one o'clock, Major Grambling came into the room, accompanied by a corporal who carried a notebook, ink bottle, and a couple of pens. Two soldiers carrying rifles followed them in and assumed positions behind the major's desk. The corporal sat down in one of the chairs beside the desk and placed his ink bottle on the desk beside him.

"Who are we missing, Captain?" Major Grambling asked.

"Sir, we're missing Corporal Walker, whose report is what this hearing is all about," Boyd replied.

"Was he informed of this hearing?"

"He was, sir," Boyd answered.

"Well, he's not making a very good impression on his reliability so far, is he?" Grambling remarked. He was about to say more, but Walker came in the door just then. "I hope we're not inconveniencing you, Corporal, if the fort is under an attack or something of more importance to you."

"No, sir. I just let the time slip up on me," Walker responded and sat down beside Captain Boyd, who told him to sit in the chair on the other side of the major's desk. He looked uncertain but stood up again. The major motioned toward the vacant chair.

Walker asked, "What? Am I on trial here?"

"Actually your report is on trial," Grambling said. "At least, the accuracy of it. Have a seat and we'll get on with it." He waited until Walker sat down, then continued. "The clerk will read the report you submitted on your assignment to intercept a special detail escorting Amy Boyd to this post, and your recommendation to discipline Crow scout, Crazy Wolf, for his disobedience of orders and refusal to help in the burial of seven soldiers killed in an ambush of that escort detail." He paused a moment to let that sink in.

"Read the report, please, Corporal Bowen."

The clerk read Walker's report to Captain Boyd. It was filled with accusations of outright disobedience, disrespect for the deaths of the slain soldiers, and a charge of desertion. It ended with recommendations to dishonorably discharge Crazy Wolf from the roles of Crow scouts from this post and all other posts in the country.

Major Grambling asked Walker, "Is that an accurate reading of your report?"

"Yes, sir. And every word of it's true," Walker said, glaring at Crazy Wolf.

"All right. Captain Boyd, he's your witness."

Boyd stood up. "Corporal Walker, is it your contention that Crow scout—"

"Is it my what?" Walker interrupted.

"I'll rephrase it. Are you saying Crazy Wolf refused to help you and Private Castle when it was time to bury the bodies of the seven soldiers who were killed trying to protect my daughter?"

"That's a fact," Walker said.

"And he rode away and never returned to the patrol?"

"That's right," Walker contended smugly.

"Major Grambling, I'm through with this witness. I'd like to call—"

Again Walker interrupted. "What about yesterday at the stables when that wild Injun jumped me and held a knife to my throat? Ain't you gonna ask anything about that?"

Boyd paused to fix his gaze on Walker, astonished by his stupidity. "All right, we'll address that altercation next. What is your memory of that incident?"

"I remember it good. We was just talkin' and all of a sudden that crazy Injun flew at me and knocked me down and held a knife to my throat. He was fixin' to cut my throat, but Sergeant Grissom over there stopped him."

"All right, thank you, Corporal. You can step down now." Boyd waited until Walker got out of the chair and sat back down in the row of chairs. "I'll call Sergeant Grissom to take the stand now."

When Grissom sat down, Boyd produced a Bible from his satchel. "Sergeant, you mind placing your hand on this Bible and swearing that the testimony you're about to give is the truth, so help you, God?"

"No, sir. I don't mind a-tall." He placed his hand on the Bible and swore to tell the truth.

"Now, Sergeant, you witnessed the incident between Corporal Walker and the accused?" Grissom said that he did, so Boyd asked, "Did the accused, Crazy Wolf, attack Corporal Walker?"

"Yes, sir. He did. He sprang like a mountain lion and knocked Walker to the ground. He held his knife up against Walker's throat and warned him not to make any more insultin' remarks about your daughter. There wasn't nothin' stoppin' him from cuttin' Walker's throat. I reckon he just didn't wanna kill nobody."

"So you're saying he acted in defense of my daughter's honor. Is that right?"

"Yes, sir. Exactly," Grissom replied.

"All right, Sergeant, you can step down." Boyd turned to the judge. "Since Sergeant Grissom was the only witness to the altercation, the prosecution has nothing more to present. I want to move along and get to the question of desertion and refusal to bury the dead. I call Private Castle to the stand."

Walker glared at Castle as he walked up and sat in the witness chair.

"Do you believe in God, Private Castle?" Boyd asked.

"Yes, sir. I reckon I do," Castle answered.

Boyd had him swear on the Bible to tell the truth. Castle did so, looking very much like he was afraid not to.

"You just heard Corporal Walker's report. Do you agree it is an accurate accounting of what took place at the scene of that ambush?"

"I reckon so," Castle answered.

"So, you agree, Crazy Wolf refused to help bury the dead."

Castle hesitated. "Well, he didn't exactly hesitate to help. He wanted to go after them Sioux warriors right away. He said he could track 'em and maybe catch up with 'em before they killed the woman."

"The woman being Amy Boyd, my daughter, right?"

"Yes, sir. Crazy Wolf said that was the reason we were sent up there, to make sure she was safe, and he wanted to go after her while the trail was still fresh."

"And it turned out to be the right call, didn't it?" Boyd couldn't resist asking.

"Yes, sir. I reckon it did 'cause he caught up with 'em and saved her." Castle grinned when he said it.

"Tell me, Private Castle," Boyd continued, "after Crazy Wolf went after the Sioux war party, how long did it take you and Corporal Walker to bury the bodies of those seven men?"

"Sir?" Castle hesitated, not sure what to say.

"I asked how long did it actually take you and Corporal Walker to dig those seven graves? Or maybe you just dug one great big grave and buried them all in that one hole. Whatever. About how long do you think it took to do that before you were finished and started back here? I wonder how long it takes two men to dig seven graves." He waited for an answer.

"Well, you see, sir, I can't tell you how long it takes. We never touched a shovel. Corporal Walker said our job was to get back here as soon as we could, so we could tell you your daughter was dead."

"Why, you little double-crossin'—" Walker blurted, before one of the armed guards silenced him with a poke of his rifle butt.

Captain Boyd turned to the major to sum up his hearing. "I think the testimony of the witnesses confirm the fact that Corporal Walker's report was grossly in error, apparently on purpose, and an attempt to besmirch the name and honor of the scout, Crazy Wolf. If you would like more information regarding Crazy Wolf's integrity and bravery, my daughter can give you a full report on how he rescued her from within the Sioux camp then fled with her and killed all seven of the Sioux warriors before bringing her safely to this post."

Major Grambling wasted no time in removing any restrictions that had been placed upon Crazy Wolf's service with the scouts. Then he considered Corporal Ben Walker. "Corporal, there has to be a punishment for such despicable attempts to slander a man's reputation. I feel like I ought to have you shot for what you tried to do to this man. If we weren't already short of men, I think I *would* have you shot. But I'm going to strip you of your corporal's stripes and bust you back to the private you were on your first day in this army. Don't make me sorry I spared you." He banged the gavel on his desk and announced, "This hearing is over. Let's get back to work."

To add a little more drama to the hearing, Major Grambling had his guards bring Walker up before him. And with the help of a pocketknife, he cut enough of the stitches for his guards to get a grip on the corporal stripes and rip them off Walker's sleeve.

Knowing he could well end up in the guardhouse, Walker fought to control the slow burn he was enduring, and kept his mouth shut. But he swore to himself this shame and humiliation would not go unpunished. He admitted no guilt in any of the results of this day. It was all Crazy Wolf's fault, and he would see that he paid the ultimate price for it. This so-called hearing had served only to make a hero out of that hated white-man-turned-Injun.

To hell with this army, he thought. It wasn't worth it at corporal's pay. He'd be damned if he would stay with it at a private's pay. *For now, hold your tongue*, he told himself. *Wait for the time and the opportunity. It is bound to come.*

"Are you done with me?" he finally asked and was told by Captain Boyd he was dismissed to return to the company. He left the room, never locking eyes with anyone.

"You watch your back," Grissom said to Crazy Wolf as he filed out of the room.

"You can be sure of that."

Outside the temporary courtroom, Private Castle was quick to catch up to Crazy Wolf before he walked away. Castle wanted to hear again about the killing of the Sioux warriors that had pursued Crazy Wolf and Amy Boyd.

He repeated how it happened, and the particular circumstances that made it possible for him to kill all six of the warriors. "It wouldn't have made much difference who was doin' the shootin'. Those Sioux were in the middle of a whole bunch of horses swimmin' to get across that river. And they didn't know what was goin' on around 'em till all but two of 'em was already hit. Your grandma coulda took care of those Sioux, if she had a good rifle."

"I don't know about that," Castle remarked. "My grandma's pretty tough, but I don't believe she's that good a shot." He saw Captain Boyd coming out the door then and decided he'd make himself scarce.

"Crazy Wolf," Boyd called out when he saw the scout turn to walk away. "I wanted to tell you Amy sends you her warmest regards. She's been busy sewing herself some new clothes, but she was ready to come to the hearing on a moment's notice if she was needed to testify on your behalf."

"Well, I do appreciate that, sir. Please tell her I said thanks. How's she gettin' along?"

"Remarkably well," Boyd answered. "I would never have thought she could ever have recovered from what she was subjected to. Oh, she doesn't tell me in detail what she went through, but I can pretty much guess. I should tell you, she credits her attitude and a positive outlook on life to you."

"That's mighty kind of her, but I think it's more apt to be because of the strong woman she is." Crazy Wolf grinned and added, "Most likely inherited it."

Boyd chuckled. "I'll tell her you said that, and she'll probably say it skips every other generation." He became serious then. "But I'm forever in your debt for what you did for my daughter."

"Well, I'd have to say you paid off that debt by clearing my name."

"That's the least I could have done," the captain said.

CHAPTER 8

Later that afternoon, Private Walker was informed to pack his gear and report to the commanding officer of F Company. The transfer was thought to be in the best interest of the men who worked under Walker in B Company, as well as for Walker, himself. For Captain Boyd, it was like pulling a decayed tooth out of an otherwise normal set of teeth.

No one was happier to see him transferred than Private Castle. With Walker's transfer, he was no longer subject to landing on work details with the man. However, he might run into him at Garland's Saloon. A little over a mile outside the fort, Garland's was a favorite hangout for the enlisted men.

As fate would have it, that night was bound to be a sure-fire occasion when the two men would feel the need for a drink of whiskey. Castle felt the day's happenings called for a couple of drinks in celebration of Walker's transfer to another company. Walker, on the other hand, was in no mood for a celebratory drink for a new start.

He had been subjected to a lengthy discourse from his new company commander—he was not happy to have Walker transferred to F Company. He was informed that

disciplinary action would be swift and stern at the first sign
of trouble from him. Although his first assignment was to
report to the mess sergeant for kitchen duty, he had not
complained. He had already made up his mind to desert
the army. But before he did, there were scores to settle, the
biggest of which was with one white-man-turned-Injun.

Those were the thoughts he was drowning with Garland's watered-down whiskey when Private Fred Castle
walked into the saloon with a couple of other soldiers from
B Company. Walker watched them chipping in at the bar
to buy a bottle of whiskey, then take it to an empty table
and sit down. *You double-crossing little snake*, he thought
as he watched them laughing and talking.

After they had taken a couple of drinks, he got up from
his table in the corner and walked over to their table,
pulled the vacant chair back and sat down. "Well, ain't this
lucky? I was hopin' some of the boys from my old company might show up here tonight. I don't know nobody in
F Company yet, not like I knew my old comrades I sol-
diered with in B Company." He grabbed their bottle and
poured himself a drink. "Now B Company, that's a company of men you can count on. Ain't that right, Castle?"

"You got no call to come after me, Walker. I didn't
know they was gonna call me up on that hearin'. And I
sure as hell didn't volunteer to do it. I was ordered to be
there, and I was ordered to tell the truth. I had to. They had
me swear to it on the Bible."

"When did you get so religious?" Walker demanded.
"You buckin' to be the chaplain? You're supposed to back
up your fellow soldiers. You yellow little snake, you cost
me two stripes. I'm thinkin' I oughta wring your neck."

"You wanna wring somebody's neck, why don't you go
wring Crazy Wolf's neck? He's the one who caused you to
look like a fool. 'Course you already had a little go-round

with him in the stable, didn't you? Didn't go too well, did it, *Private*?"

Walker hesitated, completely surprised by Castle's sudden confidence. He never had the guts to talk to him like that before. *This is some more of Crazy Wolf's work*, he thought. *Even a squeaky little mouse like Castle is mouthing off like a grown rat.* He got up from his chair. "Well, I don't wanna spoil your party here, boys. Thanks for the drink of likker. What the hell is it, anyway?" He reached down and picked up the bottle and looked at the label. "It says it's seventy-six proof rye whiskey. I doubt it. Don't let it go to your head." Then he drew the bottle back and smashed it against the back of Castle's head.

Castle's two companions recoiled backward as Castle was knocked forward, his face colliding with the tabletop in a shower of broken glass and whiskey. Walker quickly pulled out a two-shot Remington pocket pistol and held it on Castle's friends when they looked as if to retaliate. Since they, nor Castle, were armed, they backed away while Castle still lay with his face on the table and blood coming from the back of his head.

The noisy drone that had been the atmosphere of the crowded barroom, lessened at once as those closest to the altercation became aware of what had happened. The customers, almost all of whom were soldiers, were not armed, and none were inclined to risk taking a shot from the tiny pistol. Walker was not challenged as he backed out the door. Once outside, he ran back toward the fort, disappearing in the darkness.

Although Walker had already made up his mind to desert the army, he had not planned to do it that night. But after his flare-up in the saloon, he realized he had left himself no choice. He would surely be arrested and thrown into the guardhouse for assaulting Castle. He had to act immediately. As he trotted back to his barracks, he gave thought of each step he had to take to make his escape.

Only one man, who had the duty as Charge of Quarters, was in the barracks. He was sitting on his bed, reading a book by lantern light. Recognizing Walker as the new man, he asked, "What's goin' on? You run outta money?"

"You the CQ?" Walker asked.

"Yeah, I'm the CQ."

"What's your name?"

"Baker," the CQ answered.

"Baker," Walker repeated. "Yeah, that's the name. I was sent to relieve you. You're to report to the hospital on the double."

Baker jumped up off his cot. "The hospital? What for?"

"Hell, man, I don't know. They just said go relieve a soldier named Baker, pullin' CQ at F Company barracks. It was a matter of life or death. It was an order. I didn't ask no questions."

"What the hell," Baker mumbled to himself as he hurriedly buttoned up his jacket and grabbed his hat. "Will I need my rifle?"

"I don't think so. Give it to me. I'll put it away for you. Give me the key to the gun racks."

Baker dutifully handed over his rifle and the keys to the gun racks. He pointed to the rack his rifle came from in the center of the barracks as he ran out the door. Knowing he didn't have much time, Walker took Baker's rifle and threw the gun rack keys under Baker's cot. The rifle was just like his, and every other man's in the regiment, a Springfield 1873 single-shot carbine. He also took Baker's cartridge belt and handgun. At his bed he grabbed his haversack with his personal items, as well as his meat can, cup, and utensils. He reached down and pulled the blanket off his bed, thinking he might wish he had it when he was camping out on the prairie somewhere.

Keeping as much in the shadow of the buildings as possible, he left the barracks and ran down the road to the stable, stopping just before he reached it. He knew a guard would be posted at the stable. Waiting until he spotted him at the far end of the corral, obviously walking a circular route around the stables, the barn, and the corral gave Walker time to slip inside the stable and take his pick of the horses in the stalls, which were usually the better horses, favorites of the officers. He figured, if he was going to steal a horse, he might as well take a good one.

While he was at it, he stole an officer's saddle and saddlebags. Once the Morgan gelding was saddled, he slipped around inside the barn and the stables until he located the guard turning the front corner of the barn, walking toward the back. Walker gave the guard time to be behind the barn, then he opened the front stable door and rode the horse out of the stable and down the road leading away from the fort.

There was a natural urge to flog his stolen mount for speed to remove him from the scene as quickly as the big Morgan could take him. But one desire had captured his mind more than any other—to put a round from Private Baker's Springfield carbine into the center of Crazy Wolf's broad back. His best chance to take that shot would be at that time of night.

At the end of the stables road, he followed the narrow path which circled back toward the riverbank and rode a short distance up the river, then up a high bluff. Down near the water's edge, he looked down at the Crow scout camp below the bluff. As he expected, a large fire was burning in the middle of the camp, and he could see Indians sitting around it. Stepping down from the Morgan gelding, he dropped the reins on the ground, not concerned about any of the scouts happening upon him high on the bluff. The main way into the camp was by a path farther down the bluff, closer to the water.

"Now, Private Baker," he murmured softly to himself, "we're gonna see if you've been taking care of your weapon." He drew the Springfield carbine from the saddle scabbard, raised the long-range sight, and loaded a cartridge. Raising the rifle to his shoulder, he sighted on one of the figures walking in the camp. The rifle was accurate at that range, but he noticed a natural shelf about ten feet farther down the bluff that looked to be an even better shooter's platform.

He dropped down the steep brow of the bluff to the shelf below it, sliding slightly in the loose dirt. It was perfect—a shot of about forty yards with nothing in the way to block his sight of the target. He dropped to one knee and looked carefully around the fire. The bodies were fairly easy to see, thanks to the firelight, but he could not be absolutely sure of those who were seated. He continued to stare, trying to make out the faces until he found himself on the verge of panic. He couldn't be sure of his target!

There would be no time for a second shot. The first one had to count.

A couple of the scouts got on their feet to put some wood on the fire. They had been on either side of two he had thought could possibly be Crazy Wolf and his constant companion, Bloody Axe. *It's him! If he would get up, I could be sure.*

"I think I am ready for sleep," Bloody Axe said. "There is nothing more I can teach you today."

Crazy Wolf chuckled. "I think you taught me everything you know when I was five. Have you learned something since then?"

"One thing," Bloody Axe replied, still joking. "Whenever you go anywhere without me, you get in trouble."

"Let's go to bed," Crazy Wolf said. "Maybe you'll learn something in a dream."

They got up from the ground and stood looking at the fire for a moment. Crazy Wolf started to say something but hesitated when he heard a sound like that of a flat hand slap against the back of Bloody Axe's deerskin shirt. It was followed immediately by the report of the rifle.

Bloody Axe took a step toward the fire, then collapsed.

The scouts dived to the ground for cover. Frantic, Crazy Wolf crawled over to Bloody Axe, calling his name over and over. He saw the bullet hole in the back of his shirt and the blood seeping out. "Hang on, my brother, don't give in to it!" he implored. "I need you. You are stronger than the Sioux bullet."

Bloody Axe made no response.

One of the scouts on the opposite side of the fire had seen the muzzle flash of the shot and cried out, "The bluff! They're on the bluff!" Like Crazy Wolf and the others, he thought it was a Sioux war party, their natural enemies.

Their response was almost immediate. With weapons in hand, the scouts—all but Crazy Wolf—stormed up the bluff only to find no one there. With help from the moon just then rising, the few tracks seemed to indicate only one person, and that one left after taking the one shot. As it was obvious they could not track the sniper in the dark, the Crow warriors went back to the camp to see how badly Bloody Axe was hurt.

One look at Crazy Wolf told them Bloody Axe was dead.

One of the older Crow scouts, Drags Him, knew the two young warriors were like brothers, so he tried to comfort Crazy Wolf. "We will help you honor your brother and ready him for his journey. He was a brave warrior and deserves our respect."

Crazy Wolf thanked Drags Him, and they picked up Bloody Axe and carried him to his bedroll to position him before rigor mortis began. They placed the bedroll next to a thicket of small trees then Crazy Wolf took his rope and tied Bloody Axe's legs together, then tied his feet to a tree, and his shoulders to another, so the body would not draw up. This was to make sure he would lie straight in his grave.

"I will find the man who killed him." Crazy Wolf turned to look at the body of his brother. "I will avenge your death at the hand of this coward who sneaks in the darkness to do his evil." Unlike the other scouts, he no longer thought the sniper was a Sioux warrior. He felt sure it was the man Bloody Axe warned him to watch his back for. Crazy Wolf knew it was Ben Walker. And he knew the shot was meant for him, not Bloody Axe.

At the Crow camp the next morning, Cliff Freeman was surprised to find his scouts preparing to bury one of their number. He was at once concerned to discover the deceased was Bloody Axe. Knowing he and Crazy Wolf had been raised like brothers, Freeman was told Crazy Wolf had wrapped Bloody Axe in his blanket, ready to be carried to a deep grave some two-hundred yards down-river, but at the present time, Crazy Wolf was up on the bluff, inspecting the earthen shelf from where the shot had been fired.

Drags Him told Freeman about the one sniper shot that had fired into their camp on the night just past. That struck Freeman as rather odd, especially since he had learned some news, himself, that morning. He hadn't planned to pass it on to his scouts. It had to do with the soldiers and didn't expect the Crow scouts would be interested.

But he changed his mind. "I've got a couple of details I need scouts for, but I'll wait till Crazy Wolf comes back."

Up on the bluff, Crazy Wolf scouted the ledge and the path along the top of the bluff. His fellow scouts had left a good many tracks of their own the night before. But he was able to make out hoofprints on the path and the direction the sniper had gone. As he made his way back down the high bluff and into the camp Crazy Wolf saw Cliff Freeman ride into the Crow camp. *Good*, he thought, *I need to tell him I will be taking some time off to deal with this coward.*

"Crazy Wolf," Freeman greeted him. "I am sorry to hear about the death of your brother. That was very sad news to hear this morning. Some of the scouts here think the shooter was a Sioux, but I think differently. Last night, Ben Walker smashed Private Castle in the head with a whiskey bottle and put him in the hospital. Then he took a rifle outta the barracks and stole a horse outta the stable. He's a deserter, took off who knows where. If I was to bet on it, I'd say he took a quick stop here to take a shot at you. And he got Bloody Axe instead. Whaddayou think?"

"I didn't know the part about him desertin'," Crazy Wolf answered. "But I ain't surprised a bit. I'm gonna put Bloody Axe into the ground. After that, I'll be leavin' to settle up with Ben Walker."

"I figured you might. I hate to lose you, Crazy Wolf, but I understand what you're feelin' and don't blame you one bit. When you're done, if you wanna come back to work for me, I'll find a place for you. You're one of the best scouts, maybe *the best*, who's ever worked for me. And I wish you good huntin'."

"I 'preciate it, Mr. Freeman. Maybe I'll see you again."
Crazy Wolf didn't express it, but perhaps after settling
with Ben Walker, he should ride down to Red Lodge to tell
Spotted Pony his son is dead. The brothers had just agreed
they should go to see Spotted Pony soon as he was nearing
the end of his life. Giving him this news was a hard thing
to do, especially sorrowful that Bloody Axe was killed by
a man who was trying to kill Crazy Wolf but missed.

Freeman paused to study the young man and felt the
need to offer him some advice. "Cody," he started. "That's
right, ain't it? That's your given name by your birth mother
and father. Right?"

"Yes. My name was Cody Hunter, but not anymore."

"I understand that," Freeman said, "and I ain't sayin'
you ain't Crow. I'm just thinking it might be a good idea
to not look like an Indian while you're tryin' to track down
Ben Walker. He ain't gonna be runnin' to no Indian reservation to hide out. He's gonna be tryin' to lose himself
wherever white folks are. Your clothes are all right. All the
trappers and half the cowhands are all wearin' buckskins.
So that won't make no difference. You talk damn-nigh
perfect English, and that's somethin' that's always throwed
me. How in the world did you learn to talk like that?"

"What are you sayin' I need to do?" Crazy Wolf asked.
So far, it sounded like he was all right just like he was.

"Cut your hair," Freeman said. "Cut off those two
long braids and get rid of that rag you wear around your
forehead."

Crazy Wolf was shocked. His long, dark braids were a
source of pride to him. He and Bloody Axe used to compete
with each other over whose hair was the most lustrous.
Then a thought occurred to him. "I could cut my hair off
in mourning for Bloody Axe."

"Right," Freeman said at once. "That would be a fittin' thing to do. I think he'd appreciate that. But don't go choppin' all your hair off, so you'll look like you been scalped. Just get rid of the braids. You can let it hang down to your collar, if you want, but no braids." He paused then to gauge the scout's reaction. "Whaddaya think?"

"Maybe you're right," Crazy Wolf said. "I did not think about where I might have to go to find Walker. The people might try to capture me and take me to the reservation."

"That's a fact," Freeman said.

"I will do it," Crazy Wolf declared. "But now, I must take Bloody Axe to his grave."

CHAPTER 9

While the other scouts slept, Crazy Wolf, using only a short-handled mattock and an infantryman's shovel, spent almost the entire night digging Bloody Axe's grave a good five feet deep. When he finished, he returned to the camp and laid down on his bedroll next to the body of his brother and fell asleep, only to be awakened by the sound of the bugle blowing Reveille over at the fort an hour later. When the other scouts went to breakfast, he stayed in the camp to make sure no harm came to the body.

Returning after their breakfast, six warriors carried the body of Bloody Axe to its final resting place and lowered him carefully into the grave, where he would lay straight and dignified forever. When the body settled on the bottom of the grave, the blanket that had been used to carry him was folded over him. The six warriors wished him a safe journey, then left Crazy Wolf to fill in the grave alone.

When he returned to the camp, Crazy Wolf prepared to begin his search, one he fully anticipated to be long and tedious. He packed what supplies were available on his and Bloody Axe's horses, then said farewell to the friends they had made with the warriors from other villages. All wished him a safe and successful hunt.

He rode into the fort and entered the post trader's store to buy additional supplies. When he walked into the store, the owner, Milton Bush, was talking to a slender Indian woman who appeared to be looking at a bolt of cloth. Bush looked up and saw Crazy Wolf. "I'll be with you in a minute, chief." It occurred to him the two Indians might be man and wife. "Is he with you, ma'am?"

She turned to see who he was talking about. "Crazy Wolf!" she exclaimed, surprised.

He was equally surprised. "Amy, I didn't know that was you. I thought you were a Crow woman."

"So did I," Milton Bush remarked.

"I'm surprised you didn't recognize the dress," Amy said, ignoring Bush's remark. "It's still the best I've got to wear. I'm looking at what material Mr. Bush has to offer. I've already started sewing on a skirt and blouse."

"I've got a good selection of materials and some patterns, too," Bush inserted, anxious to rid his shelves of stock there was no demand for at the army post. "You're one of the Crow scouts, ain't you?" he asked Crazy Wolf.

"That's right, and I've got a list of supplies I'm gonna need." Back to Amy then, he asked, "Are you gettin' settled in at your father's quarters all right?"

"Oh, yes. I'm an old hand at living with my dad on an army post. There's no problem there. I just don't have any clothes to wear."

"And you need 'em out here in this country," Bush remarked. "Winter will be comin' on before you know it."

She favored Bush with a polite smile, then turned back to Crazy Wolf. "I wasn't sure if I'd ever see you again. Thought you might be sent out to scout on some long campaign or something. I told Papa I should at least invite you over for a nice dinner sometime to thank you for risking your life to save me."

"A big home-cooked dinner is just the thing to show your appreciation," Bush said. It struck him then. "You must be Captain Boyd's daughter."

"That's right, I am and I think I've changed my mind. I'd like to look at that bolt of denim again."

"I already took it back when I went to get this gingham," Bush said, looking a little perturbed. But he smiled and said, "I'll go get it."

"Is something wrong?" she asked Crazy Wolf at once, having sensed a somewhat serious demeanor about him that was unusual. "Now that the third party of our conversation is gone for a second, you seem sad."

"Sorry, I didn't know it showed. If you've got the time, we could wait until after we're finished in here and we can talk outside."

"That will be good. Let's do that."

When Bush came back with the bolt of denim, she said, "Go ahead and take care of his list of supplies. I need time to decide between the denim and the gingham."

"Yes, ma'am, whatever you say," Bush replied with a wink for Crazy Wolf.

Crazy Wolf called out his list of supplies and the quantity of each one in short order, keeping Bush moving quickly to place each item on the counter. The last item on his list was some canvas sacks to carry his supplies.

When Bush totaled the bill, he commented, "That's a nice order. Adds up to about a month's pay for you, don't it?" He knew the Indian scouts were paid the same salary the army paid their cavalrymen, but the scouts were cut off when they were no longer needed.

Crazy Wolf paid for his order.

"Ain't the army payin' for your supplies no more?"

"Not this time." Crazy Wolf was all right money-wise for a while. He spent so little. Consequently, almost all of his salary was tucked away unspent. He took his parcels outside to load onto his horses and was still securing his packs when Amy came out of the store. "You didn't take long," he said.

"I had already decided on the gingham. Why are you buying so many supplies?" Like Bush, she wondered. "Doesn't the army furnish all the supplies for their scouts?"

"Yes, but the trip I'm gettin' ready to take is a personal thing I have to do." He went on then to tell her about the death of his friend and brother and the obligation he felt to avenge his murder, especially since it was an assassination attempt against his life and not Bloody Axe's.

"I must avenge my brother's death and tell my Crow father his son is dead." Crazy Wolf tightened the last rope holding the packs in place on Bloody Axe's gray gelding. "I am glad we happened to be here at the trader's store at the same time. I wanted to see how you were getting along, and if everything was going well with you and your father. But I didn't think it a good idea to go to your father's private quarters."

"I think it would be all right if you knocked on my father's door. He thinks of you as a friend, a friend who saved his daughter's life." Amy was at once concerned for him, but she knew better than to waste her words trying to talk him out of his quest for vengeance. He had been too many years a warrior. "I hope you will be careful."

"I can promise you that." Then he told her of his plan to go on this trail as a white man, as Cliff Freeman had suggested. "I think he is right. I can go in many more places as a white man than I could as an Indian, so I am going to cut off my hair."

She nodded. "I agree, but it would be a better idea if I cut your hair."

"It is no trouble," he insisted. "All I will do is take my knife and cut these two braids off then I'll have short hair, and no more Indian."

She shook her head as if amazed by his thinking. "I thought so," she teased. "But what you would end up with would be an Indian with two big gaps in his hair. I will cut your hair like I cut my father's hair, and you will have hair like a white man."

His expression reflected his agreement, but he was reluctant to ask her to do it.

"Come home with me now and I'll cut your hair, and you can be on your way long before my father comes home."

"I don't know if that would be good for you. Someone would see my horses outside your house. I don't want anyone to think anything ill of you."

"If they see your horses outside, they'll know we're not trying to hide anything. If you like, I'll set a chair on the front porch and cut your hair out there, so we won't be hiding." She chuckled and added, "It doesn't really make any difference, anyway. The few women who live on the post have made no overtures of welcome to me. I think they all have a pretty vivid picture of what happens to a white woman who is taken by the Indians."

He gave her a sympathetic look, but she could tell he was thinking it over, so she pushed. "It won't take me but a few minutes to cut your hair, and you'll look like a genuine white man."

"All right. If you're sure that won't be askin' too much."

"Well, let me think about that. You tracked seven Sioux warriors who killed my guards and snatched me away with them. You rescued me and killed all seven of the warriors who took me. Then you got some clothes for me, so I could face my father when you brought me to him. And now you want me to cut your hair. I'll have to think about that. You might be asking too much."

He answered her sarcasm with a sheepish grin. "All right, you can cut my hair, but we'll do it on the front porch. I might want to work as a scout again, if I'm successful in tracking Ben Walker down." He led his horses and walked with her back to officer's row, a short line of small identical houses.

"This one?" he asked when she stopped in front of one in the middle of the row.

"Home, sweet, home," she replied. "You can tie your horses to the stair rail. I'll go in and get Papa's barbering things."

"I'll just drop their reins. They won't go anywhere."

She went inside the house and returned in a few seconds carrying a kitchen chair. He was quick to take it from her and set it down near the front of the porch. She went back inside to return again with some scissors, a comb, and a small mirror, which she handed to him.

He sat down in the chair and said, "All right. Cut 'em off."

She removed the bandanna tied around his forehead and hesitated. "When was the last time you washed your hair?"

"I don't know," he answered. "When was the last time it rained?"

She snipped the rawhide binding holding his braids together, first one and then the other. When the hair was released, she took his hand and ordered, "Come with me."

He was too surprised to resist.

"Whoa!" he exclaimed when she opened the door. "We can't go in the house!"

"Just be quick about it," she ordered, "and we'll be right

back out." She pulled him firmly until he surrendered then marched him straight through the house to the kitchen pump, where she started filling a bucket with water.

"Your hair is so thick with greasy smoke from I don't know how many campfires, you don't have a chance for a decent haircut till we wash some of it out of there." When her bucket was full, she picked it up and led him out the back door to a washtub on the back stoop. She dumped the water in the tub then told him to get her another one. She dumped that one in the tub as well. Then with him on his knees, she dunked his head in the water and started working up some suds with a bar of harsh laundry soap. When she finished her torturous assault on his head, she filled her bucket once more and rinsed all the soap out before attacking him with a dry towel. She looked at her project for a moment before saying, "Now, we can go back to the front porch."

After drying his long hair as well as she could with a towel, she used the scissors and cut it fairly even. Deciding against trying to get a barbershop effect by using her father's razor on his neck and sideburns, she handed Crazy Wolf the mirror when she finished.

At first, he didn't recognize himself. "I swear," was all he could say. "I swear," he repeated then looked at her and asked, "Do you think I look like a white man?"

She shook her head in disbelief. "Yes, you look like a white man. Crazy Wolf, you are a white man." Watching as he continued to stare into the mirror, trying to feel like a white man when he had been an Indian since childhood, she then pointed out, "Your hair should look a little more natural once it completely dries."

"I never knew haircuts could be that painful," he commented. "My people cut their hair when it gets too long, but not each hair by itself." He smiled at her. "Thank you for my haircut. It was a lot of trouble for you."

"Nothing is too much trouble when it comes to you, my friend. I thank God for you every night when I say my prayers. And I ask Him to keep you safe."

"That is a very nice thing to say, and I thank you for sayin' it. I would ask your God to give you happiness for the rest of your life, and I hope we will meet again. You are a good woman. Life owes you much happiness after what it gave you so far. And now, I will go before the people peeking out their windows send for the soldiers to arrest the white man who killed the Indian inside your house." He stepped off the porch and up onto his horse.

"You be careful, Cody, and take care of yourself," she said as he wheeled the dun gelding away from the porch and trotted off toward the river. *I should have called him Crazy Wolf,* she thought. *They'll never take all the Indian out of him.*

Because of everything that had to be done that morning, Cody Hunter started his search for Ben Walker a little past noon. He could have eaten the noon meal in the mess hall with the other Crow scouts, but he had already said his farewells earlier. In addition, he preferred not to appear before them with his new haircut. There would be a generous amount of good-natured ribbing about his new look, but there might also be some feelings of offense and insult over his decision to look less like an Indian, and he did not want that. Best to start on Walker's trail at once, and eat something when he rested his horses.

With that decided, Cody rode back up on the bluff where Walker had taken the shot. Once again, he examined the small area the path actually occupied and confirmed to his satisfaction hoofprints only went up to the top of the bluff. None went back the other way, which meant after Walker took the shot, he fled in the same direction he came up—to the west. Hoofprints Cody saw here and there along the hard dirt path told him Walker had stayed on the path as it wound in and out through the trees close to the edge of the river. As he followed the path, Cody gave some thought to Walker—a soldier stationed for duty at the fort—and decided he would not likely know the country.

So Cody tried to think as Walker might have been thinking. Following a strange path in the dark of night, he would have most likely wanted to make his way onto the road that followed the Yellowstone. But as the dense growth along the river closed in over him, probably the only thing he could see for sure was the path under his horse's hooves. He would likely have gambled on the first opportunity to head more toward the north, in hopes of striking the road.

With those thoughts in mind, Cody pulled Storm to a halt when he came to a smaller path forking away toward the northwest. He looked down at the small path and tried to imagine if it would have shone bright enough for Walker to have seen it.

"One thing would say he did," Cody announced as he stepped down from his horse and took a closer look at the fork. But he couldn't see any prints at all. Not willing to go against his gut instinct, he walked a little way along the new path and was rewarded after about twenty-five feet with a definite hoofprint, after which he found them consistently. It told him Walker had been concerned about a Crow scout following his trail, so when he finally found a path he thought might lead him to the road, he walked his horse on the grass *beside* the path a little way before riding on the path.

Cody followed that same path, and as he had figured, came out on the wagon road after about a quarter of a mile. *"That was the easy part,"* he told himself. Now he was on a common road traveled by horses, oxen, carts, and wagons. It would be much more difficult to distinguish Walker's tracks from any others, although he felt sure Walker had turned to the west, for to turn east would have taken him back to Fort Keogh.

At that point, it was like rabbit hunting, and Cody had to put himself in the rabbit's place. Walker had no packhorse. He had stolen just the one saddle horse, and probably had very little, or nothing, to eat. His situation was desperate. He would be looking for any slight chance to remedy his situation.

Cody studied each side of the road carefully as he followed it through a land of low, rolling hills barren of trees, searching for any unusual signs of disturbance of the foliage. Mile after mile, the scenery never changed as the road made its way through shallow valleys of grass between squat hills, dotted with a pine or a fir here and there. He knew the odds were not reasonable he would discover where someone had been ambushed on the road but didn't want to overlook any clue.

In spite of his careful scanning of the roadside, he saw no indication of anything that hinted of an unusual incident as he continued down the road toward the Rosebud River until time to start looking for a place to rest his horses and cook something to eat. Fortunately, he saw what looked like a sizable creek up ahead a short way. When he reached the point where the road crossed the creek, it was evident the spot was a commonly-used campsite as several remains of old campfires were visible on the banks of the creek. He crossed on over to the other side, then turned his horses upstream to find a spot not stripped of firewood. He had gone only a few yards when he spotted a wagon in the trees ahead.

From what he could see through the bushes, it appeared to be a freight wagon, and he decided to let them know of his presence before he picked his spot. A horse acknowledged his horses' presence and Bloody Axe's gray answered.

They know I'm here now, he thought, *so I might as well announce it*. "Hello the camp!" he called out. There was no answer. He waited. It occurred to him he saw no sign of a fire. He called out again. "Hello the camp! Mind if I come in?" There was still no answer.

Cody drew his rifle from his saddle sling and dismounted. Leaving his horses where they were, he made his way carefully along the bank until he reached the small grassy clearing and the wagon. Although he saw no sign of life in the ashes of what had been a healthy fire, he did notice a horse standing near the water, watching him approach. Cody glanced at the wagon. It was rigged for a team of two horses. His first thought was that Walker had acquired a packhorse for himself, unless the other horse was wandering around up creek.

Walking around to the other side of the wagon, he found the owner lying on the ground in nothing but his underwear. One large buzzard sat on the dead man's chest, picking away at the shirt of his long handles. Several other buzzards were on the ground close by, watching the large one carefully. Cody lifted his rifle, thinking to scare the grisly beasts away, then decided to let them alone to do what nature put them there for.

So, Walker had a packhorse, likely a sorrel, and he was no longer wearing his army uniform. It appeared things were going his way right from the start. He'd even been lucky enough to find a victim who must have been about the same size. Cody took a few moments to look in the wagon, not expecting to find anything of value and he was not disappointed. The dead man had hauled a wagonload of something to Fort Keogh, perhaps, and he had been on his way home with his empty wagon when it had been his misfortune to cross paths with Ben Walker.

A wife and children waited and wondered, maybe. Cody hoped not.

He went back to his horses, rode back to the road, then continued downstream for a couple dozen yards to put some distance between him and the scene at the wagon. As his horses rested, he built a fire and sliced some strips of bacon to eat with a couple of pieces of hardtack. The trader's surviving horse followed along to their camp behind Bloody Axe's gray. As he sat drinking his coffee, Cody contemplated the horse. A fairly sturdy looking sorrel, he wondered why Walker had left it behind. Evidently, he had not wanted to bother with an extra horse. But if that were the case, he could have sold the horse and pocketed some extra money.

Maybe it's going to be harder to think like this man than I figured, he thought, half in jest.

CHAPTER 10

After his horses were rested, Cody set out on the road west again with the intention of reaching a small settlement he had been to once before while on an army patrol. A man named Alexander had been sent to set up a steamboat landing on the Yellowstone, about forty-five or fifty miles west of Fort Keogh. The purpose of the landing was to unload ammunition and supplies for the troops in the Indian wars after Custer's defeat at Little Big Horn. A little settlement had grown up around the steamboat landing, with a trading post and saloon soon to follow.

As far as Cody knew, no other settlement existed on the Yellowstone before reaching Coulson, and he wondered if Walker might stay there a little longer before moving on to wherever he was heading. He would have to load his new packhorse up with supplies enough for a long trip, no matter what direction he started out.

As he alternated the dun's pace between a walk and a trot for much of the way to the steamboat landing in order to shorten the time it would take to reach it before dark, Cody turned his thoughts to what Walker might do next. After coming up with several, he rejected all but one. Since finding the victim he badly needed, Walker would most likely be content to ride on in to the boat landing and buy necessary supplies.

Settling on that, Cody was not as concerned about overrunning his target as he had been before finding the wagon.

Soon he came upon the first of several rude dwellings that signaled the fledgling town and reached the center of the little settlement a couple hours before dark. Looking around he saw some obvious growth since he had last been there. The trading post and saloon had expanded and was now two separate businesses, although still side by side. Several horses were tied at both places but none were the dark Morgan and a sorrel he searched for. He also noticed a blacksmith's forge that hadn't been there before.

"How do?" Howard Glazier greeted him when he walked into the store. "What can I do for you?"

"Howdy," Cody replied, finding it interesting the man didn't realize he was a Crow. "I was supposed to meet a friend of mine here this mornin', but I didn't make it as fast as I thought I would. Although I hope he didn't make it here when he said he would, I'm wondering if he mighta gone on without me. He's ridin' a Morgan and leadin' a sorrel, and he's plannin' to buy some supplies here. Have you seen him?"

Glazier didn't answer right away. He took a moment or two to study Cody, giving the impression he was deciding whether or not to answer truthfully, which was the first sign that he was not. "No, sir. I don't recall nobody like that so far today. Reckon he just ain't got here yet. How 'bout you? You needin' supplies?"

Walker must have given him one helluva story, Cody thought. Figuring it would be a waste of time asking any more questions, he decided to try his luck at the saloon next door. "Nope, but I appreciate your help. I guess I'll have to wait for him to show up."

He walked next door to the saloon but paused before he went inside. As a Crow warrior, he had never been in a saloon but once in his whole life. And on that occasion he'd been informed he could not be served. Taking a deep breath, he pushed on through the door and found the saloon empty except for the bartender and one old man who was eating at one of only two tables in the room. Cody wondered if the bartender had also swallowed Walker's story.

"Howdy," Howard Glazier's brother, Walter, greeted him. "You need a drink of likker?"

"No, what I'd really like is something to eat," Cody answered. "I notice that fellow over there is eating. Can I buy some supper here? Or is he just part of the family?"

Walter laughed. "He's part of the cook's family, and that's part of her salary. She feeds the old man. But I'll sell you some supper, same as what he's eatin', deer meat butchered this mornin'. Give you some coffee to wash it down with. It'll cost you fifty cents."

"Fifty cents, huh?" That was about twice what he would have expected to pay for a plate of food. "You say it was butchered this mornin'? Well, I guess for fresh deer meat it's worth it. "I'll try some."

"Set yourself down at the table, and I'll tell the cook to fix a plate for you," Walter said, then yelled, "Mae! Bring a plate of food for a customer!"

Cody walked over, sat down at the table, and nodded to the old man at the other table.

In a couple of minutes, a tired looking woman of perhaps middle age came out of the kitchen with a plate of venison, cooked up in a stew. Two pieces of cornbread were on top of the stew. She placed the plate on the table, then asked, "Do you want coffee?"

He smiled up at her. "Yes, my sister. You are Apsaalooke, are you not?" He spoke in the Crow tongue.

Her eyes came alive at once. "Yes," she answered, also in the native tongue. "Why do you ask?"

"I am Crow," he answered. "My father is Spotted Pony. I have been working as a scout for the soldiers at the fort."

"But you look like a white man," she said.

"I know. That is my burden to bear. I was born to a white woman, but I never knew her. I have been a Crow since I was five."

Walter saw that the stranger and Mae were talking, so he walked back over to join them. "That's pretty good stew, ain't it?"

"Yes, it sure is," Cody said, switching back to English. "It sure hits the spot right now. Maybe you can tell me something. I was thinkin' to meet another fellow here." He went on to tell him the same story he'd told his brother.

And like his brother, Walter immediately said he had seen no such man.

"The fellow next door said the same thing when I asked him," Cody remarked. "So, I reckon he hasn't showed up here yet."

"I reckon not," Walter said. "You might as well make your camp and wait till he does."

"Reckon so. I'll have to finish my supper and take care of my horses. I expect they are wondering what's keepin' me." He glanced at Mae and caught her gazing at him as if concerned. "May I have just a little bit more coffee?"

She turned at once and went to fetch the coffeepot. Evidently losing any desire to talk anymore, Walter walked back behind the bar as she returned with the coffee.

Cody watched her carefully as she filled his cup. "He

does not lie very well, does he?" he asked softly in the Crow tongue.

She looked up at him quickly and stopped pouring lest she spill the coffee. "No," she answered even more softly.

"The man I am after killed my brother, Bloody Axe, thinking it was me. That is why I am chasing the man. He is a soldier who has run away from the army."

She took a quick glance toward the bar to make sure Walter wasn't watching her closely, then she whispered, "The man you look for left here early this morning. He said someone might come looking for him because he saw them kill a man. He said they might be wearing buckskins."

"I thought it might be something like that," Cody said, still speaking in the Crow tongue. "Thank you, my sister. Did he say where he was going?" He'd asked, just on the chance, and as expected, Walker had not said.

Cody would have been surprised if Walker even knew where he was going. There was nowhere to go in the direction he had fled. The closest thing to a town on the Yellowstone would probably be Coulson, and that was a hundred miles from the settlement. Any place north or south of the Yellowstone, where Walker might disappear, would be just as far. Cody concluded that Walker would just continue to run, following the Yellowstone until he decided he was clear of anyone chasing him, or decided to wait in ambush. Regardless, Cody's only choice was to pursue him and kill him.

He got up to leave. "Thank you," he said to Mae in English.

"Good luck," she answered in Crow.

He nodded and left two quarters on the bar when he passed by Walter. Feeling an urge to get back on the wagon track and go after Walker immediately, he knew he had to set up his camp for the night, rest and graze his horses, and start again first thing in the morning.

Cody started out the next morning on what would be a two-and-a-half-day trip before he reached the town of Coulson. Behind him, he led the gray gelding that had belonged to Bloody Axe. Behind the gray, the sorrel left behind by Ben Walker followed along on a lead rope. At first, he thought to find a pack saddle somewhere along his journey and split the load between the sorrel and the gray. On the other hand, the gray wasn't carrying that much of a load. Maybe he might sell the sorrel, if he found a buyer. The likelihood of that seemed highly unlikely considering the fact that he met only one other traveler during the first day of the trip. He was a gruff-looking old fellow dressed in skins, as was Cody. His rifle was out of his saddle sling and lying across his thighs, just as Cody's was.

Passing level with each other, Cody said, "Howdy. Run into anybody back that way?"

"Howdy," the other rider answered. "One feller leadin' a packhorse. Anybody back your way?"

"Nope, not a soul," Cody answered. "Good day to ya."

The other fellow nodded, and they continued on their way. That was the extent of his progress for that day.

He began to see signs of civilization on the morning of his third day away from the Glazier brothers' trading post and saloon when he came to the first of a few cabins on the bank of the river. They were dwellings of the workers in a sawmill owned by a man named John Alderson, he was told at one time. Coulson was a much bigger town than the simple settlement he had last seen. The oldest-looking building was a general store and trading post whose sign proclaimed it to be HEADQUARTERS.

An odd name for a general store, he thought.

Other shops and businesses as well as several saloons and dance halls had sprung up, and it occurred to him the town offered a lot of temptation for a man of Ben Walker's tastes. He thought it a good idea to check the town thoroughly before deciding to move on up the river. As he weighed that decision against the possibility of getting even farther behind Walker in the event he was not tempted by Coulson's evil pleasures, Cody knew there was no way he could ride away from the town unless he had searched every crack where a rat could hide. His plan was to go from one end of the town to the other and hope to spot Walker, preferably before Walker spotted him.

With that settled in his mind, the next thing would be the welfare of his horses and belongings. He paused for a moment when he heard a gunshot, followed by a second one a few seconds later. It seemed to have come from a dance hall halfway down the street. He watched the door to see if anyone ran out. No one did.

A couple of men walked into the dance hall, but other than those two, no one on the street appeared to notice the shots. He waited a few minutes more until two men dragged a body out of the building and left it on the boardwalk. Evidently, it was a typical day in Coulson.

He turned around and took his horses to the stable he had just ridden past. Although not partial to putting his Indian ponies into a stable, judging by his first impression of the town, there was a real possibility they might be stolen while he was snooping around the saloons.

"Yes, sir," Red Puckett called out from the corral. "Can I help ya?"

"I think I would like to leave my horses here, if you don't charge too much," Cody said.

Red came out of the corral and closed the gate. "Well, I reckon that depends on what you think is too much, and what I think ain't enough. Let's see if we can cut a deal that don't upset either one of us. Why don't you tell me what you've got in mind. You talkin' about overnight? Or are you gonna be here a month? That'll make a difference in what I'll charge."

"I ain't sure how long I'm gonna be in town," Cody said. "Overnight for sure, but I might be here a couple of days. So how much for keepin' my horses overnight?"

"I charge fifty cents a day for each horse. So that'd be a dollar and a half for all three."

"Then I'll probably only stay for one night. And I'll sleep in the stall with my horses."

"There's an extra charge for you to sleep in the stable," Red countered.

"Why? You don't have to feed me any hay. I'm not even sure my horses will eat hay—maybe the sorrel, but the dun and the gray only eat grass. And sometimes I give them some grain. I will sell you the sorrel. How much will you give?"

"What?" Red asked, confused. "You talk like an Injun. What are you talking about? Why do you think I'd want that sorrel?"

Cody pointed to a board nailed over the stable door. WE BUY HORSES.

"Oh," Red responded, surprised that Cody could read. "Why do you wanna sell him?"

"I don't need him. What will you give?"

"I don't know," Red answered. "Let me look at him." He walked back to look the sorrel over. After he looked at his teeth and his hooves, he noticed that Cody's other two horses were not shod, while the sorrel was. "Where'd you steal this horse from? Weren't close around Coulson were it?"

"I didn't steal him," Cody replied. "He decided he wanted to follow me. I'm looking for the man who shot the horse's owner. I found the horse a day-and-a-half east of here. How much you give?"

Red shook his head and chuckled. "Fifteen dollars."

"Twenty would be better," Cody said. "A dollar for my other two horses to stay overnight, and nothing for me to sleep with them."

Red chuckled again. "Mister, you drive a hard bargain, but that horse is in pretty good shape. So, you've got a deal." He figured he just paid twenty dollars for a horse he could sell for forty. And if the young man had to stay in town a day or two longer than he figured, he would recover some more of his twenty dollars in boarding fees. "Come on, we'll bring 'em on in the stable and get their saddles off and I'll show you the stall you'll be payin' for."

When that was done, they turned them out in the corral. Red noticed that the tall man wearing buckskins stood for a while looking at the horses in the corral. He wasn't sure if it was the smart thing to do to ask this man many questions, but he was curious enough to risk it.

"You said you were lookin' for the man who killed the feller that used to own that horse I just bought. Are you some kinda lawman or somethin'?"

Cody looked at him as if amazed by the question. "No, I'm no lawman. I just happened to find the dead man and his wagon, and the sorrel was runnin' loose. After it followed me for a long time, I put a rope on him."

"If you got there after the killer was long gone, how do you know you're followin' the right man?"

"Because I was already following him and his trail led me to the wagon and the dead man." Cody then asked the question he needed an answer for. "Maybe you've had more new customers than me today and yesterday. Maybe a man riding a Morgan, leading a packhorse that maybe looks a lot like the one you just bought?"

"Nope," Red answered. "I ain't had nobody leave a Morgan the last few days. Can I ask why you was already chasin' the man you're sure killed that feller?"

"He killed my brother," Cody answered.

"Oh . . . well, I hope you find the son of a bitch!"

"If you give me the money for the horse, I can go find something to eat." Cody wanted him to think he didn't have any money, so maybe he wouldn't stall him for the payment.

"Sure thing," Red responded. "Lemme go get it for you." He went into the tack room where he had his little metal cash box hidden, got the money, came back, and counted out nineteen dollars. "I know you ain't ever been here before, so if you want a good dinner, go to Tuggle's. Bob Tuggle's wife is about as good a cook as you'll find anywhere, and the price is fair." When Cody looked as if interested, Red said, "It's right down the street next to the Boatman's Saloon."

"Much obliged. I'll try it out." Cody took his rifle and walked out of the stable to the street, where he paused to survey the town. It seemed to him unusually busy for that early in the day. He walked toward one of the two-story buildings with a large sign that read, THE BOATMAN'S. *Probably named to attract the men who worked the puddleboats on the river,* he thought. Since there was no railroad, the fastest way to transport freight to Coulson was by way of the paddleboats up the Yellowstone River.

At the restaurant, he paused to take a look over the batwing doors to see what it looked like inside. Since he had lived as a Crow Indian practically all his life, he was not familiar with saloons. Now, in the last few days, he was looking into his second one. Of course, he knew what a saloon was—the place where the white man went to get the firewater he called whiskey. The room he saw in the Boatman's was much bigger than the one Walter Glazier owned, and there were more tables. But other than that, it looked about the same.

"You goin' in, or comin' out?" A gruff voice behind him interrupted his thoughts.

Cody quickly took a step away from the door and turned to encounter a short, stocky little man grinning up at him.

"You're standin' in the way of a powerful thirst," the man said.

"I beg your pardon," Cody said. "I reckon my mind was wanderin'."

"Maybe you oughta wander on inside and get you a drink of likker. That's what I always do when my mind starts to wander."

"No, I think it would be better if I go get something to eat," Cody told him,

"Probably a good idea, big'un. It ain't a good idea to drink on an empty stomach." He pushed on through the door and went inside.

Cody continued on past the saloon to Tuggle's, a small building wedged in between the Boatman's and the big store named Headquarters. Still very much the Crow Indian, he was experiencing extremely odd feelings walking alone in the white man's town. It was not a world he was familiar with, and he had to remind himself these people do not know he is a Crow. The Crow woman, Mae, back in the first saloon, didn't even recognize him as one of her people.

These people in this town don't think I look like an Indian, he reminded himself then walked on inside Tuggle's.

The few customers, as well as Bob Tuggle and his wife, Rosie, turned to stare at the tall man dressed in buckskins and carrying a Henry rifle standing in the doorway, seemingly undecided what to do.

"Welcome to Tuggle's," Bob greeted him. "Come on in and set yourself down anywhere there ain't a fanny."

Cody looked at the one long table in the little room. It was like the tables in the mess hall at Fort Keogh. Most of the places at the table were empty, as it was well past noon. The empty spots had plates turned upside down. Assuming they were still clean, he went to the chair at the end of the table instead of sitting on one of the benches on each side.

Seeing that he was going to sit at the end, Bob said, "You can just prop your rifle up against the wall behind you, so it won't be in your way."

"Right." Cody did so then settled himself in the chair and looked at the faces all turned his way. A couple of the heads nodded politely, and he responded with a nod in turn.

Bob's wife, Rosie, appeared at his elbow then, holding a heavy iron pot in one hand and a big serving spoon in the other. She didn't say anything but stood there waiting.

One of the customers who had nodded to him said, "Turn your plate over."

Realizing what she was waiting for then, he quickly turned the plate right-side-up, and she immediately started spooning out his dinner. "It's beef stew today. You want coffee?"

"Yes, I want coffee. Thank you."

"You're welcome," she said with a chuckle. She cocked her head to one side and gave him a close look. "You've been in the mountains or somewhere a long time, ain't you?"

"Yes, ma'am, I have." He looked at the stew, not sure if he should attack it with the spoon beside his plate or not. He noticed then that the other people were using the fork, so he picked his up, too. He had forgotten about using a fork when he was a small boy but had become acquainted with it since eating in the army mess halls, so it was not a problem for him. Everyone else at the table looked to be relieved for him.

The stew was good, and so were the biscuits and coffee. Red Puckett had not lied when he had recommended it.

Finished, Cody got up from the table, picked up his rifle, and went to the counter in the front of the room where Bob Tuggle was sitting on a stool. "How much for my dinner?"

"Twenty-five cents for the stew and five cents for the coffee," Bob told him.

"That is a reasonable price," Cody said, pulling some change from his pocket. "The man at the stable told me to come here to eat. I'm glad he did. It was very good."

"Red said that, huh?" Rosie spoke up, overhearing Cody's remarks. "Well, we're glad you enjoyed it. Come back to see us, if you're gonna be in town awhile."

"Thank you, I will, but I don't know if I'll be here long or not."

"Well, we serve three meals a day," Bob said, "so maybe we'll see you at supper. What are you fixin' for supper tonight, Rosie?"

"I'm gonna be baking that ham we got today. And I can't wait to have some of that, myself."

"Me too," Bob said. "We don't get a good bakin' ham very often."

Cody just nodded politely and went out the door. He was anxious to start looking in every door on the chance Ben Walker was still in town.

"There's somethin' wrong with that young feller," Bob commented to Rosie after Cody disappeared from in front of their door. "He's been kicked in the head or somethin'."

"He's a fine-lookin' young man," Rosie said, "but he acts like he don't know how to talk to people. And when he does talk, he talks as good as a schoolteacher. Maybe he's just been alone up in the mountains too long."

"He said he had," Bob reminded her. "He better get his mind back here on earth 'cause this town will shear him like a sheep."

Bob was partially right. Cody did have some deep concerns on his mind. His only purpose in this white man's town was to avenge his Crow brother's death. Other things were also on his mind, however. He had sworn to follow Ben Walker no matter where he led. After he killed Walker, he intended to go tell Spotted Pony about Bloody Axe's death. What he had not foreseen was the fateful coincidence that in Walker's flight, he was getting closer and closer to Red Lodge, the little settlement close to Spotted Pony's village on Rock Creek.

Spotted Pony had taught him and Bloody Axe the spirits of great Crow wise men had influence on men's lives. Cody believed this. There could be evil spirits as well as those of good intention. He and Bloody Axe had talked of the possibility when they were young boys. Could some evil spirit be guiding the evil man who'd killed Bloody Axe directly to Bloody Axe's father?

Cody told himself to think such things as that was childish nonsense and actually, Walker's frantic attempt to escape was simply making his execution more convenient. After it was done, he wouldn't have a long journey to carry the sorrowful news of Bloody Axe's death to his father. Coulson was an easy two-day ride from Red Lodge.

CHAPTER 11

Cody stood outside the big building next door to Tuggle's and debated whether it was worth the time to go in and look around just on the chance Walker was buying more supplies. He looked at the hitching rail in front of the store and saw no Morgan or sorrel packhorse tied there and decided the saloons and the dance halls would most likely be the bait for someone of Walker's character. Continuing in the direction he had started, he looked in every door till he reached the end of the street.

The first was a barbershop—no one in it but the barber, who was dozing in his chair. Next was a dance hall. Although he had never been in one, he understood it was a place where men could go and drink firewater and dance with a woman, which would sometimes lead to a tussle in her bed. The only difference he could see between the dance hall and what the soldiers at the fort called a "Hog Ranch" was the opportunity the dance hall women had to tire their customers out, so they wouldn't have to fool with them for too long in the bed.

Determined to look in every door, he went inside and found himself in a large empty room with a bar at one end and a group of tables along the sides. A raised platform stood at one end of the room with half a dozen empty chairs on it. The place was quiet—no customers, no music.

At a small table next to the bar, a man sat, smoking a cigar. "You lookin' for a drink?" he called out.

"No," Cody answered. "I just wanted to look in here."

"You're too early," the man said. "The musicians ain't even here yet. There ain't nothin' to see. Come back in a couple of hours."

"Much obliged," Cody replied and went back outside.

On the street, he realized he knew very little about how things worked in a town like Coulson, and came to the conclusion the only places he had a remote chance of running into Walker were the saloons. Of the four, he had already looked inside the Boatman's, although he did not go inside. The next closest was Maxwell's.

Carrying his rifle in his right hand, he stepped inside and walked around the few tables near the back, then came back by the bar where seven men were standing and drinking.

"Can I help you?" the bartender asked as he walked toward the door.

"No, thanks," Cody answered. "Just lookin' for somebody." He went out the door, and on to the next saloon.

It was the same story at number three and number four, striking him with the realization he had guessed wrong when he'd thought the odds were good that Walker stopped there.

Still in hopes that Walker's lead had not lengthened, Cody started looking in every business along the street, but he accomplished only one thing. People were talking about the crazy man who had walked all over town looking for somebody.

Left with no trail to follow, he could only assume Walker had continued on the road west.

Discouraged, Cody walked slowly, giving thought to what to do next. To make matters worse, it was getting late—almost suppertime. He headed for the stables, but as he hurried along, he wondered how much time would he actually save by saddling his horse and loading up the gray again? A couple of hours? He would have to stop to rest the horses before riding very far, and that would mean an all-night camp. There was no thought of giving up and going back to Fort Keogh. Ben Walker had to be traveling the road following the Yellowstone, leaving Cody no other option but to start out again.

As he approached the stable, Red Puckett walked out to meet him. Cody heard a snap right beside his ear just before he heard the sound of the rifle shot behind him somewhere.

Red yelled as the bullet smacked into the stable door beside him and Cody dropped to the ground immediately, rolling over behind the watering trough in front of the stable door. A second shot smacked into the side of the trough as he struggled to get to a firing position.

"The Boatman's!" Red yelled. "He's shootin' from a window on the second floor!"

"Which window?" Cody yelled back.

"Second from the front! It's the only open window!"

Lying on his back, Cody levered a round into the Henry, then rolled back over on his stomach. Drawing his knees up under him as far as he could without exposing his head, he waited for the next shot. When he heard the bullet strike the trough, he popped up and fired two quick rounds into the open window before ducking down again.

Approximately fifty yards away, Ben Walker dropped flat on the floor of Darlene Futch's bedroom after two shots ripped through the curtains and imbedded in the opposite wall. Darlene hovered in the corner behind her bed, screaming hysterically.

"Shut up, damn it!" he yelled at her. "He ain't hit nothin'."

Darlene had told him about some stranger walking all over town, looking for someone. She'd said the man was wearing buckskins and carrying a rifle. Walker knew he was who the man was looking for. Standing by the window a few minutes ago, she saw the man going toward the stable, and called Walker to come look.

As soon as he had seen the familiar form of the man, he knew it was Crazy Wolf, and he grabbed his rifle. Raising the window and set to shoot, he hesitated. He was sure it was Crazy Wolf, but at that distance, something didn't look right. He didn't know what it was, but the way the man was dressed, the way he walked and carried the rifle, it had to be Crazy Wolf. Walker had seen that walk enough times to know he was right. He pulled the trigger. He missed and cursed for having doubts and waiting too long. He couldn't risk getting back up to the window to shoot again. Crazy Wolf had the window in his sights, waiting for him to pop up.

"I've got to get outta here. That maniac has found me."

"What about me?" Darlene cried.

"What about you?" Walker returned sarcastically. "He ain't after you. You just stay in that corner for a while. You'll be all right."

"What about the money you owe me for last night and this evenin'?" She whimpered pitifully. "You almost got me killed."

"I didn't get nothin' to pay you for. And I sure ain't gonna pay you nothin' for tonight. I'm leavin'."

"You sorry dog," she spat, "I hope he catches you."

"I'll miss you, too," he said and crawled to the door, reached up, grabbed the knob, and opened the door. After he crawled out into the hall, he scrambled up onto his feet and ran to the stairs, thanking his lucky stars that he had staked his horses behind the Boatman's, instead of paying to put them in the stable. He didn't stop to give anybody downstairs in the saloon any explanations but ran straight out the back door to his horses.

At the stable, the watering trough was the only cover before Cody could get to the stable where Red was watching. He stayed hidden until finally convinced Walker had run, then rose up on one knee, and aimed his rifle at the window. When no rifle appeared on the windowsill, he got to his feet and ran toward the Boatman's, his rifle ready to fire. He ran into the saloon to find a startled group of customers wondering what had caused the shots they'd just heard and the flight of Ben Walker out the back door.

As Cody headed for the stairs, a man standing beside them pointed toward the back of the room. "He went out the back!" the man exclaimed,

Cody veered toward the back door without hesitating and with no thoughts that the man might be setting him up for an ambush. He ran out the back door of the saloon in time to get a glimpse of Walker racing away on the black Morgan, leading a sorrel packhorse behind him.

Too late for a reasonable shot as Walker galloped past the backs of the buildings, Cody threw one shot after him, anyway. It struck the corner of the post office. Running across the yard behind the Boatman's, he had time to get one last glimpse of his target before it disappeared past a clump of small firs. His choice had just been made for him. He walked around the side of saloon and headed back to the stable to get his horses.

"Did you see who it was?" Red asked at the stable.

"No, I didn't get but a glimpse of him, but I know who he is. He's the man I've been tracking," Cody said. "The one I told you about. I don't reckon I'll be stayin' here tonight. I'm leaving as soon as I get my horses ready to go."

"Well, I'm sorry you ain't gonna be with us a while, but I hope you can settle up with that feller." Red hesitated before remarking, "I reckon you're lookin' for your money back, since you ain't gonna be here like you said you was."

"No, we both made that deal in good faith. I don't expect any money back. You kept my horses most of the day, so I didn't have to worry about them, so we're even."

"That's mighty neighborly of you, friend. I 'preciate it." Red brought Cody's packhorse out and held the reins while Cody arranged his packs.

When Cody stepped up on his horse, Red backed away and asked, "What's your name, friend?"

"Cody Hunter. What's your'n?"

"Red Puckett. Next time you're back this way, I owe you for a night's board."

"Much obliged." Cody gave Storm a nudge with his heels and guided him toward the back of the buildings on the main street.

He rode across the grass plot behind the Boatman's and headed toward the clump of fir trees where he'd caught the last sight of Walker. Reining Storm to a halt, Cody slid out of the saddle to take a close look at the ground. Since there was no grass, as there had been behind the saloon, he saw distinct hoofprints of Walker's galloping horses in the hard dirt. They showed a sharp turn around the clump of trees, then a straight line toward the road that followed the river west.

He's got nothing on his mind but putting some miles between us as fast as he can, Cody thought. He followed an obvious route back to the road, pausing briefly when he reached the road to make sure the tracks he followed went to the west. The hoofprints on the road showed Walker's horses were still galloping in an effort to put as much distance between them as quickly as possible. Cody knew the horses couldn't keep that pace very long, so he resisted the urge to gallop after him. Instead, he alternated Storm's pace between a walk and a trot, thinking he might overtake Walker in the long run.

As he'd expected, Walker's horses maintained the gallop for a little over two miles before their tracks indicated they had cut back to a slow walk in an effort to recover. Cody expected to gain ground by continuing his alternating pace.

Up ahead of the white Crow warrior, Ben Walker knew he was being pursued, even though he had seen no sign of a horse and rider behind him. Finally forced to let up on the big Morgan gelding when the willing horse had begun to show signs of failing, he slowed his pace. His packhorse looked close to the point of collapse. He'd thought by galloping as far as the horses could, he might gain enough lead on Crazy Wolf then he could let his horses recover just enough to increase their pace again.

He had not gone ten miles when he reached the confluence of Clark's Fork with the Yellowstone River. Since he was riding in country he had no prior knowledge of, he assumed it was just another nameless river, and he had as good a chance of striking a settlement on that river as he did on the Yellowstone. He believed his chance of beating Crazy Wolf was better in a town of any size than he had out in the wild country. If he could find himself a good defensive spot in town, he could see him coming.

He cursed himself for running away from Coulson. He should have sat right there in the back of the saloon and shot him down when he walked in the door. But instead, Walker was standing at the fork of the rivers, trying to decide which one to take. Crazy Wolf will think I stayed with the Yellowstone, he decided, and turned his horses onto the one that forked off to the south.

Had he chosen to continue along the Yellowstone, he would have come to the little town he wished for in less than ten miles. Settlers had begun making homes in the area and a fledgling town was already developing. The railroad had not come yet, but now that the threat of the Sioux Indians had been broken, white men felt safe in the Yellowstone Valley. Many of those who'd come to the valley were prospectors who thought there might be gold in the headwaters of the Clark's Fork. Government surveyors were already mapping the future route of the railroad from the east. In anticipation of its coming, a station house and post office was built, and the settlement was named Carlton.

Unaware of all this, Walker prodded his weary horses along the Clark Fork of the Yellowstone, seeing no sign of civilization ahead. He was walking beside the Morgan, and he knew he was going to have to rest his horses soon, but he kept them moving as long as he thought he could. Finally, when the river took a sharp little turn, he decided it a good place to lie in wait for his pursuer. He placed the reins over the Morgan's head and laid them on his neck, then pulled his rifle from its scabbard. The two horses went down to the water's edge immediately. He knew he would have to camp there. The sun had already dropped below the line of mountains to the west, and it would be only a short time before the last dying rays of light would go out, leaving the river canyon in heavy darkness. He was hungry but was afraid to build a fire that would lead the wild Indian right to him.

"We'll see if the big Crow scout can track as good as he thinks he can," Walker mumbled to himself. "I'm gonna lay right here on this bank and wait for him. And if he shows up, I'll shoot him down like I would any crazy wolf." He checked his rifle to make sure it was ready.

Deciding he was going to be there until morning, regardless, Walker hurried to unload his horses while he still had a few minutes of daylight left. He used his packs and saddle to build a protective bunker to shoot behind as the last few minutes of light faded away. Content with the ambush he had waiting, he found himself hoping Crazy Wolf would continue to come after him. The former soldier was certain he would be able to see a man on a horse before that man could see him lying on the bank of the river.

Back at the confluence of Clark's Fork with the Yellowstone, Cody was hurrying to make use of the fading light of day as anxiously as Walker was. To be sure which way Walker had gone when he had reached that point, Cody searched both trails for a short distance, and realized Walker had chosen to follow Clark's Fork, instead of continuing along the main body of the Yellowstone River.

Where could the cavalry deserter be headed in that direction? Cody wondered. It didn't make sense, unless Walker did it in a desperate move to throw him off his trail. The thought Cody had remembered earlier about the evil spirits came to his mind since the Clark's Fork route was the way to Spotted Pony's village at Red Lodge. He immediately put that out of his mind.

But if I track him as far as Rock Creek, I'll go straight to Spotted Pony's village, he thought.

He started out again, following Walker's trail along Clark's Fork. It was a trail he had ridden many times, going back and forth on hunting parties as well as war parties against the Sioux and the Cheyenne. He knew every curve the river took, so much so, that he could almost feel his way along in the darkness.

Knowing Walker had to be thinking about ambushing him, Cody took extra caution when he approached places in the river that lent themselves to prime ambush spots. Just as he did whenever approaching a sharp curve in the river, he dismounted and led his horses. As he neared the curve in the river, a horse down by the water issued a call for identification and Bloody Axe's gray answered the call.

Both men stopped to listen.

Ben Walker felt a sharp stab of panic. The Crow devil had found him! Then he reminded himself that he still had the advantage. He was secure behind the rampart he had fashioned. Crazy Wolf had to come to him, and Walker was loaded, cocked, and ready to fire. One squeeze of the trigger and it was the happy hunting ground for the Crow scout. Walker took his hand off the trigger guard for a quick moment to wipe the sweat from his palm, quickly returning it, ready to pull the trigger. It seemed like an eternity since the horses had nickered.

Come on, he urged, knowing that any second Crazy Wolf would ride right up to him. What if he'd heard the horses and stopped? "Damn you. Where are you?" Walker whispered impatiently.

"I'm here, Walker," were the ghostly words he heard as his head was jerked back and the knife slashed his throat.

In reflex, his finger locked down on the trigger and he fired his final shot off into the darkness of the night.

While he still had a handful of hair, Cody used his knife once more, taking the rapidly dying man's scalp. He would give it to his father as proof that Bloody Axe's death had been avenged. Then he quickly got off the body and dragged it a few feet away before Walker bled out over his packs and saddle, which took only minutes.

Cody decided to leave him where he was as the buzzards would find him quickly in the morning. He stripped Walker of his guns and ammunition as well as a modest sum of money he carried in his pocket. No doubt that had come from the same source that had provided him with a pack-horse. Cody would keep the money and some of the ammunition. Everything else, he would give to Spotted Pony.

Finished, he went back to get his horses and brought them to water with the Morgan and the sorrel. He gathered enough wood to build a fire and cooked something to eat.

In the morning, he would visit his father in the Crow village.

CHAPTER 12

The first evidence that the heavy darkness was surrendering to the new day were the slender fingers of light finding their way through the leaves of the cottonwoods beside Clark's Fork of the Yellowstone. Moments later, a ray of sunshine darted across the face of the lone individual sitting beneath the tree, watching the group of four deer as they came from the grove of trees on the opposite bank and walked down to the water to drink. Cody let the deer drink.

When they started to leave, he slowly raised the Henry rifle, laid the front sight on a young doe, and squeezed the trigger. She dropped and the buck and the other two does bolted up into the trees. Fortunate he'd seen the crossing the deer had been using, now, he could take food to Spotted Pony's little village of old people and women.

After he prepared the carcass for travel, he loaded it on the sorrel packhorse Walker had stolen, and set out for the two-hour journey up Rock Creek.

Spotted Pony sat by the fire in front of his tipi, a blanket wrapped over his bony shoulders.

"A rider comes!" one of the women tending the fire called out. "He is leading three horses. It looks like a deer on one of the horses!"

"Who is it?" Spotted Pony asked. "Can you tell?" The old chief was almost totally blind when looking at distant objects and was not a great deal better up close.

Another woman cried out, "It is Crazy Wolf! And he is bringing a deer!" That was enough to summon the rest of the two-dozen residents to gather to welcome Crazy Wolf.

One of the two older boys in the village, Lost Turtle, came out to join them. "It is Crazy Wolf, but he looks different." As he stared at the approaching rider, he realized what made him look strange. "He has cut his hair!"

"Is Bloody Axe with him?" Spotted Pony asked.

"No," Lost Turtle answered. "He is alone."

As he'd expected, Cody was welcomed with shouts of "Crazy Wolf!" and "Welcome!" It had been quite some time since he had returned to the village on Rock Creek. He dismounted and walked through the small crowd of friends there to greet him to stand before his father.

"It is good you have come to visit us, my son," Spotted Pony said. "The light in my eyes has gone out, so I cannot see you clearly. I hear them saying you have cut off your hair and you look like a white man."

"That is true, Father," Crazy Wolf answered. "I did it because I had to look for something in the white man's world, but it will grow back. It is not important. I am still a Crow warrior."

"Then it is a happy occasion today to have you come to visit," Spotted Pony said.

"I am afraid it is not really a happy occasion, for I have come to bring you sorrowful news."

"Bloody Axe?" Spotted Pony guessed at once. "I was afraid when they said you were alone. He is dead?"

"Yes, Father, he is dead. He was shot in the back by one of the soldiers who was trying to shoot me. I have killed the soldier who killed him, and I have brought you his scalp so that he will wander lost in the next world."

Spotted Pony didn't speak for several seconds while he absorbed the tragic news. "Death waits for all of us," he finally said. "I think maybe I will be with Bloody Axe soon." He shook his head sadly while he thought of Bloody Axe. Then he raised his head again and asked, "And now the soldiers are looking for you?"

They were interrupted by one of the women then who asked what Crazy Wolf wanted to do with the deer.

"I want you to butcher it, Sunflower, and cook it, so everyone can eat," Crazy Wolf said, which generated a cheer from the crowd as they took charge of the feast.

Turning back to Spotted Pony, he said, "No, I am not in any trouble with the soldiers. The man I killed was a bad soldier. He deserted the army and stole the two horses I brought to you. I especially want you to have the black horse. Many white chiefs ride horses like that one. They call it a Morgan horse, and it is fitting that you should own one. So I give it to you, along with a fine saddle."

"I will ride it when they come to move us to the main reservation in the Powder River country," Spotted Pony said. "They say we can no longer stay here."

"Why do they say you have to leave here?" Crazy Wolf asked, genuinely surprised.

"I think because they want us all to live in one place and hope we all learn to be farmers," Spotted Pony said.

Sunflower came back to them again to apologize to Crazy Wolf. "I am sorry we have no coffee to make for you to have with your deer meat, but the creek has good water."

"I have coffee. I brought it just for this feast." Crazy

Wolf went to his packhorse and got the sack of ground coffee he had bought for himself as well as a sack Walker had in his packs. "I think I have enough for everybody." Giving her the two sacks, he grinned at how happy that made her.

She took them and ran to round up several coffeepots.

It wasn't very long before cuts of fresh venison were roasting over the fire and everyone had a cup of hot coffee. It was a sad celebration, however, due to the news of Bloody Axe's death, and the despair in knowing the village was going to be forced away from their long-time home. After he had eaten his fill, Spotted Pony asked Crazy Wolf to sit with him again to talk.

They moved away from the fire where there was less noise of the feast. "Are you going to go to the reservation to live?" Spotted Pony asked.

"No," Crazy Wolf answered. "I don't plan to live on the reservation."

"Where will you go then?"

"I don't know. Maybe I will go farther west, maybe to the Washington country. Maybe there is still room for a Crow warrior there."

"I have been thinking about the move to the big reservation and I have decided I will not go. My body and my brain are telling me the circle of my life has been completed. It is time for me to go and I am ready. It has been a good life.

"When they said you look like a white man, it made me realize you have completed your circle of life as a Crow warrior. You are too young to end your life on a reservation. It is a wise thing you are thinking to do. Ride to the far country where I first found you but go as a white man. No one can tell you that you must go to the reservation. You are the same as the soldiers, the settlers in their wagon trains, and the people who build the towns. You are young and strong. I am proud of the man you have become, Crazy Wolf. Go now and complete your circle of life as I and Bloody Axe have done."

Crazy Wolf had not expected to hear that kind of talk from the old chief who had always preached his pride in being born a Crow. And he sincerely believed Spotted Pony still felt the Crow to be superior to all other men. It was obvious the old man was being realistic. He could see the Native Americans were unable to stop the advance of the white man upon his homeland. In effect, Spotted Pony was telling Crazy Wolf he could forgive him for taking advantage of having been born of a white mother and father.

"I have always respected your wisdom, Father. So I will do as you say."

"Good, my son," Spotted Pony responded. "Now, I must rest. All this talk has made me weary. Tell Sunflower to come here for me."

Crazy Wolf got up and went back to the fire where the others were still eating. He told Sunflower that Spotted Pony asked for her. "I think he is tired and needs to rest."

"I thought he might be before much longer. I will take care of him." She turned and called Lost Turtle to help her. They went at once and took the old man back inside the tipi.

Sunflower and Lost Turtle came back out of the tipi shortly.

"Spotted Pony is resting. Lost Turtle helps me move the old man around," she said. "I can't always do it by myself. But he is getting so skinny, I can almost manage him by myself. It was good to see him eat something for a change. Usually, he doesn't want anything, but I think he just says that because he is afraid there is not enough food for everyone. Lost Turtle hunts for game, but he has no shells for Spotted Pony's old single-shot rifle. He says he cannot get close enough to a deer or an elk to shoot it with his bow."

Crazy Wolf watched the boy while Sunflower was talking. He guessed he was thirteen or fourteen and was evidently a responsible young man, judging by her comments regarding his help. "Lost Turtle, is there still meat to hunt between here and Clark's Fork?"

"Yes, there are deer, white tail and mule. Sometimes some antelope pass through the valley. I wish I could get close enough to try a shot with my bow."

"Do you think you could hit one with an 1873 Springfield carbine?" Crazy Wolf asked. "That's the same weapon the army uses. It's a single-shot rifle, but it's breech-loading and it fires a powerful bullet."

"I would like to try," Lost Turtle responded.

"Come with me and I'll show you one." Crazy Wolf led the very interested young boy to the edge of the camp where he had left the saddles. "This is the saddle and blanket that was on the black horse I brought to Spotted Pony." He pulled the carbine out of the saddle scabbard and held it up for Lost Turtle to see. Seeing the wide-eyed look of excitement on the boy's face, he handed it to him.

Lost Turtle took it as if taking a precious instrument.

"You load it here," Crazy Wolf said and showed him how the hinged breechblock worked like a trapdoor for loading. "That's all you do. Once that's done, you're ready to shoot."

Lost Turtle brought the rifle up to his shoulder and aimed it at a tree about thirty yards away.

"Here is a cartridge. See if you can hit the tree." Crazy Wolf handed Lost Turtle the cartridge and the boy loaded the rifle, just as he'd been shown.

"Good," Crazy Wolf said. "Now squeeze the trigger slow and steady."

The weapon suddenly fired, causing a whoop of surprise from the people still around the fire. They all ran over to see what the shooting was about.

"I hit the tree!" Lost Turtle exclaimed. "I saw the bark fly."

"So did I," Crazy Wolf said. "It was a good shot." He held up a cartridge belt full of cartridges for the weapon. "I brought the horses as a present for Spotted Pony. The rifle is for you to hunt with. Don't be wasteful with your cartridges. And take good care of your rifle. I will show you how to take it apart to clean it."

Lost Turtle was too happy to speak. To him, and this small camp of people, the rifle was a wonderful gift to help feed them. Crazy Wolf could not completely enjoy their enthusiasm for the weapon, since it was a bullet from that very weapon that had taken Bloody Axe's life.

"I will hunt for meat tomorrow," Lost Turtle declared, "and we can smoke the meat, so we will have plenty to eat when there is no game."

"I think maybe I'd better go to the tipi and tell Spotted Pony the shot he heard was Lost Turtle killing a tree," Sunflower said. "His eyes are dim, but his hearing is still good. He might think we are under Sioux attack."

"It is my fault if his rest was disturbed," Crazy Wolf said. "I should have told him I was going to give the rifle to Lost Turtle."

She went inside the tipi to tell the old chief about Lost Turtle's excitement over the gift Crazy Wolf had given him. Upon her return, Crazy Wolf waited for her report, but she said nothing.

"Did he hear the shot?" Crazy Wolf asked.

"No, I don't think so," she replied softly. "Spotted Pony is no longer here. From the touch of his face, I think he left right after Lost Turtle and I laid him on his blankets. Well before Lost Turtle shot the gun."

The joyful reunion became an occasion of mourning for the death of their longtime chief. They all knew that he was ready to leave this world, so it was not unexpected, just sad that it happened on that day.

Sunflower, who'd spent more time with him than anyone else during the last painful years, expressed her thoughts. "He was just hanging on to life in hopes of seeing his sons, Bloody Axe and Crazy Wolf, at least one more time." She looked at Crazy Wolf. "He was so happy when you came, and when he learned of Bloody Axe's death, he was ready to go to meet him on the other side. When you talked with him, did he tell you what he wanted you to do?"

"Yes, we talked about that. I told him I would not go to the reservation, and he said that was what he hoped I would say. We decided my path was to the far west. He said it would make no difference what happened to you and the others here in this small camp if I went with you, or if I didn't, and I agreed with him. I will be leaving right after we bury him."

"I think that is a wise decision," she said. "Because of your birth, you can live in the white man's world."

"I don't plan on living in anyone's world but my own. I will live with what the forests and the mountains have to offer me and claim kin to no man." He smiled at her. "And once in a while, after I've killed a deer and filled my belly with fresh venison, I'll think about this day and hope that your bellies are full, too."

She laughed. "Lost Turtle will grow into our chief, and those of us who are left after the soldiers have given up looking for us, may follow him into the mountains to live." She paused to give Crazy Wolf a stern look. "I am glad you are not going to the reservation. It would be a waste of a strong young man like you."

The women prepared Spotted Pony's body for burial the next day, dressing him in his best deerskin shirt and leggings, and what jewelry he had saved over the years for this occasion. Crazy Wolf, Lost Turtle, and a couple of the younger boys dug a deep grave on a little knoll overlooking the camp. They lowered Spotted Pony carefully into the grave and all took part in the filling-in of the grave. The women cried and Sunflower announced that the old man had given her instructions. There would be two days of mourning for his death and no more. Crazy Wolf assured Lost Turtle that Spotted Pony wished for him to inherit the dark Morgan gelding, which made the young boy extremely proud.

Crazy Wolf stayed one more day after they buried Spotted Pony then said his goodbyes for the final time, and wished for them the government would never find their little pocket of Crow freedom.

He saddled Storm, fixed his packs on the gray, and rode back up Rock Creek until it met Clark's Fork of the Yellowstone, then followed that to its junction with the Yellowstone River. He wasn't really sure where he was going, just that it was in the general direction of the high mountains of the west. He would look for a town or trading post right away, however, for he had left most of his supplies with Sunflower and the others. He counted himself lucky, though, as he had the rest of Walker's stolen money and would need it to replace all his basic supplies.

Having reached the confluence of Clark's Fork and the Yellowstone, it was time to rest his horses. After taking care of them, he built a fire just big enough to make some coffee with the tiny handful he had saved for himself for this one breakfast. He would drink it with the small amount of smoked venison he had brought from the village. As he waited for the coffee to boil, it crossed his mind that while he was riding down Rock Creek earlier, he had heard no sound of that Springfield carbine. And wondered if Lost Turtle was finding any sign of deer. He had left the village to go hunting before Crazy Wolf had started out. The thought brought a smile to his face. Circumstances were forcing the boy to become a responsible man overnight, but Lost Turtle seemed capable of handling it.

As for Crazy Wolf, his circle of life was over. There was only Cody Hunter from now on and he would be ever grateful to Spotted Pony for teaching him to live with what the earth provided.

When he thought his horses were ready, Cody loaded up again and started out toward Big Timber, a trip of two days at most.

Unaware of the seemingly overnight creation of Carlton Station, Cody was justifiably amazed when he came to the first log cabin after a ride of only about eight miles or so from the fork in the rivers. He was amazed to find an already growing settlement when he rode on, and best of all, what appeared to be a trading post. Having anticipated a ride of a day and a half from that point to reach the trading post at Big Timber, he was happy to head straight to it.

"Mornin'," Luke Hudson greeted Cody when he pulled up in front of the steps.

Luke stepped out of the doorway and walked out on the porch. While he had been watching, he'd thought Cody was an Indian. As he got close enough to see he was probably a hunter or a trapper, Luke became more interested in the packhorse. The man had just one packhorse and it wasn't packed high with hides, so it didn't appear he was coming to trade. Luke hoped he wasn't hoping for a handout.

Cody looked up and returned the greeting. "Mornin',"

"It's a fine mornin', ain't it?" Luke offered. "What can I do for ya?"

Cody paused and considered that, then answered, "Yes, sir. It is a fine mornin' at that. I'm needin' to buy some basic supplies, if you're in the business of selling such." It occurred to him it was the first day of the rest of his life.

"You're in the right place," Luke said with a chuckle. "Come into the store and I'll see if I've got what you're needin'."

Cody casually looped his reins over the hitching rail and followed Luke into the store. "The first thing I'm needin' is coffee," he said at the counter. "Have you got any roasted coffee?"

"I sure do. I roast it, myself, and grind it, too."

"How much you charge for it?"

"How much you thinkin' about buyin'?" Luke countered.

"Ten pounds. Maybe twenty pounds, depending on the price," Cody responded.

"Twenty-seven cents a pound," Luke said.

"The last I bought in Coulson was twenty-six cents a pound, but twenty-seven ain't bad, I reckon. I'll take twenty pounds. I'm gonna need some flour and . . ." He talked about the price on the first couple of items, then after he found that Luke was dealing fairly, he just called them off. And Luke put them on the counter. By the time they were finished, Cody had run up a bill that amounted to over fourteen dollars.

"I reckon that's all I can think of," he said "How much you gonna need?"

"Do you know your numbers?" Luke wasn't sure Cody knew how big a bill he had amassed.

"Some," Cody answered, "enough to get by."

"Here's what I make it out to be," Luke said, turning around the piece of paper he wrote it on so Cody could see it. Then he went down the list, showing the cost of each item. "And that's the total," he said when he got to the bottom.

Cody followed along with each item, then read the total he saw at the bottom of the page. "Fourteen dollars and forty-seven cents. That looks about right." He pulled out some money and started counting it out.

Luke released a sigh of relief. "That's a mighty fine order. Just make it fourteen and a quarter. I'll give you some help carryin' this stuff out to your horses."

"Much obliged," Cody said.

Feeling some guilt for having misjudged the buckskin clad stranger, Luke said "I surely appreciate the order. I reckon I forgot my manners. My name's Luke Hudson, and it's a pleasure doin' business with ya."

"Cody Hunter. Pleased to meet you."

"Are you set up somewhere around here, or you just passin' through?"

"I'm just passin' through," Cody answered.

"Where ya headed?"

"West."

Luke paused, waiting for more than that.

"No place in particular to the west in mind, but I'll know it when I find it. I think I was almost there once when I was just a little fellow. Things got turned around, and I ended up spending most of my life in the prairie country. Now I think it's time to go back to look for those mountains."

Luke was touched by the young man's sincerity. "Well, I hope you find what you're looking for young feller. You look strong enough to handle whatever you run into. Good luck to ya."

CHAPTER 13

Cody left Carlton Station with supplies to last him many days, even if he had only fair luck in finding suitable game along his journey. He hoped to save the rest of the money for cartridges for his rifle when he needed them. With no source of future income, other than animal hides he might accumulate, he would be very cautious with his cartridges and use his bow whenever hunting small game. He could live off the land, and easily learn to live without luxuries like coffee and molasses.

As he rode along, he remembered his earlier years when he had taken a spirit journey for days without any food at all, until he was visited by his vision. It came to him but made no sense. Many of the young boys of the tribe took their warrior names from their visions.

Awaking from his vision, he was lying on his back being pelted by a pouring rain. He remembered nothing except how good the rain tasted as he gulped it down. Ashamed not to have a vision to relate, he went back to the village and told Spotted Pony his vision had told him to keep the name his father gave him, Crazy Wolf.

He chuckled thinking about it. "Now as a white man, I laugh at the foolishness of an immature Indian boy."

Then he thought of the foolishness of some of the young men of the village—those who learned to like the firewater the white men were eager to sell them. They often had visions two or three times a night. He was glad neither he nor Bloody Axe were ever tempted to try the evil water. It occurred to him he had not really thought of Bloody Axe as gone from his life forever. They'd been like blood brothers, always together.

Somehow Cody felt Bloody Axe would show up again. "You would be a welcome sight, my brother, even though it might mean I was dead, too," he said, half in jest.

He traveled for two days before he met anyone else on the trail up the Yellowstone valley. Thinking to camp overnight at Big Timber Creek, he was surprised to find a camp already there. Two men were camped on the bank, close to the confluence of the creek with the river. From the looks of the camp, Cody figured they had been there for several days.

He decided it was still early enough in the evening to continue on up the river to camp. Since it had not been a hard day on his horses, he could put a couple of miles between his camp and theirs without asking too much of the horses.

When they spotted him, both men walked out to meet him.

"Howdy, neighbor," one of the men, a heavy-set brute with a bushy black beard, called out to him. "Ain't seen many folks on this trail all day. Where you headed?"

"I'm headin' up to Fort Ellis. I'm supposed to meet a cavalry patrol comin' this way to pick me up." That was the first thing Cody could think of to say that might change their minds, if they had any ill intentions. From the look of them, he thought that a good possibility.

"Is that a fact?" the other man, as lean as his partner

was heavy, replied. "The cavalry comin' to meet you? You must be somebody important, or you're packin' somethin' important."

"We was just gittin' ready to cook us up some supper," the heavy-set man said. "You're welcome to use our fire, if you want to. A whole lotta folks like to camp here by this crick, and we're glad to share it. Good idea to camp with a friend in this part of the country any time."

"That's mighty neighborly of you to offer," Cody said. "But I got a late start this mornin', and my horses just got a rest a few miles back. I don't want 'em to get lazy on me."

"I see what you mean," Bushy Beard said. "Well, you know where we are, in case you change your mind. Have a good evenin'."

"Thank you, kindly. The same to you fellows." *I don't expect any of us will get much sleep tonight,* Cody thought as he rode away, halfway expecting a bullet in the back.

"Do you believe that crap about the cavalry comin' to meet him?" Rafer Batson asked as the two men stood watching Cody ride away.

"Hell, no," Quincy Kite responded, tugging away at his heavy black whiskers while he tried to imagine what was packed on that gray horse toting the packsaddle. "That's just all he could think up to fool us into thinkin' we'd best not get any ideas about messin' with him."

"You reckon he's been up there in the mountains at the headwaters of Clark's Fork? Lotta folks think there's gold up there, just like there was at Virginia City."

"I don't know where he's been," Quincy said. "He don't look like no prospector to me. Dressed like a damn Injun. I expect if he's carryin' any gold, he stole it from the feller that dug it up."

"You might be right," Rafer said. "That means it rightfully belongs to us. Right?"

"That's a fact. It's about time he came along. I was gittin' tired of waiting for somebody to show up."

"Young feller," Rafer declared. "Looks like he might be able to handle hisself pretty good. I shoulda brought my rifle out here with me. Sure woulda made it a heap easier to just put a bullet between his shoulder blades before he rides outta range."

"Maybe," Quincy allowed. "But more'n likely if we walked out to meet him carryin' rifles, he'da most likely took off at a gallop. And he might notta stopped anywhere to camp."

"Maybe so," Rafer insisted, "but I'da still knocked his behind outta the saddle if I'da had my rifle."

"You talk like you've got some kinda important meetin' to go to tonight," Quincy japed. "If you're too busy to take care of business, I reckon I can take care of it by myself. 'Course I'll only be able to cut you in for about five percent of the take."

"I expect I'd best go with you," Rafer came back, "to keep you outta trouble."

"Let's go get some supper cooked up. We're workin' tonight, and there ain't no tellin' how far that feller's gonna ride before he decides to stop. And I don't work so good on an empty stomach."

"I hope to hell he's got some chawin' tobacca," Rafer said as they walked back to their campfire. "I ain't had a chaw in I don't know when. A chaw and a drink of likker, that's what I'm needin' right now."

Both parties had a fair estimate of what the coming night was going to bring. Cody was sure he had read the true intent of the welcome to join in their campfire. Not only did he feel he was sized up, but he also felt their eyes had left tracks all over his packhorse. It had been a fairly easy day on his horses, but he would push them a little farther while searching for a place that would lend itself to the standoff he knew was coming.

He continued riding along the river road for a couple of miles before he found a spot that would work for him—a short bluff with several large cottonwood trees close to the edge of the bluff. A small clearing stood between two of the largest trees and he picked that as the best place for his fire. He relieved his horses of their saddles and packs and placed them on one side of the small clearing, then spread his bedroll beside them. Then he led the horses down off the bluff and hobbled them near the edge of the water. He wanted them out of the way of any gunfire that erupted in the camp. Although sure the two men would steal the horses, he also felt sure they would want to kill him first. They would want whatever he had on his person and in his packs.

His camp was as ready as he could get it for his guests. Down at the edge of the river, he filled his coffeepot with water, confident his visitors would wait until dark before making their call. He could see no reason for him to go without supper when they would most likely wait until he was asleep.

He made his pot of coffee and ate the last of the smoked venison he had brought from the Crow village. He didn't plan on getting any sleep.

"There he is," Quincy said softly as he pointed toward some tall trees on a short bluff above the river. "I swear,

I was startin' to think he mighta rode all the way to Bozeman before he made camp."

"I see it," Rafer whispered and pointed toward the small fire, too. "Where's his horses?"

"Down by the water," Quincy replied. "But he's up on the bluff by the fire, so he can see anybody comin' from the road before they get close enough to get a shot at him. Pretty smart, and with all them short bushes between them big trees and the road, I reckon he figures he could hear ya comin', too."

"How we gonna sneak in there, then?" Rafer wondered.

"It'd be pretty damn hard to walk into that camp without him knowin' you was comin' unless you don't go in the front door. We'd best go in the back door."

"Back door?" Rafer responded. "What are you talking about?"

"We leave the horses right here," Quincy explained. "We get any closer and the damn-fool horses will start talkin' to his horses, anyway. We'll leave 'em here and cut right straight through them trees to the river on foot. Then, we walk up the river till we get to his horses, and we can crawl right up that bluff to his camp. And he'll be dead before he knows he's got company."

"You sure that'll work?"

"Sure, I'm sure," Quincy said. "He ain't worryin' about nobody crawlin' outta the river after him."

They tied their horses by the road, took their rifles, and walked through the brush and trees until they reached the beginning of the low bluff. Instead of walking up onto the bluff, they walked along the edge of the water until they came to Cody's two horses. They paused a few moments to give the horses some attention in an effort to keep them quiet.

After listening for sounds of snoring from the direction

of the campfire, and hearing no sound at all, Quincy walked up to the lip of the bluff, which was about as high as his neck. Peering over the lip, he could just make out what appeared to be the sleeping figure. He had made his bed on the other side of the fire, close up under the big trees.

Quincy watched for several long moments. When there was still no motion from the sleeping figure, he was sure the man was fast asleep, then turned his head to smile at Rafer. As he had predicted, they had gotten into the camp undetected.

Though neither one voiced it, both were certain they could lead the two horses away without waking the sleeper, but . . . as they had decided beforehand, they wanted whatever the sleeper had on him and in his packs. Aside from that, they always held to the rule that a dead man wasn't likely to give chase.

"It's time to wake him up," Quincy whispered.

After looking the situation over, he propped his rifle against the face of the bluff and drew his handgun, thinking the .45 would be less awkward to handle. Then he moved up onto the bluff and slowly crawled on his hands and knees toward the fire and the sleeper on the other side of it, keeping his .45 in hand, ready to fire. Rafer copied his every move and crawled up behind him, also on all fours.

Advancing as far as the edge of the faint firelight, Quincy stopped when he heard a thud behind him. Rafer grunted painfully.

"Quincy, I'm hit!" Rafer cried out.

Shocked by Rafer's outcry, Quincy fired two shots into the roll of blankets on the other side of the fire, then turned to find out why Rafer had blurted out.

"What the—?" That was as far as he got before he felt a hard blow and looked down to see the arrow protruding from his chest. He screamed out in pain, looking around him frantically to see where it came from, only to be hit by a second arrow. He screamed out again, dropped the pistol from his hand, and grasped the arrow shaft in an attempt to pull it out. He cried out when his efforts brought only excruciating pain. Behind him, Rafer pushed himself up from his hands and knees to a position on his knees, trying to turn his head around to see the arrow in his back.

Too stunned to realize what was happening, he recoiled with nothing more than a grunt when a second arrow plunged into his stomach. He tried to back away when Cody suddenly dropped lightly to the ground from the large cottonwood above them and picked up the .45 Quincy had dropped. He cocked the pistol and put one shot in Quincy's head. He cocked it again and put a shot in Rafer's head as well, for he had no desire to extend their suffering.

He left the bodies where they lay, thinking he would take care of them in the morning when he could see what he was doing. He did go back to the road, however, to look for their horses. He found where they had left them tied to a tree, and led them back to his camp, leaving them with his two horses. Assuming the two would-be assassins had left their packhorses in a decent situation, he would go back for them in the morning, since it was over two miles back to their camp. What little bit of night was left, he would use to sleep.

Well past first light, Cody woke the next morning to the sounds of ducks on the river. His immediate thought was *coffee* before he sat up and saw the two bodies lying between the ashes of his campfire and the river bluff. He decided maybe the first thing he should do was saddle

Storm and go get the packhorses from his visitors' camp. He forgot about the coffee and rode back to the camp where he was happy to see the two horses had been hobbled close to the water, so they were all right. Quickly, he went through the packs, keeping everything he could use, and discarding the rest, then he led the horses back to his camp and left them with the other horses by the water.

Recovering his arrows, he found two of the four had to be broken to get the shafts out of the bodies, but he took the other two to the water's edge and washed them with sand to remove all the blood. He then searched the bodies for anything of value, finding nothing other than their gun belts and weapons. The rifles would be of value as trade items, especially the Winchester 73 Quincy had carried. Finished with the bodies, he dragged them over to one side of the clearing, so the buzzards would have no trouble locating them.

Then he evaluated his horse stock. The packhorses looked to be average and about six or seven years old. Both of the deceased had been riding good horses with decent saddles. He guessed by the length of the stirrups that the heavy-set man with the full black beard rode the bay, and his slim partner rode the red roan. Cody hoped to sell both at a good price.

He was happy to find that both men had carried a coil of rope, just as he did. He would fare better on that particular road if he trailed the horses. It would be easier than trying to drive them as he had moved the horses after rescuing Amy Boyd.

Realizing he hadn't thought about Amy Boyd in a while, he chuckled when he wondered who was going to give him a haircut next time. "I reckon I'll have to cut my own," he declared.

If he remembered correctly, and he usually did when it

came to distances, Fort Ellis was a good day and a half's ride. Since he was already late starting out for Bozeman, he figured he would wait until the horses needed rest before having that first cup of coffee and something to eat. That would then count as the half day's ride. When everything was packed up, he took one last look at the two corpses that would have robbed and killed him, hoping there were not two more like them waiting ahead for him.

The trip to Bozeman was, happily, an uneventful one. He arrived before suppertime of the second day after the ambush at Big Timber Creek. As he'd passed Fort Ellis three miles east of the town, he'd decided to see if he could get rid of some of his string of horses and rode all the way through the thriving little town until coming upon a stable at the end of the main street. He pulled his string of horses up in front of the stable and stepped down from the saddle.

John Tyler, a lanky man with a bald head and a bushy mustache, walked out of the stable door. "Howdy, stranger. Whatcha got there?" he asked, looking at the string of horses, some wearing saddles, some carrying packs. "You lookin' to board all them horses?"

"No," Cody answered. "I'm lookin' to sell all but two of 'em, and I figure you're in the business of buyin' and sellin' horses. Is that a fact?"

Tyler went on the defensive right away. "Well, I do buy some horses from time to time, but I ain't buyin' any lately. Money's kinda tight. Where'd you get them horses, anyway? Couple of 'em look like somebody just stepped down from the saddle to go squat behind a bush."

"I didn't steal 'em, if that's what's botherin' you," Cody said. "The last two fannies that sat in those saddles are feedin' the buzzards back near Big Timber Creek. They visited my camp in the middle of the night with the intention of slittin' my throat and stealin' my two horses, that dun, and that gray." He pointed his horses out. "Now, I aim to sell the horses they left for me, and I came to you first because I know that's the business you're in. You can look them over and you'll see the two saddle horses are in good shape, and the two sorrels are in fair to good shape. The saddles go with 'em. All I'm askin' is a fair price for both of us." He waited while Tyler thought about what he'd said.

When he didn't respond after a few seconds, Cody added, "If you ain't interested in 'em, I'm goin' to auction them off in the middle of the street. I have no use for this many horses." When Tyler still remained silent, Cody said, "Well, thank you for your time," and turned back toward his horse.

"Now, hold on a minute!" Tyler exclaimed. "I ain't even had a chance to look 'em over that good. I ain't used to dealin' like this. You tellin' me there ain't no lawman, soldier, or private citizen who is gonna come here and say these horses belong to them?"

"If they do, I wouldn't pay 'em no mind. They'll most likely be ghosts," Cody said.

Tyler sucked air in sharply through his teeth and shook his head. "I ain't never done business this way before. Lemme look 'em over."

"If you wouldn't mind, I'd like to let 'em visit your water trough. They just got done walkin' about eighteen miles."

"They don't look none the wear for it," Tyler commented. "Sure, let's take 'em to water."

"I expect they'll appreciate it." Cody felt he had exaggerated only a little. The horses had gotten water just the other side of Fort Ellis.

After Tyler looked them over thoroughly, he was ready

to deal. "So that there ain't no misunderstandin', I'm gonna tell you how much I can pay for four horses. And that's them four right there, the two saddles included. Right?"

"That's right," Cody said, "but it don't include what's in the packs. The packs ain't for sale."

"All right," Tyler agreed. "Just give me a couple of minutes to work up my figures, and I'll be right back." He went inside to his secret place to see how much cash he had on hand and to do his figuring.

Cody waited outside the stable and after about twenty minutes, Tyler returned. He was holding a stack of paper money in his hand. "I figured it as close as I could 'cause I have to turn around and sell 'em to make a profit. The best I can do is give you one-hundred-and-fifty dollars for the four of 'em. That's figurin' twenty-five apiece for the two sorrels, which I figure ain't really worth more than twenty. And I figure fifty apiece for the bay and the roan."

"One-fifty, huh?" Cody responded. "That's about the price for one good saddle horse like either one of those other two. That sounds like a good deal for you. All you have to do is sell one and you'll have all your money back."

Tyler was a little surprised to find that the buckskin-clad young man knew the price of a good horse. "Well, I know you'da liked to got more, but there ain't a lot of folks come lookin' to buy a good horse lately. I figured what I thought—"

"Don't misunderstand," Cody interrupted. "I'll take your offer. I expected a little more than that, but not much more. I would not have had the horses to sell if I had not been attacked by the men who used to own them. We both got a good deal, but I have one counteroffer."

"Oh? What's that?" Tyler asked, concerned.

"One-hundred-fifty, plus my other two horses and myself sleep in your stable tonight at no charge. I will be leaving tomorrow."

Tyler's face relaxed to form a grin. "You gotta deal." He counted out the money so Cody could see it was all there then extended his hand. "My name's John Tyler. It's a pleasure to do business with you."

"Cody Hunter," he said, shaking his hand. He put the money in the pocket sewn inside his buckskin shirt. "I'll help you take care of your new horses."

They took the horses inside and removed the saddles and the packs from all four packhorses, which amounted to a load that was easily what one horse could carry, especially a horse like Bloody Axe's gray. Tyler showed him a stall for his horses and packs and Cody asked what time he closed the stable, so he could be sure he got back in time.

"Nothin' to worry about," Tyler said, "unless you're plannin' to spend that money in the saloon tonight. I don't go home till seven o'clock."

"No saloon," Cody stated. "But since I can afford it now, I'll go somewhere to get some supper. Can you recommend a place?"

"The Dinin' Room," Tyler said without hesitation.

When Cody reacted as if he'd been japed, Tyler laughed and explained. "That's the name of the place, The Dinin' Room. It's the best food in town, if you want somethin' that tastes like home cookin'."

"That sounds like what I'm lookin' for." Cody thought he could have told Tyler *home cooking* to him was more like freshly killed game of some kind with pemmican or corn cakes.

Tyler told him where The Dining Room was and Cody said he would be back in plenty of time. He walked down the main street, which was still fairly busy, even at the supper hour. Reaching the first side street with The Wagon Wheel saloon on the corner, he turned and followed the street a short distance to The Dining Room.

CHAPTER 14

"Good evenin', young feller," Clem Hopkins greeted when Cody walked in the door. "This your first time at The Dinin' Room?"

"Yes, sir. It is," Cody replied.

"Thought it was. This is a family restaurant, and we like to ask our customers to leave their firearms at home when they eat here."

"Oh." Cody looked puzzled. He had left his Henry rifle in the stable with his saddle. "Oh, the six-gun. I forgot I was wearin' it. I'm sorry."

He must have seemed sincere, for when he started to leave, Clem said, "You don't have to leave. If you'll just let me take that pistol, I'll stick it right here under this counter, and you can pick it up when you leave. All right?"

"Thank you, sir." Cody drew the pistol from his holster and handed it to Clem, handle first. "The man at the stable, John Tyler, told me this was the place to eat. I'm glad I don't have to go back and tell him you wouldn't let me in."

Clem laughed. "No, sir. We wouldn't want that. You walk right in and pick out any table you like and one of the girls will take care of you."

Cody walked into a large square room with one long

table that seated about a dozen people. Only four people were seated and eating, and they weren't sitting together. He decided on one of the small tables lined up against the walls. With no experience eating in nice restaurants, he preferred not to be in an obvious spot. It was but a few seconds before a young lady came to his table and introduced herself as Amanda.

"Pleased to meet you, ma'am," he responded, not certain it was the proper thing to do. "My name's Cody Hunter."

Her facial expression told him she hadn't expected his response, and he told himself he was going to have to learn how to behave as a white man.

She smiled at him and said, "Well, I'm pleased to meet you, too. What are you drinking?"

"Ma'am?" he replied, confused.

"What would you like to drink with your supper?"

"Oh. Can I get a cup of coffee?"

"You surely can," she answered cheerfully. "Do you take anything with it?"

Again, he looked confused. "Supper was what I was thinkin'."

His reply confused her as well for a moment, then she said, "I meant, do you put any sugar or milk in your coffee?"

"Oh. No, ma'am. I drink it just like it comes outta the pot," he said.

"Good," she said, totally convinced the young man must have come from another planet. "I'll go get you a cup of coffee, and when I get back I'll help you order your supper. You have your choice of two things tonight"—she pointed to a chalkboard on the wall—"and you can decide which you want. I'll read you your choices when I get back with the coffee."

He watched her disappear into the kitchen and was tempted to get up and walk out before she returned, knowing he had come off as a half-wit. It was only his second restaurant visit as a white man, and he had expected this experience to be much like his visit to the first place. Tuggle's in Coulson hadn't been a great deal different from eating in the army mess hall. You sat down at a big table and Tuggle's wife came around with a pot and spooned food on your plate. He looked at the chalkboard she had pointed to and realized then what it was for. He was still looking at it when she came back with his coffee.

She placed it before him and said, "Now, let's see which you want for your supper."

He surprised her when he said, "I think I'll take the pork chop and mashed potato. I don't get much chance to eat either one of those."

"You read the board?" She said it before she caught herself then tried to recover. "What I mean is that board is hard for some people to read from the tables on this side of the room. You must have really good eyesight."

He smiled. "Yes, ma'am, I do."

"I'll be right back with your supper," she said and returned to the kitchen.

"That was quick," Ethel Reilly said when Amanda came back in the kitchen and went to the stove to fill a plate. "From the way you talked about him, I thought you'd be a while before he decided what he wanted."

"He read the chalkboard while I was getting his coffee," Amanda said. "I'da bet five dollars he couldn't read. I promise you, Ethel, that is the most innocent man I've ever seen in here. He acts like he's never been in a public eating place before."

"Maybe he hasn't," Ethel replied with a chuckle. "He had to kill a deer to make a shirt to wear. You reckon he knows how to use a knife and fork?"

"I can't wait to see," Amanda answered. "I just hope I don't have to clean him up after he finishes."

"Let me know if you do," Ethel said. "I'll be glad to give you a hand. He ain't that bad looking in sort of a mountain-lion-looking way."

"Ethel Reilly, bite your tongue," Amanda scolded as she started toward the door with Cody's supper. "I might have to tell Clem you're having impure thoughts about our customers."

"Hell, Clem already knows that," Ethel called after her.

"Here you go, Mr. Cody Hunter," Amanda announced cheerfully as she placed the plate before him on the table. "I picked the biggest pork chop in the pan. How's that look to ya?"

"You didn't have to do that, but it's a mighty nice thing to do, and I thank you."

"You're welcome. I'll be back to check on you in a little bit." She looked at his coffee cup. "Your coffee okay?"

"Yes, ma'am, it's very good coffee," he answered, making every effort to be a gracious guest.

She stood there for a few moments, waiting to see if he was going to use the knife and fork on the pork chop, but he paused as well, waiting for her to leave. She said she'd be back with more coffee in a little while and went directly to the kitchen door where Ethel was standing, watching Cody's table.

"Move back inside the door," she said to Ethel. "He's gonna know we're watching him."

As a matter of fact, he was aware that he was being watched. The two women were not very secretive in their surveillance of the wild man. He was not aware that their surveillance was strictly for their personal entertainment, however. He was concerned that if he appeared to be too uncivilized, he might be asked to leave. With that in mind, he made deliberate motions to grasp his knife and fork, cut bite-size pieces from his chop, and stab them with the fork to transfer to his mouth.

Amanda was filling his coffee cup when they heard the first shot. He was at once alert, much more than she. It didn't sound that far away.

When she saw him pausing to listen, she said, "The Wagon Wheel Saloon up at the corner. Every once in a while some drunk shoots a hole in the ceiling."

In a few minutes, however, there were more shots in rapid succession.

"That was more than one gun," Cody said. "Maybe bad trouble."

"You may be right," Amanda said. "Just as long as they keep it in the saloon. The marshal will be down there right away." She looked toward the front door. "Clem went out to take a look."

While she and Cody watched, Clem came back in the front door. Another man followed behind him. Suddenly a startled gasp went up when those closest to the door noticed the man was holding a gun to Clem's back. Then everyone in the restaurant became aware of it, and a wave of frightened murmuring descended upon the room.

A stocky brute of a man wearing the clothes of a rancher, the gunman gave Clem a shove in the back toward one of the small tables. "You set your ass down in that chair and don't you move outta it." Then he looked around the room at the few customers eating supper. "Who wants to die tonight? Who's gonna be first?" He looked around the whole room again, his gaze settling on Cody as he pointed his six-gun at him. "You, there, wild man. Stand up so I can see you."

Cody stood up.

"Where's your gun?"

"I don't have one," Cody answered.

"The hell you don't," the gunman responded. "You're wearin' a holster. Where's the damn gun?"

"I had to leave it at the stable. You can't bring a gun inside if you want to eat here."

"Nobody in here has a gun," Clem said.

"Keep your mouth shut!" the gunman ordered. "Now, everybody, pull out your guns and lay 'em on the table." Nobody moved. "Come on, I wanna see them guns on the tables."

"You're the only one who's got a gun, you damn fool," one gray-haired old man finally said. "Get outta here and let us eat!"

The gunman raised his pistol and fired a shot in the wall directly behind the old man's head, the bullet passing inches from his ear. The younger couple at the table with the old man begged the gunman to spare him.

"He opens his mouth one more time, it'll be the last time," the gunman roared. "I shot a man down in that saloon for cheatin' at cards. And I shot his partner down when he tried to help him. So I ain't got nothin' more to lose if I shoot one or two more. I told that two-bit marshal of yours to bring my horse and the money I left in that saloon to this place in thirty minutes. And if he don't, I'm gonna shoot one of you nice people every fifteen minutes after that. And folks, I'm a man of my word, so you better hope that marshal gets up here with my horse."

"Macy!" The call came from outside the front door. "I got your horse out here, just like you said!"

The gunman moved over beside the window, his six-gun still pointing toward the diners. He took a quick look out the window to see his horse standing in front of the restaurant. "Where's my money?" He yelled out.

"It's in your saddlebag. There ain't no use in anybody else dyin' tonight. If you're smart, you'll give yourself up. Save yourself a lotta trouble."

"If you don't clear outta that yard right now, I'm gonna start killin' these folks in here, one by one till I can't see hide nor hair of you," Macy yelled.

"All right, all right," the marshal yelled back. "I'm leavin'."

"And in case you got somebody set up somewhere with a rifle, when I come outta here, I'm gonna be wearin' one of these ladies in here like a shirt. She's gonna ride outta town with me in case you're fool enough to get a posse after me. You think about that, Marshal."

"Macy, you don't need to do that. I give you my word, there ain't no sniper waitin' to take a shot. Leave the woman be, and just get on outta town."

"You give me your word, huh?" Macy said scornfully. "I wonder what that's worth. Damn it, I'm tired of playin' around with you." He cocked his .45 and fired a shot into the ceiling. It brought the results he thought it would— a scream of fright from the women in the dining room and a withdrawal by the marshal.

"All right, Macy, you win. I'm leaving. You don't have to kidnap no woman."

Macy eased up beside the window again and watched the marshal and his deputy backing away from the building. He walked back to stand near the entrance of the restaurant and surveyed the hostages, all staring back at him with ghostlike faces. He pointed to Amanda. "You, come 'ere. You and I are gonna take a little ride."

"Oh, no," Amanda responded. "I'll be damned if I'm going anywhere with you."

"You are, or I'm gonna leave you here with a bullet in your brain," Macy declared. "You might as well get that in your head right now." He walked over and grabbed her wrist, unaware of the explosion about to occur.

She resisted, causing him to turn upon her in anger. By the time he looked back toward the tables, it was too late to stop the missile that was Crazy Wolf, charging like a wild bull head down and angry. As he collided with the startled gunman, he almost ran through him, driving his body against the front wall and knocking the wind out of Macy's lungs. It was an identical re-enactment of the attack upon Corporal Ben Walker. However, it was called for because Cody had no gun. The six-gun was knocked out of Macy's hand and went sliding across the floor to stop at Ethel's feet. She reached down quickly and picked it up.

When Cody, seated on Macy's back, reached out for it, she placed it in his hand. He cocked it to make sure it was ready to fire, then pressed it hard against Macy's skull. "Don't you move," he commanded. He looked up at Clem who had come to help if help was required, and asked, "Have you got some rope?"

"I sure as hell have," Clem said and hurried to fetch it.

When he returned with the rope, Cody said, "Here," and handed him the gun. Taking the rope, he hogtied Macy, making sure he was tied good and tight, then said, "I reckon somebody needs to go get the marshal. I doubt he's very far away."

Clem volunteered. "I'll get him." He stepped out onto the front porch and called out, "Marshal Cox!"

Within seconds, the marshal, his deputy, and two volunteers stepped out of their hiding places at various points around the yard.

"You can come get him now," Clem said. "He's changed his mind about leavin'."

Inside The Dining Room to take charge of the prisoner, Marshal Cox exclaimed, "Dang. I kinda wish you'da let him leave, and we woulda shot him down in the front yard."

"And shot Amanda down, too, I suppose," Clem said.

"Well, there's that possibility, all right," Cox admitted.

Standing off to the side, Cody was surprised when Amanda suddenly appeared beside him and said, "You're just gonna have to deal with it, because I'm gonna have to hug your neck." She wrapped her arms around his chest, laid her head on his shoulder, and almost crushed the life out of him. "I think you saved my life today, Cody Hunter. How can I ever repay you?"

"I don't know," Cody replied, then smiled. "More coffee?"

She gave him an extra hard squeeze in response before she released him. "You can have all the coffee you want."

"One more cup oughta do it," Cody said. "I was just fixin' to finish it off when that fellow walked in, but it got cold and I like it hot."

She looked at him in disbelief, not sure if he was japing her or not. All of the other customers were up from the tables and milling about the room, jabbering to each other about the incident that just happened. Marshal Cox and his deputy were talking to Clem while they untied Macy's feet, so he could walk to the jail. Amanda looked at Cody again, and he gave her another smile. It was general confusion in the room, and he wanted a cup of coffee.

"All right," she said, "you're having me on. But if you

want a cup of coffee, I'll go get you one right now. You want a slice of apple pie with it?"

He hesitated a moment. "I didn't think about that. Is it an extra charge?"

"Not tonight, it isn't," she answered, amazed that he would ask. "Go back and sit down, and I'll bring you pie and coffee."

"Yes, ma'am," he said and returned to his table although he had some concern about the time. He didn't see a clock anywhere and he wasn't sure now how much time had been wasted with the gunman. He had to get back to the stable before Tyler locked it up for the night.

Amanda was back in a couple of minutes with hot coffee and apple pie. She left him to finish his supper while she joined the spectators watching the marshal and his deputy march the gunman out of the building. They stopped on the porch, and the marshal left his deputy to guard the prisoner. He wanted to talk to Cody.

Only halfway into his slice of pie, Cody looked up to see the marshal approaching his table, less than subtle in his outright appraisal of the stranger dressed in buckskins.

"Mr. Hunter," Cox addressed him. "Clem and the others told me how you took care of that fellow when he tried to abduct Amanda Clark. Said you took one helluva chance to take him down like you did. I wanna thank you for takin' a risk like that, and I know Amanda is mighty grateful. You being a stranger and all, I can't help wonderin' why you put yourself at risk like that."

"I had to make sure nothin' happened to Amanda," Cody said. "She brings me coffee."

The marshal wasn't sure if he was joking or not until Cody grinned. Then he grinned in response and said, "Well, thanks again for steppin' in when somebody like you was needed."

"You're welcome," Cody said. "Have you got a watch?"

"Yeah, I've got a watch. You need to know the time?"

"I do. I'm sleepin' in the stable tonight, so I wanna get back there before Mr. Tyler locks it up. He said he was gonna be there till seven."

Cox reached in his pocket and pulled out his watch. "Well, you've got plenty of time. It ain't but ten minutes after six. You gonna be in town a while?"

"No, sir. I'll be ridin' out tomorrow."

"Where you headed?" Cox asked.

"I ain't sure," Cody answered truthfully. "I'm just headin' west, try to find me a mountain to climb and a fresh spring to take a drink of water, I reckon."

Cox shook his head in envy. "Well, good luck to ya. Wish I could go with you." He hurried back outside to help his deputy.

Cody finished his pie and coffee, then got up and went to the front counter where the other customers were still standing around discussing the incident they had experienced. They parted to give Cody room when he approached and stood gaping at him. When Clem smiled at him, Cody said. "I need to pay for my supper, and Amanda mighta forgot to tell you, I ate a piece of pie, too. How much I owe you?"

One of the customers spoke up. "I'll pay for his supper, Clem." His offer prompted offers from several others.

"There ain't no charge for your supper," Clem said with a wide grin. "There ain't no tellin' what mighta happened, or who mighta been killed, if you hadn't done what you done." Then he pretended to reconsider before saying, "Of course, we coulda got rid of Amanda, but I reckon you can't have everything." He paused for the chuckling that remark caused, then continued. "So, you don't owe me anything, and I hope you'll come back to see us, if you're back this way again." He continued grinning at Cody, expecting him to walk out the door. But Cody continued to stand there in front of the counter as if waiting for him to say more until it became awkward.

Clem asked, "Is there somethin' else I can do for you?"

"Reckon I could have my .45 back?" Cody asked.

"Oh, hell, I forgot all about it," Clem confessed. He reached under the counter and retrieved the pistol. "Sorry."

"'Preciate the free supper," Cody said. "It was mighty good cookin'."

"If you're back this way again, I think I'll let you keep your gun," Clem joked.

Returning to the stable, Cody found John Tyler talking to Marshal Cox's deputy and holding the reins of Macy's horse. When he walked up to them, the deputy turned to leave, paused long enough to say, "Cody," in greeting, then walked away.

"You know Jimmy?" Tyler asked, referring to the deputy.

"I know he's the marshal's deputy," Cody answered. "I didn't know his name till now."

"How'd you like The Dinin' Room?" Tyler asked, expecting to hear Cody's version of the altercation at the restaurant, after just hearing Jimmy's version.

"It was good," Cody said. "I had a pork chop and it was fried just right. And the service was real good, too. If I was gonna be in town a while, I'd go back there to eat."

"According to what Jimmy just told me, they had a kinda unusual supper tonight." Tyler tried again to get him to open up.

"Yeah, that's right. It was pork chops," Cody repeated. "But that was only one of two things they cooked. You could take your pick and eat beef if you didn't want a chop. It was a nice place, and the people who run it were nice. I'm glad you recommended it."

"I reckon they're glad I recommended it, too," Tyler said.

"Oh, you mean that little business with the fellow the marshal arrested. I reckon that was kinda unusual. At least I hope it was. You want me to give you a hand with that horse?"

"Yeah, if you want to," Tyler replied. "And you can tell me your side of what happened in The Dinin' Room between you and Max Macy."

"All right," Cody agreed, "but there really wasn't that much to talk about."

CHAPTER 15

"I thought you said you was headin' west," John Tyler said when Cody finished checking his packs and stepped up on Storm, then turned the dun gelding back toward town.

"That's right, I am headin' west. Before I do, though, I decided to go back to Fort Ellis to see if I could run up on a fellow I used to scout for when he was ridin' outta Fort Keogh. That is, if he ain't out in the field somewhere. He was a fine officer to work for and, I don't know for sure if I'll be back this way again."

"Well, I hope you find him," Tyler said. "You take care of yourself, young man."

"I'll do that. And you do the same." Cody touched Storm with his heels and the big dun reacted immediately, settling into a comfortable lope he knew his master favored, to be reined back to a walk once they cleared the town.

Back on the road to the fort, he met a couple of patrols starting out on some duty call. As he passed them, he took a good look at the officers in command to make sure neither one was Lieutenant Ira McCall. They weren't, so he continued on, hoping Ira had duty at the fort today.

Cody assumed his odds of catching him on base were low, but it was worth a try.

Riding into the parade ground of the fort, he looked for the post commander's building, thinking someone there could send him in the right direction. He didn't know if McCall was still in the same troop as when Cody rode for him, but it would have made things much easier. He pulled his horses up in front of what appeared to be the head-quarters building and walked inside.

The two desks in the room were manned by two men wearing sergeant's stripes. They both regarded the buckskin-clad stranger as someone surely in the wrong place.

"Somethin' I can help you with?" one of the sergeants asked.

"Beggin' your pardon, Sergeant," Cody said very respectfully, "I'm hopin' you can help me find Lieutenant Ira McCall."

"What do you want him for?" First Sergeant Davey Graham asked, older than the other one by a few gray hairs.

Cody turned to talk to him. "I'm just passin' by Fort Ellis on my way west and I know Second Lieutenant McCall is stationed here now. I thought I'd stop and see if I could visit him again. You see, I used to scout for Lieutenant McCall when he was at Fort Keogh. He was in Troop D of the Second Cavalry back then, but I don't know if he's still in that troop out here or some other outfit. I figured maybe you could tell me where to look for him. He's a mighty good soldier and a fine man. I just hoped I could say hello before I leave this part of the country."

The two sergeants exchanged glances, trying to decide if there was some reason not to help the young man out.

They decided at the same time that it was a problem McCall could handle himself.

Sergeant Graham volunteered the information. "Lieutenant McCall is still in D Troop, but now we're all back with the rest of the Second Cavalry. Come on and I'll show you." He walked outside with Cody and pointed to another door in the same building. "First Lieutenant Pitt and Second Lieutenant McCall have desks in there. Just go in and tell the corporal on duty you're lookin' for Lieutenant McCall. Whether he's there or not, I couldn't tell you. But that's where he usually is when he ain't in the field."

"Much obliged, Sergeant," Cody said, "I figure there's a good chance he's in the field somewhere, but I might get lucky and catch him in at his desk."

"If he ain't in, they oughta be able to tell you when he'll be back."

"Thanks again, Sergeant." Cody took Storm's reins and led his horses a few yards down in front of the door with no identification markings on it. He dropped Storm's reins on the ground and walked into the office to confront a clerk who looked as if he was created to be a company clerk in the army.

Corporal Raymond Slaughter looked up in surprise when Cody walked into the room. "Can I help you?"

"Yes, thank you, Corporal," Cody replied. "I've come to see Lieutenant McCall. Is he in?"

Slaughter hesitated. "Well he's in, but the lieutenant is extremely busy right now. Is he expecting you?"

"No," Cody answered politely. "He's not expectin' me. I didn't know I was gonna be here myself."

"Does he know you?"

"Yes, he knows me."

"What is your name?" Slaughter asked, thinking he might remember hearing the lieutenant mention it.

"Cody Hunter."

Slaughter couldn't recall ever hearing the name before. He decided to let the lieutenant get rid of him. "Wait right here, and I'll check with Lieutenant McCall."

Cody thanked him and the corporal went into an inner office and closed the door behind him.

McCall looked up. "What's going on, Slaughter?"

"Sir, there's a fellow in the orderly room who wants to see you. Says you know him."

"Did he give you his name?"

"Yes, sir. Cody Hunter. He says you know him," he repeated.

"Cody Hunter," McCall repeated. "It sounds kinda familiar, like I heard it somewhere before, but I can't remember where. He didn't say what he wanted?"

"He acted like it was just a friendly call, but I swear, he doesn't look like anybody you'd know. Looks like he just came out of the woods."

"I've gotta get a patrol ready to move out north of here in the morning, I ain't got time to talk to everybody who wanders in out of the woods. Get rid of him."

Slaughter did an about face.

"No, wait a minute," McCall said. "Cody Hunter," he repeated again. "Hell, send him on in here. Maybe I'll remember who he is."

"Yes, sir." Slaughter went back to his desk in the orderly room. "Lieutenant McCall said to go on in."

Cody walked into an office with two desks. Lieutenant McCall was standing up behind one of them to receive him. No one sat at the other desk. McCall was astonished. Slaughter hadn't said anything about the man being dressed in buckskins. A stranger, yet he looked familiar somehow.

Then it struck him! "Crazy Wolf!" he blurted out. "Crazy Wolf," he repeated, "but you look different!"

Cody stood there grinning, then he pointed to his hair.

"Your hair," McCall said. "You cut off your hair. Well, I'll be. If you ain't a sight for sore eyes. What are you doing out here? Where's your brother, Bloody Axe? Is he out here with you? Cody Hunter" he said then. "I swear, I'd forgotten that name." He laughed and added, "You'da gotten in here a lot quicker if you'd said *Crazy Wolf*. I declare, this calls for a drink." He reached behind him and opened a cabinet.

"Oh, I forgot, you don't drink." He paused. "You haven't started, have you?"

Cody shook his head.

McCall started to close the cabinet, then stopped and pulled out the bottle. "It calls for me to have a drink. You want some coffee? Lemme see if Slaughter has got any coffee made. If he doesn't, he can fire us up a fresh pot." He didn't give Cody time to refuse but went to the door and yelled for Slaughter to make some fresh coffee.

Cody was overwhelmed by the reception he'd received. He had been fairly confident McCall would welcome his visit, but he had not been prepared for reactions like a family reunion. He waited until McCall settled down a little and began repeating the questions he had showered him with when first realizing who he was.

Cody answered one question. "No, Bloody Axe is not with me. He is dead and that is the real reason I am out here." He went on to tell McCall the whole story that led up to this morning in Bozeman.

"Damn," McCall swore. "That's a helluva tragic story. I'm awful sorry to hear about Bloody Axe. I know how close you two were. And now your father, old Spotted Pony, has passed over, too. So now you are going to walk the white man's path. I thought you would never leave the Crow world. What made you decide to do that?"

Cody explained that, originally, it was a move of convenience, and was to be but a temporary change, so he could move more freely in the white man's world while tracking Ben Walker. But when so much of his Crow world was no more, he decided in order to remain a free man, he was going to have to learn to live as a white man.

They were interrupted when Corporal Slaughter brought in fresh coffee. For his efforts, he was entertained by the lieutenant for twenty minutes with stories about the "best damn Crow scout in the whole country."

Cody insisted the lieutenant might be exaggerating just a bit.

When the corporal managed to escape, McCall started asking questions again. "Where are you headin' now? You never said. After you settled up with that fellow that shot Bloody Axe, you coulda gone back to work for Cliff Freeman, couldn't you?"

"Yeah. Cliff told me he had a job for me any time I decided to come back. You know, I thought about that for a long time. And like I told you, I feel like it's time I went back to my roots as a white man for the selfish reason that I can do a lot more without the restrictions placed on the Indian. I wasn't gonna do it as long as Spotted Pony was alive. But now that he's gone, and Bloody Axe is gone, I don't have to prove myself to anybody. I was born white. I might as well take advantage of it."

"Well, for what it's worth, I think you're makin' the right decision," McCall told him. "But if you're just headin' off up into the mountains by yourself, what difference does it make if you're a white man or a Crow Indian?"

Cody paused a moment to consider that. Then he said,
"When I run into that patrol from the Second Cavalry, they
won't make me go live on the reservation."

"You've got a point there," McCall allowed. "Listen,"
he said, abruptly changing the subject, "since you ain't in
any particular hurry to lose yourself in the mountains, why
don't you ride on a patrol with me in the mornin'?" Seeing
an expression of doubt on Cody's face, he sought to
persuade him, and the more he talked, the better he liked
the idea. "It'd be like old times, havin' you along as a
scout. You know I tried to take you with me when D Troop
was transferred outta Fort Keogh. But Colonel Miles put a
whippin' on that request. But, hell, you're a free white
man. I can hire you as a scout if I want to. Captain Grace
leaves it up to his officers to hire the scouts, anyway.
Whaddaya say, Crazy—" He caught himself. "Cody?
I'll put you on the payroll, fifty cents a day, same as a
seasoned, re-enlisted soldier." He shook his head again
in disbelief. "I swear, it's a damn lucky thing you got here
today. If you'd waited till tomorrow, I'da been gone for
fifteen days."

"What about the scouts you've been using?" Cody
asked. "I don't want to knock anybody out of a job."

"We don't have but about a dozen scouts, and some of
them don't work all the time. It ain't like it was at Keogh
where I didn't use anybody but you and Bloody Axe. If
you're concerned about causin' trouble with the other
scouts, you don't have to worry." McCall could see Cody
was still reluctant to change his plans to move on to the
west, so he played his ace. "We're going up in the Big Belt
Mountains to try to find a boy and a girl who were taken
from their home by Blackfoot raiders."

As he'd expected, that captured Cody's attention.

"A boy and a girl?" Cody asked. "How old are they?"

"I think the boy is about ten, and the girl is twelve, brother and sister. Their farm was struck by a war party that burned the house down and killed the mother and father. Ran off with all the stock, except what they couldn't use, then shot them. We're gonna take rations for fifteen days. We'll ride up to Three Forks. That's not but about a day's march from here. Then we'll take a look north of there, along the river. There's a couple more families trying to make it with farms up that way, and they've been hit a couple of times by what they think are Blackfeet." McCall paused again, trying to judge Cody's inclination. "How 'bout it, Cody? I'd appreciate your help."

"I'll go with you as long as it won't cause any problems for any of your regular scouts," Cody finally decided.

"You have my word," McCall said. They were interrupted then by the sound of a bugle. McCall glanced at the clock on the wall and announced, "Twelve o'clock, time for dinner. Let's go to the mess hall and you can be my guest. You're not an Indian now."

"Ain't I supposed to eat with the scouts?" Cody asked.

"I ain't hired you as a scout yet," McCall replied. "This will be a job interview. Might as well get you accustomed to army grub again."

"I'm looking forward to it," Cody said. "I didn't eat any breakfast yet. But I'm not sure I wanna hire on as a scout, so I'll just ride along on this patrol at no pay. I'll be glad to help with the scoutin'. I just don't wanna be paid for it, and you can use your regular scouts. Is that all right with you?" He'd made that decision on the spur of the moment when he realized he did not want to obligate himself to the job of scouting for the army. He wanted to see the country his real father and brothers had died in quest of. But when McCall told him about the two children being abducted, he could not say no.

McCall shrugged, trying to show indifference. "Sure. You can just ride along as my guest, and an observer. I'll just leave it up to you how much you want to help." He figured Cody's real reason was because he didn't want to possibly knock one of the regular scouts out of a job. "Let's go see what the cooks are offering today."

"I have to do something with my horses," Cody said, "especially the one I'm using as a packhorse. That was Bloody Axe's horse, and he's standing outside packed up ready to start out to the mountains."

"We'll take 'em to the cavalry stables," McCall said. "Sergeant Webber owes me a favor or two. He'll take care of 'em. I'll walk over there with you."

Sergeant Webber proved to be as accommodating as McCall said he would be. He gave Cody an empty stall to use as he saw fit. Cody took the saddle off Storm and unloaded the gray of its packs, then asked if he could sleep there.

Webber grinned and asked, "Didn't the lieutenant tell you there's empty bunks in the barracks?"

"Yeah, he did," Cody said, "but I thought I'd best sleep with Storm tonight in case he gets homesick and makes a fuss."

"Since you've rode with Lieutenant McCall before, I reckon you know that in a cavalry troop we have two horse calls every day," Webber said. "We're mighty particular about our horses 'cause if something happens to your horse, you're walkin'. You let me know if you need anything for your horses and I'll take care of it if I can."

"Thank you, Sergeant. I 'preciate that," Cody said. "I noticed those sacks of grain in that back stall. I'd like to give my horses a portion of grain if I could. They haven't had any in a pretty good while."

"Yes, sir," Webber replied. "Feel free to help yourself.

There's a bucket hangin' on a nail on the side of the stall."
When Cody went to feed his horses, Webber commented
to McCall, "Unusual friend you got there, Lieutenant. I
don't reckon you met him at the officers' Christmas Ball.
He looks like he'd be right at home in the woods."

"You'd be right about that, Sergeant," McCall declared.

"I noticed his horses ain't wearin' no shoes, and he car-
ries a bow on his saddle sling. He's spent some time with
one of the Indian tribes."

"You're very observant, Webber," McCall remarked.
"Just between you and me, he's spent his whole life as an
Indian. He was one of the Crow scouts at Fort Keogh."

"He don't really look Crow, except for the buckskin
clothes. And he talks better English than I do."

"It's a long story," McCall said. "I'll tell it to you sometime. But he was born to a white man and woman, so he
ain't pretending to be white. He really is white, and you
can count on him when you get in a tight spot. I know a
couple of times I owed my life to his quick thinking." He
laughed purposely. "Now, I'm gonna go to the mess hall
and see if I can convince the mess sergeant that Cody ain't
an Injun."

He felt a little guilty when he caught himself wondering
if Cody used a knife and fork. He'd never eaten with him
anywhere except on patrol when everybody was seated on
the ground, eating with their hands and maybe a spoon.

Cody returned to encounter questioning expressions on
both their faces. He unconsciously looked quickly behind
him, in case he had left a stall open or a latch unlocked.

"Come on, Cody," McCall said. "Let's go see if they'll
let us eat in the mess hall."

"Right," Cody replied, then thanked Sergeant Webber
for his help and followed McCall out the stable door.

They were among the late arrivers, so plenty of eyeballs

were on Ira McCall and his guest, but the mess sergeant couldn't care less about a wild savage in his mess hall. If Lieutenant McCall said he was his guest, that was good enough for the sergeant. While they ate, McCall told Cody that his afternoon would be spent getting ready for the patrol to leave the fort right after breakfast the next day. "We'll get a good breakfast before departing because it's not a long day's march to Three Forks where we'll bivouac that first night out. I'll have the men detailed for this patrol for a briefing and weapons inspection this afternoon. After breakfast in the morning each man will draw fifteen days' rations in his haversack. I would do that tonight, but if I did, a lot of the men would eat half their rations tonight. It's up to you if you wanna be there for the briefing. I know you never attended a briefing and weapons inspection at Fort Keogh, but it might give you a chance to see what kind of men you'll be riding with. Like I said, that's up to you. Otherwise, I'll meet you back here for supper."

"Glad to see you showed up for supper," McCall said when he found Cody waiting for him in front of the mess hall. "When you didn't show up on the parade ground, I thought you mighta changed your mind about going on this patrol and took off for those high mountains you were talkin' about."

Cody chuckled. "I considered it, but I thought I wouldn't get to eat free in the mess hall, if I took off. And I sure don't wanna miss gettin' that haversack with fifteen days of food in it," he joked. "You said you ain't gonna hand those out till in the mornin' so I reckon I'll be here ready to go at first light."

"I figured I'd join some of the other officers tonight over at the canteen for a couple of drinks of whiskey after supper. You're welcome to join us, even if you don't drink any whiskey." The lieutenant knew what his answer would be to that.

"I thought scouts weren't allowed in the officers' canteen," Cody said.

"I didn't hire you as a scout," McCall came back. "Remember?"

"Oh, that's right," Cody replied. "I forgot about that. I already told Storm I'd be back right after I ate supper. He's a little nervous around all those army horses."

"At least one of us will get a good night's sleep," McCall said. "I was gonna introduce you to Hank Fry this afternoon, if you'd showed up. He's the only scout I'm takin' on this patrol tomorrow. He's usually the only one I take, unless we're headin' out on a big campaign when I'll take two or three. But you can meet him in the morning. He'll tell you that he's usually the only scout I take on a regular patrol, so you'll know you aren't knockin' anybody out of a job. All right? Now, let's go in and get some supper."

To the few officers seated close to them in the mess hall, McCall introduced Cody as a friend he served with at Fort Keogh. If they were curious about in what capacity he'd served, they didn't ask, which suited Cody fine. He ate his supper and drank all the coffee he wanted, then abruptly said he would see McCall in the morning.

It was not until he had gone that the lieutenant was hit with questions about him. McCall would inform him the next morning at breakfast that he had told his fellow officers, over drinks, that Cody Hunter was a renowned Indian Warfare Specialist. As for Cody, he made a comfortable bed for himself on the extra hay Sergeant Webber had pitched in the corner of his stall for him.

CHAPTER 16

Cody was awake and ready to get started when the bugler sounded Reveille at five-thirty the next morning. He saddled Storm and led the dun gelding outside the stable. When the bugle sounded Stable and Watering Call, he led the dun and Bloody Axe's gray to water while most of the soldiers were just getting to the stable. After his horses were watered, he took the gray back to the stable and put him in the stall. He stroked his neck and face and said, "I'm gonna be gone for a couple of weeks, but I'll be back for you. So don't forget who you belong to. Sergeant Webber will turn you out with the other horses, so you won't have to stay in this stall all the time."

Feeling he and the horse understood each other, he left the gray and led Storm out of the stable just as he heard the bugle sounding Mess Call. He shook his head and mumbled to himself, "Seven o'clock. Half the morning's gone."

At the mess hall, he found a stack of haversacks waiting close to the enlisted men's mess being guarded by a sergeant. Cody smiled when he thought of McCall's explanation for not issuing rations for the patrol until morning and led his horse over to the stack. "Good mornin', Sergeant. Have you got one of those for me?"

Sergeant Barnes, who had been watching the buckskin-clad stranger carefully, returned the greeting. "Good mornin'. You must be Mr. Cody Hunter."

"That's right, I am. How'd you know?"

"Just a lucky guess." Barnes held one of the haversacks out toward Cody. One of these is for you. Lieutenant McCall said to tell you to come on over to the officers' mess. He's already inside."

"I brought a parfleche with me," Cody said. "I'll just empty that bag into mine. Don't wanna run off with the army's property." As he took a few minutes to empty the army's bag into the buffalo hide parfleche given to him as a present from one of the women in his village, he inspected the contents—bacon, hardtack, beef jerky, sugar, some coffee, a meat can, and a metal cup to make the coffee in. He saw nothing that could tempt him and decided it would have been safe to issue the bags to the men last night. He hung the parfleche back on his saddle, thanked Sergeant Barnes, and led Storm over to the officers' entrance.

Inside, he saw McCall sitting at a table close to the door. The mess sergeant remembered him and motioned him on through the line.

"Mornin'," McCall greeted him as he brought his tray over to the table. "Did you get your field rations?"

"Yes, sir. I did," Cody answered as he sat down. "It reminded me why I haven't missed being a Crow scout for the army."

"You probably also understand why I'm not starting out before breakfast," McCall returned. "You didn't see Hank Fry outside, did you?"

"Well, I don't know," Cody answered. "Is he a sergeant?"

"No," McCall replied. "Hank Fry, he's my scout. I told you about him."

"Oh, that's right, you did. I knew the name sounded familiar. So, no, I didn't see him. Nobody out there but the sergeant."

While they finished their breakfasts, McCall filled Cody in on some background information that had to do with the reason for that morning's patrol. "Three Forks was named for the three rivers that flow north to come together at that point to form the Missouri River. Now that settlers and prospectors from back east feel like they can safely travel up the Yellowstone without being attacked by the Sioux, they're coming west. Towns like Miles City, Coulson, and Bozeman are springin' up. That land to the south of Three Forks has attracted quite a few settlers, so there's already a good-sized settlement growin' up.

"A pocket of Blackfoot Indians ain't been rounded up yet, and we think they've got a camp somewhere in the Big Belt Mountains to the northeast of Three Forks. In the last couple of months, some of the settlers that live north of the town, like the one on the Gallatin River we're responding to today, have lost livestock and suffered damage by small raidin' parties. They're pretty sure it's some of those Blackfoot in the Big Belts. Our patrol is to see if that's really where they came from, and maybe get an idea how many are holed up in those mountains. Of course, our primary mission is to hopefully find those two kids, if they're still alive."

"There's a good chance they're still alive," Cody said. "The Blackfeet often take slaves when they raid. And the girl is close to the age of breeding."

"What we find out might decide on a major campaign by the whole regiment." McCall paused to gauge Cody's reactions to the purpose of the mission. When he couldn't tell for sure, he said, "And I knew you'd wanna take part in something that important."

"You were goin' up there with just one scout?" Cody asked, knowing most officers would take two or three.

"Well, you said you would help out," McCall insisted.

Breakfast finished, they finally prepared to leave when the bugler sounded Assembly and Roll Call. McCall's men went to get their horses and those troopers who had not picked up their haversacks did so at that time, leaving two figures waiting at the assembly point.

Cody nudged Storm and the horse carried him slowly over to the other figures. "Hank Fry?"

"That's right," Hank replied. "Cody Hunter?"

"Guilty," Cody responded.

"The lieutenant told me you was gonna ride along on this one," Hank said. "You're a lot younger than I thought. McCall said you used to ride for him when the troop was back down the Yellowstone."

"That's right." Cody was aware Hank was looking him over the same way he might look over a horse he was considering.

McCall hadn't gotten around to telling Cody much about Hank Fry. From the streaks of gray in his mustache and short beard, and what hair Cody could see protruding out from under a weathered Boss of the Plains Stetson, he appeared to be well into middle-age.

Cody had a feeling Hank might consider him as competition, so he set to dispelling that notion right away. "I'm just passin' through Bozeman on my way west of here. Maybe even going to Washington Territory. Happens I just got here the day before McCall was ridin' out on patrol, so

he talked me into goin' on patrol with him . . . and you."
He waited for Hank's comment.

It didn't come.

"I'm not in any hurry to get where I'm goin', anyway.
I'll try not to get in anybody's way."

Hank seemed to wait patiently, then he said, "Glad to
have you along. Maybe I can learn a few things, myself."

Cody did not want to hear that response from the older
scout. "I expect you could teach me a helluva lot about the
business of scoutin'," he said. "Let me set you straight on
one thing. I ain't lookin' for a job as a scout, so I'll try to
keep outta your way." Hank started to respond, but McCall
rode up at that point.

"I see you two got acquainted," McCall said as he
pulled up beside them. He called out to Sergeant Barnes to
get the patrol lined up and perform a Roll Call. He then
gave the men a quick introduction to the stranger in buckskins. He told them Cody was an old friend passing
through, and he was riding along on this patrol just to see
what they would do if they did run into some Indians. That
got the laugh he was after.

McCall turned to the scouts. "Hank, you two can just
ride along with me up front. There's no need to send a
scout out today, since we're just gonna ride the road to
Three Forks. You can sharpen up all your scoutin' skills for
tomorrow."

When everything was to the lieutenant's satisfaction,
they moved out.

After walking the horses for an hour, McCall ordered
the patrol to break into a trot for the next hour. To cover
the thirty-six miles to get to Three Forks in one day, and
because of the late start from Fort Ellis, they were going

to have to alternate the horses' walking pace with an occasional trot. Having made the trip several times before, he planned to stop to rest the horses when they struck the Gallatin River about halfway to the town.

When they reached the river, the horses were taken care of first and then the men built a couple of fires to cook their dinners. They could have simply followed the river until they reached the farm that had been struck, but the man they had to contact lived in the town of Three Forks, and that was quicker by way of the road.

When the horses were rested, they set out again under the same marching orders—walk for an hour, then trot for an hour before reverting to a walk for two hours. By that method, they reached Three Forks in eight hours and went into camp for the night. McCall threatened to hang any man who tried to slip out of camp to visit the one saloon in the town.

The report of the Blackfoot raid had been made by Ernest Blanchard, who owned the general store in Three Forks. As one of the first inhabitants of the little town, he was the unofficial mayor and the man the other citizens went to for help. The lieutenant would contact Mr. Blanchard to get an idea of the distance to the farm that was raided. Mainly, he just wanted to make him aware that the army had responded to his telegram. Since it was well past closing time in town, he would go first thing in the morning.

Hank Fry was prompted to tell the lieutenant they didn't need to get directions to the farm. "Just stop at the one that was burned to the ground."

The morning broke clear and sunny and while the camp was cooking breakfast McCall left Barnes in charge and rode into Three Forks. He took his scout and Cody in with him, since he thought they should also hear the directions to the farm.

"Good mornin', Lieutenant," Ernest Blanchard called out from the back of Blanchard's General Store when the three men walked inside. "You get my message about the Indian raid the other night?"

"Yes, sir," McCall replied. "We got the message yesterday and we got here just a little while ago."

"I hope you brought more men with you than these two fellows," Blanchard said, hoping he was joking.

"I did, indeed. I've got a fifteen-man patrol camped about a mile north of here. I'd like an idea how far this farm is from here. I understand it's on the Gallatin River."

"Well, you're camped on the right side of town," Blanchard said, "'cause the farm is about a mile up that river from where it joins the Missouri. Fellow's name who owned it was Franklin Lassiter. Damn Blackfoot struck him in the middle of the night, killed him and his wife and stole his two children. They ran off with all of his cattle, as well as a shoat just weaned and on solid food. They even stole his dog. They just scattered the rest of his stock. Frank and Carolyn were two fine people, their children always polite. I reckon he never heard them Indians until it was too late.

"Blackfeet don't make much noise when they wanna move quiet," McCall agreed. "Are you sure the Indians took the children?"

Blanchard gave him a questioning look. "We're pretty sure, seein' as how they're gone."

"Right," McCall replied, realizing it was a dumb question. "Wonder why they took the dog?"

"To eat him," Hank interrupted. "Same as they did the shoat. Warn't no Blackfoot, anyway. Blackfoot don't never come down this far."

The other three men turned to look at him in question.

"What makes you say that?" Blanchard asked. "Those other raids we've had were all Blackfoot."

"I doubt it," Hank maintained. "Maybe Flathead. Blackfoot don't come down this way."

Blanchard shook his head, skeptical.

"Why do you think they were Blackfoot, Mr. Blanchard?" McCall asked.

"Everybody knows that chain of mountains has been a favorite hideout for two or three bands of Blackfoot," Blanchard insisted.

"It's hard for a lotta people to tell one Injun from another'n," Hank maintained. "Blackfoot don't come down this far."

Cody couldn't understand why the man wanted to argue the point but kept his mouth shut, with no intention to join in . . . until he was given no choice.

"Cody, what do you think?" McCall asked.

"I didn't see the Indians in question," Cody answered. "We just got here, so we haven't seen any sign left by the raiders. Right now, I don't know who they are. Could be a raidin' party of Mormons for all I know. I say let's see if we can pick up enough sign to track 'em. Then maybe we can follow them to their camp and we'll know for sure what tribe they're from."

"Well, that sounds like what I was hopin' to hear from the army," Blanchard declared. "Don't let me hold you up any further. I'll tell you how to find Franklin Lassiter's place. It's the first ranch you'll hit when you ride up the river from where it joins the Missouri. I reckon that's the reason he's the one that got hit. Anyway, it ain't but about a mile up the Gallatin." He hesitated, just then remembering his manners. "Can I get you fellows some coffee or something?"

"No, thank you very much," McCall answered. "I expect we'd best get about doing what we rode up here to do. You can just wish us luck."

"I surely wish you that," Blanchard said and walked them out the front door. He stood and watched them ride away. Hearing someone behind him, he turned to find his wife.

"I was listening to you talking," she said. "I don't know what chance they have of tracking those Indians down. But I hope they listen to the young one, dressed like an Indian."

Blanchard shook his head and chuckled. "Are you sure? He said it mighta been a band of Mormons that hit Lassiter's place."

"You're right. I forgot about that."

He put his arm around her shoulders and walked her back into the store.

Coming to the town of Three Forks seemed like an awful waste of time to Cody as they rode back to the camp. Unlike Hank, however, he kept his thoughts to himself.

The camp was still at least an hour's ride south of the confluence of the Madison and Jefferson Rivers. It would be a little farther still before the Gallatin joined them to create the Missouri headwaters. As a consequence, it was quite late in the morning by the time the patrol finally struck the Gallatin River.

Suggested by Blanchard, they had taken a trail east of the snakelike winding of the Madison River, which took them almost straight north until striking the Gallatin. At that point, it was a guess which direction they should go to find Lassiter's ranch.

Hank immediately said it was downstream, toward the

confluence with the Missouri. Cody agreed, so they followed the river for a little over a quarter of a mile before coming to the burnt ruins of the Lassiter family dream.

"I swear, that's a heart-wrenching sight," McCall uttered when they rode past the charred timbers that had supported the roof of the house and into the barnyard.

Like the house, the barn was reduced to a pile of black rubble. The only structure that had not been set afire was the outhouse, and it was lying on its side as if someone had lassoed it and pulled it over.

"They didn't just come to steal cattle," McCall remarked. "They came to wipe the settlers out." He looked around him, thinking maybe he would see a couple of graves, dug by someone from a neighboring farm. But there were none. "Might as well take a look around the place while we let the horses rest a little. Then we'll start up the Missouri and see if we can see where the raiders went." He gave the order to dismount.

As they expected, tracks were found around the burned barn rubble and the hog lot. Most of them were boot prints, but there were also moccasin prints, although very few. Cody and Hank inspected the ruins independently, inside the barn and house. The question McCall had about the absence of graves was answered when Cody found the bones of two bodies under a pile of burned timbers. Evidently the Indians had killed them and dragged their bodies into the middle of the house to be burned with their home.

McCall told Sergeant Barnes to detail some of the men to dig a grave and bury what bones and remains they could find and put them in one grave. "Might as well let them spend eternity together," he told Barnes.

Barnes asked for volunteers to dig the grave, and all fifteen troopers volunteered and dug the grave in shifts of two men each.

Satisfied there was nothing more to gain from the burned buildings, Cody stood in the barnyard, looking all around him. His eyes lingered on one spot behind where the barn had been. A stand of young pines seemed an obvious choice and he walked directly toward them. It took less than a minute to find the faint prints of the unshod Indian ponies. Following on through the trees, he found the tracks coming into the barnyard as well as those leading away from it. He had the starting point to track the raiding party.

He called McCall over to the pines and showed him what he had found. "I figure there weren't but about five or six of 'em, and it looks like they came down the Missouri from the Big Belts, all right. At least they came into the pasture from the north. It doesn't take much scoutin' to see where they drove some cows away from here. They didn't steal the dog, like Blanchard thought. I found him under a bush near the pine thicket with an arrow stickin' outta both sides of him. I reckon that was as far as he could run before he died. Maybe Hank is right when he says they're Flatheads, but they're using arrows with Blackfoot markings on 'em."

They both looked to see where Hank had gone and saw him circling around south of Lassiter's house, searching for tracks of the Indians approaching from that direction. Cody was sure Hank was hoping to find tracks that would show the Indians went up the Gallatin when they left. He probably figured that would prove they were not Blackfoot, as he claimed.

McCall called out to him a couple of times before he looked up. Realizing he was being called, he came to them.

As he walked up, he explained his frustration. "They've got to have left some tracks to tell us which way they left."

"Right here," McCall said. "This is where they came in and where they went out."

Hank looked surprised, but he quickly recovered. "Right. That's what I was thinkin'. I had to be sure I was right, though. There oughta be tracks leadin' in and outta here." He took a few steps toward the south and the town, searching the ground. When neither McCall nor Cody followed him, he realized he must be wrong, turned around, and pointed down the Gallatin, toward the Missouri. "My money says they went that way."

"You're dead right," McCall said. "Looks like you've got some of 'em trackin' downriver, but it ain't that river. It's down the Missouri, just like everybody around Three Forks figures."

Although there had been much discussion over the tracks as to where the raiders had come from, there was no debate on where they were heading when they drove the cattle from the pasture.

CHAPTER 17

Since the horses had not been worked but an hour or so that morning, McCall had given the order to move out as soon as the Lassiters were buried and the patrol followed the tracks left by the war party. They followed the obvious trail along the Missouri River about twelve miles before stopping to rest the horses and eat some of the bacon and hardtack they brought. Several small fires were built to heat up water for the coffee, so critical for the success of every patrol. The meat cans served to carry the bacon and cook it and the hardtack in the grease.

Hank Fry brought his coffee and ration of bacon over to sit down with McCall, Barnes, and Cody. "Whaddaya plannin' to do with these bucks iffen we was to catch up with 'em?" he asked McCall. "You gonna arrest 'em and take 'em to the reservation?"

"I suppose that'll depend on what the situation is when we catch up with 'em," McCall replied.

"Whaddaya think we oughta do with 'em, Hank?" Sergeant Barnes asked, always entertained by Hank's perspective on various subjects, especially when the subject was Indians.

"Hell, ain't no doubt what we oughta do with 'em,"

Hank answered at once. "Line 'em up and tell 'em we're gonna take 'em back to the reservation. Then shoot 'em down like the wild dogs they are and take 'em back to the reservation. 'Cause if you don't, they'll be right back stealin' and killin' again."

Cody couldn't help thinking Hank and Ben Walker would have gotten along so well had they known each other.

Deciding the horses had rested and grazed enough, the patrol mounted up and set out again, following the tracks along the river valley. Rugged hills were scattered along the east side of the river. Cody and Hank were riding out ahead of the patrol, keeping an eye out for anything unusual. After about eight miles, McCall spotted them waiting at a stream for him to catch up.

Hank pointed to the narrow canyon the stream was flowing from. "They cut in here and followed that stream up into them hills. So now, we gotta be watchin' out we don't ride into no ambush."

"Why would they be set up to ambush us?" McCall naturally asked. "It was days ago when they rode up that canyon."

Hank hesitated, evidently having not thought of that. "Right," he said after a few moments, still trying to think of how to undo his remark.

Cody came to his rescue. "Hank's right. We're gonna have to be careful we don't ride into a camp. They might have lookouts in these hills on both sides of that canyon."

"Oh," McCall said, looking at the steep hills on both sides. "Well, that makes sense. That would be a bad place to get caught in a crossfire."

"I reckon there ain't but one way to find out," Cody said. "Come on, Hank. I'll help you check it out." He wheeled

Storm and started up the stream, and Hank followed after him.

Cody was not really worried about any lookouts on the hills north and south of the canyon. He was of the opinion the raiders could very well have a camp back in those hills, but not that close to the entrance to them.

Once inside the hills, he and Hank found the canyon led to a whole range of steeply sloping hills and narrow valleys, but the tracks of the horses and cows plainly showed which valley to follow. He signaled McCall to bring the patrol forward.

They followed the obvious trail deeper into the hills until Cody spotted the buzzards circling over a hill up ahead of them. He and Hank advanced cautiously until reaching the valley attracting the buzzards. They followed the valley as it curved sharply to meet another valley with a small stream. Cody guessed it was the same stream they had entered the hills in, and it was now the setting for a feast for vultures. The screeching, quarreling birds were feasting on the remains of the cows the patrol had been following. A count of cow heads told them Lassiter had owned ten cows. The Indians had made camp there, probably for a day or two, and it was where they had butchered all ten of the cows.

While Hank went back a way to wave the patrol forward, Cody rode into the noisy valley where the obnoxious birds were picking every morsel of meat from the skulls and feet and anything else that was left of the cows. He could see where a small quantity of the meat had been cooked to eat, but could find no evidence to show they had smoked any of the meat to preserve it, meaning the village they were going to was not so far away that the freshly butchered meat would spoil. Maybe they were not going to the Big Belts.

Cody shared his thoughts with McCall when the patrol came into the valley.

"The question now, I guess, is how far is the main camp and how big is it?" McCall pondered.

"Well, there are still tracks to follow," Cody said. "Trailin' 'em sure ain't a problem. I guess we should be able to find out where they are and then decide if we need to go back and get help." Even as he said it, he couldn't help hoping they would not have to withdraw because of the size of the camp. He knew McCall could not risk the lives of his men in an unwinnable situation. But he also knew that every additional day those two children were held captive was one day closer to death or insanity. It would be especially hard for the boy. He could be subjected to any amount of ridicule and physical punishment. It would also be a nightmare for the girl. But she was almost of an age where she could be of some use to them. The important thing was to get to her before she went out of her mind with fear. He thought of Amy Boyd and the hell she had suffered. But in her case, she was already a woman in the eyes of the Sioux warriors, and she was taken strictly for their immediate pleasure with no plans to keep her alive afterward.

He could only speculate on this war party's reasons for taking the twelve-year-old Lassiter girl. It was his guess they intended to use her as a slave and breed her when she was a little older. His thoughts were snapped back to the present when McCall asked which valley they were going to follow.

"That one," Cody said, pointing to another narrow valley leading into the higher hills.

They left the noisy birds to clean up the scene and drove on into the rugged hills. Thinking the raiders would not have stopped to butcher the cattle where they had unless it was close to home, Cody and Hank were more cautious. No doubt the raiders had no desire to butcher the meat in their camp and attract the large flock of buzzards there. It turned out the party they followed were satisfied with keeping the buzzards a little over a mile from their village as it was almost at that distance when Cody signaled Hank and pointed to smoke drifting up from beyond one of the largest of the hills ahead of them.

Hank verified it and they went back to tell McCall to hold his men in a defensive position, ready to defend or retreat, whichever was necessary while his scouts climbed up that large hill to get a look at what was on the other side.

Cody and Hank left their horses at the base of the steep hill and made their way up through small clumps of ponderosa pines here and there until reaching the almost bald top. With only knee-high grass for cover, they crawled far enough forward to see into the valley on the other side. It was easy to see why the Indians had picked that valley to locate their village. It was broader than the typical valleys in the range of hills, and included a running stream and grass for their horses. Cody guessed the stream forked off from the one where they had done their butchering.

The smoke they had seen came from a large fire in the center of a camp of fourteen tipis.

A pretty good matchup, he thought, *if there's a warrior in every one of them.*

Four of the tipis had a horse tied beside it.

Knowing an Indian warrior often tied his favorite horse beside his tipi didn't mean only four warriors were in the camp. Cody looked beyond the tipis to a grassy meadow where a dozen or more horses were grazing, indicating more than four men were in the camp. He'd been certain

more than four had attacked the Lassiter farm and driven
the cattle to this valley

Quite a few people mingled around the fire set up to
smoke the meat. It appeared they were preserving most of
the meat just butchered in the valley of the buzzards.

The next thought that came to Cody's mind was that
the village was getting ready to move. Most of the people
around the fire were women and many of them were older
women. He realized he saw no children. Maybe, he
thought, this was why the raiders had taken the boy and
his sister.

Seconds later, he saw one of the women tending the
meat turn to call to someone behind her. At the top of the
high hill, he was too far away to hear what she'd said, but
about a minute later, another woman came to the fire
from the other side of the closest tipi. She was driving
ten-year-old Billy Lassiter as one would drive a pig—
using a stick to guide him over to a pile of tree limbs that
had been cut for firewood. The boy picked up an armload
of wood and started toward the fire but was stopped
abruptly by a sharp crack of the woman's stick across his
back. He stood still while she increased his load of firewood with several large pieces, then drove him back to
the fire where the woman who had called for more wood
berated the boy for his slowness.

Atop the hill, Cody felt his body growing tense with
anger and empathy for the boy. He could imagine the
torment the child was suffering on top of the murder of
his parents. He contrasted Billy's fate to that of his own.
His father and brothers were killed by Blackfoot warriors,
too, but he'd been saved by the Crows and treated as one
of their own. Whatever action the patrol took, they must
try their best to rescue the children.

His thoughts were distracted when Hank crawled over close to him. "I ain't seen the girl. Have you?"

Cody shook his head no.

"Blackfoot," Hank announced simply. "Just like we figured."

"Right," Cody said.

"Yonder!" Hank whispered suddenly, pointing toward the stream.

Cody saw Joy Lassiter carrying a water sack. As she walked up from the stream beside a woman also carrying water, the scouts could see a short rope tied around her ankle. The other end was tied around the ankle of the woman beside her.

"They're already trainin' her to be a squaw," Hank commented. "The lieutenant is likely gonna demand her and her brother's release. He's gonna wanna know how many men they've got. I don't know how we're gonna tell him that unless we see some of 'em."

"You're right about that," Cody said. "Judgin' by the horses grazin' out there, they could have more than we've got. A lot depends on how well they're armed. If there's a man in every one of those tipis, they've got fourteen. And if they all have a brother," he joked, "there are twenty-eight of 'em. I reckon we oughta go back and tell Lieutenant McCall what we've seen and let him decide what he wants to do."

Hank agreed, so they eased back away from the crown of the hill and returned to their horses.

McCall listened to their report, and as they expected, he was disappointed when they were unable to give him a close approximate number of warriors his men might be facing.

Cody spoke first. "All we can tell you for sure is there's most likely four warriors in their tipis. Their favorite horses are tied right outside each tipi. Two or three fairly young-lookin' men were walkin' around the fire where the women were smokin' the beef. But enough horses were grazin' beyond the camp to suggest there's quite a few more men around somewhere."

McCall paused while he considered the report. "And you saw the two Lassiter children?"

"Yes, sir. We did," Hank answered. "Women was leadin' 'em around on ropes, but the young'uns seemed to be all right."

Young Lieutenant Ira McCall had a decision to make, and it was not one even an old battle-scarred officer would find easy to decide. If he confronted the Indian camp, and they chose to fight, the odds were good he would have the advantage in firepower. But he would also risk putting the lives of the two hostages in danger. In fact, it was not out of the question the hostages would be purposefully murdered in an act of retaliation. McCall could withdraw, but he considered that out of the question.

He finally made a decision based on his moral concern for the two children. "Sergeant Barnes!" he ordered. "Get the men ready to ride. Find a piece of white cloth—a rag, an undershirt—something to make a white flag with. We're going to approach that Indian camp—" He paused and looked back toward his scouts, then asked, "What are they? Flathead? Blackfoot? What?"

"They're Blackfoot," Hank answered him.

"We're gonna approach that camp under a flag of truce," McCall continued, "and I'm gonna tell 'em we've come to get those two children. We'll give them the opportunity to surrender, to be taken to the reservation where they will be taken care of. And only those who participated in the murder of Mr. and Mrs. Lassiter will be tried for their crime."

Hank turned to give Cody a look in the eye to see if he was as astonished as himself. "I'd be mighty surprised if them Blackfoot would just surrender and hand them young'uns over," Hank said to McCall. "What's your plan if they say, 'go to hell?'"

"Then I reckon we'll open fire on 'em, and keep shooting until they have to surrender," McCall answered. Then said to himself, "And hope those children don't get hit."

"If it was me givin' the orders, I'd start with that last plan," Hank saw fit to comment.

Cody didn't like McCall's plan, either, but he understood the dilemma the lieutenant found himself in. If hostages were not involved, the order of the day would simply be to hunt down the hostiles and punish them for the crimes of murder, arson, and cattle rustling. Their women and children would be taken to the reservation.

Unfortunately, the innocent often paid a penalty as severe as those who perpetrated the crime. As far as his personal feelings were concerned, the Blackfoot was an enemy of the Crow. To deepen his hatred of them, it was Blackfoot warriors who'd killed his father and his brothers, and shot him in the back when he was but a small boy. For all those reasons, he would stand with McCall and fight the Blackfoot.

After Hank's comment on the subject, McCall asked Cody if he had any questions regarding the orders he just gave.

Cody answered him. "No, I have no questions. You are in command, and I understand the difficulty of your job. I will stand and fight and hope the women and children can be spared. I think you must not delay giving them your terms. It is my opinion they are getting ready to leave the valley and go up into the mountains where they will be much harder to find."

McCall nodded his understanding.

"It is also my opinion they will not surrender," Cody added.

"Here you go, Lieutenant," Sergeant Barnes said as he walked up with the white flag he had fashioned using a slender tree limb and a white hand towel one of the men had with him.

McCall took the flag and hefted it a couple of times while thinking about what Cody had said then handed it back to Barnes. "That'll do nicely. I want you to carry it and throw it away when the shooting starts."

Barnes had given the men the command, To Horse! as if at a formal parade.

Seeing the men were all standing at the head of their horses, McCall gave a little talk to ready them for the coming confrontation and to remind them they were all soldiers.

When McCall finished, Barnes commanded, "Prepare to Mount! Mount!"

The fifteen troopers all mounted sharply, wondering what had gotten into the sergeant. One or two wisecracks were made near the rear of the column. With Cody and Hank up ahead as usual, McCall led the patrol through the narrow valley before reaching the first of the higher hills, the one the two scouts had climbed and watched the village from. Barnes ordered the men to load their carbines and hold them at the ready but not to fire until commanded to.

As the men filed around the hill, a few of the women tending smaller fires smoking slabs of beef saw them riding slowly around the base of the large hill. Confused, they squealed in fright. "Soldiers! Soldiers!" And they ran toward the center of the village.

Soon, all the women saw the soldiers, but they did not

run as they would have if the soldiers had come at them at the gallop. Instead, they milled about nervously calling the name of their chief, Bucking Horse, until he came from the tipi in the center of the village. Other warriors appeared from other tipis to join him. As puzzled as his people by the non-aggressive-approach of the soldiers to his camp, he nonetheless made a show of bravery with a powerful pose in front of the people around the big fire. In a matter of a few seconds, he was joined by eight fierce-looking warriors, some with rifles and a couple with bows.

"I'm countin' nine, including the chief, so far," Cody said to McCall. "Here comes two more, that makes eleven. One of them has a rifle." Within the next few minutes, two more appeared, carrying bows. They stood defiantly backing their chief, all in one tight little group. Cody was amazed. McCall had been right in his assumption the warriors might not give battle if his soldiers sauntered up casually, instead of charging full bore on the camp.

"You can see your targets, all standing by the chief, if I give the order to fire," McCall said to his men. "Sergeant, tell them to get more space between themselves. We don't want to give them a good target group, too."

While Barnes stretched his line of troopers, McCall took his white flag and rode out in front of them. "Chief," he called out. "Can you talk white man talk?"

His question caused the chief and the warriors around him to hurriedly argue whether they should or should not. Finally the chief decided and replied. "We talk some white man talk."

"My name is Lieutenant Ira McCall. What is your name?"

"I am Bucking Horse."

"Bucking Horse. I have heard of you," McCall lied. "I have heard Bucking Horse is a reasonable man. I like to be a reasonable man, too. That is why I have not attacked your village. I have come for the two white children you have in your camp."

His statement caused a lot of anxious murmuring among the people standing around the fire. Bucking Horse was not sure what to reply.

Finally, he said, "We have no white children. We are preparing to leave this place. Go and leave us in peace."

"Release the boy and the girl at once," McCall replied, still speaking calmly, "so we may take them back to their people. Then we will talk about peace between us."

"If the chief falls for that one, I might fall off my horse," Hank commented softly to Cody.

"How do I know your word has iron?" Bucking Horse called back. In the Blackfoot language and a lower voice, he said to the woman who had been tending the meat at the big fire, "Lone Dove, tell the women to start taking the meat off the fires and start packing it to travel. As soon as the horses are loaded, we will lead them through the canyon behind us. Do not strike your tipis. There will not be time."

"I speak with the iron of the great chief, Ulysses S. Grant," McCall shouted back to Bucking Horse, unable to think of anything more noble at that point. "He has reserved special land for the Blackfoot to have forever. But first, you must send the two white children to me."

"Take the word back to Chief Grover that we have no white children and are already in the land given to the Blackfoot forever," Bucking Horse answered. "Go and leave us in peace."

"All right, Sergeant," McCall ordered, "tell the men to get ready to charge into that camp on my command. And try not to hit any women or children." He meant it when he said it, knowing full well in the chaos that followed a charge into an Indian village, people were running everywhere. Women would be hit, children, too. But he felt he had no choice but to stop the camp.

"Bucking Horse!" he shouted out again. "Tell your warriors to drop their weapons!"

He was answered with a couple of rifle shots, both misses but enough to trigger a rapid exchange of rifle shots between the line of troopers and the scurrying Blackfoot braves as they ran for the horses behind the camp. McCall gave the order to charge, and the soldiers followed him as he galloped into the camp full bore, his pistol out as he tried to pick his shots to keep from shooting women.

Cody looked around desperately for sign of the boy or girl, afraid they might have gotten a quick slash of their throats by the bitter Blackfoot. But in the confusion of the close combat, he caught a glimpse of Joy Lassiter, a rope around her neck, being led by a young Blackfoot woman toward the narrow canyon mouth beyond the camp. The whole combat of the battle was taking place between him and the canyon, leaving him no way to reach her. He saw no sign of the boy as he was left with no choice other than to fight beside the troopers as they gradually fought their way through to the entrance to the canyon.

That was as far as they got before having to abandon their charge and take up defensive positions. The entrance to the canyon was like a funnel to the valley beyond it, narrow enough to provide cover for the Blackfoot warriors to kill any soldier trying to enter. They formed a rear guard able to hold off the cavalry troopers until what was left of their village was well up the valley.

McCall had no choice but to count his losses and take control of the members of the village who had not escaped—mostly women and wounded men who had not had time to reach the canyon before the soldiers. The battle had not been entirely one-sided, for McCall lost four men in the confusion of the hand-to-hand melee that had women fighting as well as men.

Four Blackfoot warriors, all young men, had been wounded, but none of the wounds were life-threatening. They surrendered only after running out of ammunition and arrows. The other six captives were women. McCall found himself with only one option, and that was to give up on his pursuit of the rest of the Blackfoot camp. He could not very well continue to chase Bucking Horse's band into the hills with ten captives in tow, four of them wounded. It was going to be difficult enough to march ten captives all the way back to Fort Ellis for confinement until they were transported to the reservation. The only saving development was the supply of smoked beef sufficient to feed his prisoners, as well as his soldiers, all the way back to Fort Ellis.

With Cody and some help from sign language, McCall was able to inform his captives of their immediate future. After burying his four dead troopers, he would have access to four horses. They would be used according to the most serious needs. The first one was assigned to an old woman, who could not make the walk. The other three were assigned to a warrior with a hip wound, another warrior with a shoulder wound, and a young mother with a baby. Everyone else would walk. They remained there for the night and would start back in the morning.

CHAPTER 18

The prisoners were allowed to take whatever they could carry from the abandoned tipis. At Cody's suggestion, they removed some hides from the tipis to make two tents to be used on the trip to Fort Ellis. The warrior with the shoulder wound volunteered to give up his horse so it could be used as a packhorse to carry the tents, as well as much of the smoked beef.

McCall designated two of the tipis—one for the women, one for the men—to sleep in that night, and ordered his men to pull the remaining tipis down to make it easier for them to guard the prisoners all night. When he figured he'd taken care of everything for the night, he sat down with Cody and Hank to drink a cup of coffee.

Cody took that opportunity to tell him what he had been thinking. "Looks like it's gonna be a long walk to Ellis for these folks. I might wanna stay here and see a little bit more of this hilly country."

"What are you talking about, Cody?" McCall responded. "I thought you were so all fired up to ride into the Rockies and the country on the other side. Besides, you left a horse and all your packs in the cavalry stable back at Fort Ellis."

"Oh, I intend to go back there and get 'em, but Lieutenant, I saw that little girl bein' led like a dog with a rope around her neck. I've been thinkin' about trailin' that bunch of Blackfeet just in case they get careless about her. I didn't see the little boy, though. Did you?"

McCall shook his head.

"I know you've gotta go back with your prisoners, but I'm not on the army's payroll. I might as well follow ol' Buckin' Horse to see where he's goin'. Maybe I could tell the army where he's holin' up for the summer. Then they could send a whole regiment up there if they wanted to."

"You sure you wanna stick your neck out that far?" McCall asked. "'Cause I've got a feelin' that wherever he's heading, there'll be a helluva lot more Blackfoot warriors to greet him."

"I reckon I kinda hate to give up on those two children," Cody confessed. "We were the only hope they had. I can imagine how hopeless and afraid they feel after today."

"Well, I could tell you you're crazy as hell to even think you might get a chance to rescue those kids. But if I had to pick a man I thought had half a chance, I'd pick you. And I'll wish you luck. You're a good man, Cody Hunter. When are you thinking about startin' after 'em?"

"Right after I finish this cup of coffee. There's a nice moon tonight, almost full."

Hank Fry sat through their conversation, nursing his cup of coffee and thinking he was a witness to how a man starts talking when he's in the first stages of going stark raving mad. He could keep his silence no longer. "I reckon it's a good thing it ain't a full moon, or you'd be howlin' at it all night. Better not howl too loud. You might let them Blackfeet know you're comin' after 'em."

"You mean those Flathead, don't you?" Cody responded. "Blackfeet don't come down this far."

"Go to hell," Hank grumped.

"Eventually," Cody returned.

"You'd best be careful," McCall warned. He got to his feet when Cody did and shook his hand. "Good hunting."

"Thanks. I'll be seein' ya. Take care of him, Hank." He walked by some of the smoked meat the men had stacked up, pulled out his skinning knife and cut off a sizeable piece for himself. Looking back at McCall and Hank, he said, "So I won't have to hunt right away." Then he disappeared into the darkness beyond the campfire.

"You know he's crazy as hell, don't you?" Hank asked after they heard Cody's horse trotting away. "You can get yourself in a heap of trouble trying to think like an Injun thinks."

"You're right about that, but he's been a Crow Indian all his life, ever since he was five years old. When he worked for me at Fort Keogh, he was one of the Crow scouts. His name was Crazy Wolf."

Hank didn't say anything for a long moment before responding. "I figured that."

Cody guided Storm through the narrow opening of the canyon, letting the dun gelding find his footing in the darkness at his own pace. Once the canyon opened wide enough to permit a little moonlight to filter down between the steep slopes of the two hills it separated, the horse settled into a casual walk. Cody was in no hurry and the dun knew it.

Bucking Horse's band had been moving fast when they

fled up the canyon, but they would have had to slow down before going too far. Because several people were on foot, it would be a matter of a steady walking pace man and horse could maintain. With that in mind, Cody figured he might possibly stumble onto their camp for the night sometime before midnight.

Due to the long canyon and the natural trail leading into the valley beyond, he was not concerned with trying to follow tracks. With only one way to go that made sense, he continued on that path. When the moon finally climbed directly overhead, the obvious tracks of the fleeing village told him he was right.

He let Storm pick up the pace to a comfortable lope for as long as the moon lit his way. In a little while, he reined the dun back to a steady walk when he saw the hills ahead took on a darker cast due to the presence of more trees on the slopes. Then he heard the sound of the water ahead. *Good timing,* he thought, *for Storm needs water.* As he waited in the stream while his horse drank his fill, Cody cautioned himself. Thinking he should be catching up to the Blackfoot village pretty soon, he became more alert for any sounds of horses ahead of him.

As if on cue, he heard a greeting from one of their horses, and didn't wait for Storm to answer it before climbing up the slope until he reached a ledge half covered with pines about three-quarters of the way to the top. Even with the help from the moonlight, he could not tell exactly where the camp was but felt sure it was close to the stream. Confident he and Storm were well hidden from the camp somewhere below him in the small valley, he decided to catch a couple of hours sleep. To be fair, he pulled Storm's saddle off, used it for a pillow, and laid down under the big dun, knowing Storm would alert him if anything approached them.

* * *

Awakened by sounds of the Blackfoot camp waking up, Cody didn't move until he listened for sounds of anyone approaching his hiding place on the ledge. Satisfied all was well, he saddled his horse and moved cautiously along the length of the ledge until reaching a point where he could see the stream below the hill. As he had guessed, the camp was on the other side of the stream about fifty yards away. Now able to see the camp and the hillside below the ledge, he could work his way a little farther down the hill to get a closer look into the camp.

Before moving, however, he spotted a warrior on a paint horse come out of the camp and ride back the way they had come. Watching, Cody figured the man was a scout Bucking Horse had sent to check their back trail to look for any sign of pursuit.

Cody moved down from the ledge from one clump of trees to the next until it was as far as he could risk then knelt in a stand of short firs about twenty yards from the stream. While he waited, he heard sounds of the camp ready to get underway again. Then he saw Joy Lassiter. Still with a rope around her neck, she was being led by the same young Blackfoot woman he'd seen earlier. Joy was taken down to some bushes near the creek where she was allowed to answer nature's call. Standing beside the bushes for only a few moments, the woman yanked impatiently on the rope.

Although it was a golden opportunity seemingly presented him, he forced himself to wait. He could easily take the girl from the young woman while they were apart from the rest of the camp but only if he gave up on her brother. Also in question was the whereabouts of the scout who'd ridden out to check the back trail.

He would have to have some luck, otherwise, a lot could go bad with that plan. It was a hard decision to make, especially when he was not even sure the boy was still alive. He, nor Hank, nor McCall had seen the boy during the escape, but he was not among the captives who were left behind. Cody figured Billy had to still be with the Indians.

Be patient, Crazy Wolf, he told himself, recalling the words of Old Spotted Pony when trailing a herd of deer.

Ten-year-old Billy Lassiter was very much alive, although not for very long, according to Iron Claw, if the defiant little coyote didn't soon accept his capture. Billy had been placed under the training and supervision of Iron Claw's wife, Blue Willow, whose first task was to break his spirit. So far, the stubborn little puma was resistant to any amount of whippings and threats.

"The boy is strong," Chief Bucking Horse said to Iron Claw in the Blackfoot language. "It is tempting to cut his throat and be done with him. And I would not blame Blue Willow if she decides to do that. On the other hand, if she is able to break the spirit that lives inside him, he will make a hard-working slave to do many chores for our village."

"I will tell Blue Willow to keep working the boy hard, and maybe by the time we reach the high mountains, he will grow tired of feeling the bite of her whip."

"I think that is wise," Bucking Horse said. "Then if he is still untrainable, she can cut his throat. I must tell her we are proud of her patience with the little coyote so far." He turned then when he heard a horse approaching. "Many Scalps is back. He doesn't seem in a hurry, so I think we are ready to go."

Many Scalps rode into the center of the camp and confirmed Bucking Horse's assumption, and the Blackfeet started out again, unaware of the Crow warrior watching them depart.

From the little clump of short fir trees just short of the stream, Cody had seen the scout return and realized it had been the right choice to remain patient, proving it would have been highly questionable if he could have rescued Joy Lassiter in time. Staying where he was, Cody watched the village people cross the stream and follow a narrow valley north. He spotted the ten-year-old boy in the middle of a group of women. He had been fitted with two poles under his arms tied together by a rope that hung across his neck to form a travois upon which some blankets and packs were stacked.

"They're breakin' him like they would a wild horse," Cody muttered to himself, now aware he had to figure some way to free the boy.

Remaining where he was until the last Blackfoot was out of sight, Cody then climbed back up the hill to Storm, rode back down to the stream, and dismounted to let Storm graze on the grass. Since there was no reason for him to hurry, he filled his cup with water, took it to the ashes of the big fire the Blackfeet had left to die, and stirred up enough live coals to heat his water. Wishing he had brought the little coffeepot he carried on his packhorse, he dropped some ground coffee into his boiling cup. When he guessed it was close to being fit to drink, he pulled it out of the coals and raked as many of the grounds out of the cup as he could. "It ain't real good," he announced, "but it'll do on a mornin' like this."

He cut a healthy slice off of the hunk of smoked beef he had brought, which helped make the coffee taste better. It would not be long before he'd have to take his bow hunting.

Deciding Storm was ready to travel, Cody stepped up into the saddle and started out after the Blackfoot.

It was a routine he would repeat for the next two days—sightings of the two children but no real opportunity to get both of them apart from their captors—until something totally unexpected happened.

Since they had been free of any pursuit for a few days, Cody sensed the Blackfoot had a general feeling of being free of any concern about the US Army. Although they were traveling through what seemed an endless land of rolling hills, they continued to follow a trail that kept them going in a generally northern direction, which seemed to indicate they were definitely headed for the Big Belt Mountains. The relaxation in their daily travel caused him to move in closer at night when they had rolled up in their sleeping blankets around the fire.

Based on that observation, he often tried to determine where the two children were sleeping. Some nights, the boy was tied hand and foot to a tree, and the girl was tied by her ankle to the ankle of one of the women. On this particular night, however, he couldn't spot the boy. Growing tired of watching, Cody decided to withdraw from the gully where he had been hiding.

He stopped dead still, however, when a movement out of the corner of his eye distracted him. He realized at once it was a moving object, likely an animal of some kind—a dog maybe, or a coyote. Whatever it was, was in the gully and moving his way.

Knowing he couldn't afford to startle a coyote and cause it to howl, he rolled out of the gully and laid as still and as flat as he could manage. In a matter of seconds, the animal passed by him, following the gully which ran away from the camp and down toward the creek below the camp. Cody knew he was lucky. The coyote hadn't even smelled him when he was that close.

Realizing that didn't make sense, he raised up high enough to look down the gully. It struck him like a bolt of lightning. *It was the boy!* Crawling on his hands and knees as fast as he could, he was making his escape.

Moving swiftly and as silently as a Crow Indian, Cody raised up again and took a quick look at the sleeping camp. Seeing no indication anyone knew the boy was leaving, he rolled back into the gully and went after him. The boy gave no indication of knowing he was being followed. Cody stayed right behind him until the gully ran out and the boy stopped crawling to get up and run.

Before he could take a step, however, he was wrapped up in one powerful arm while Cody's other hand clamped down over his mouth.

Picking up his squirming captive, Cody trotted into the trees where his horse was waiting before he said a word.

Finally he said, "Billy Lassiter, I'm from that cavalry patrol that came for you and Joy. I've been tryin' to rescue you both. Do not make a sound. I'm going to put you down and take my hand away. I didn't know you were gonna come to me." He took his hand away and set him on the ground.

"Oh, Lordy, Lordy, Lordy," Billy exclaimed over and over. "I thought I was dead for sure when you grabbed me. How did you know I'd be crawlin' down that gully?"

"I didn't. I just happened to be there. How did you get away? Every night I've spotted you, you've been tied to a tree."

"I was tied to a tree tonight, too," Billy said. "But they wasn't watchin' me and I finally got that rope loose enough to get my hands on the knot. And I got away."

"Well, you did a damn good job, and now we have to make sure they don't find you again. The first thing we've got to do is find us a place to hide, because as soon as they find out you're gone, they're gonna be lookin' for you."

"I don't think they'll bother lookin' for me," Billy said. "They already told me, if I didn't quit fightin' 'em, they was gonna cut my throat."

"Maybe you're right, but I still think there's a good chance they'll come lookin' for you just to punish you for runnin' away."

"I didn't wanna leave Joy with 'em, but they was trying to make a donkey outta me and I told 'em I weren't no donkey."

"I don't plan to leave Joy," Cody assured him, "but I was havin' problems getting to both of you. Now, you've just made it a lot more possible to get both of you back. Right now we've gotta get you away from their camp without letting 'em know I'm still trailin' 'em. I want them to think you took off back the way they just came. Are you ready to get goin'?"

"Yes, sir. I'm ready," Billy replied, eager to get started.

"Good. First thing I wanna do is go back to the end of that gully you crawled out of and get rid of my tracks." Cody broke a small branch off one of the pines. "You follow right behind me and make sure you step in the grass and leaves where I do. We don't want to leave any tracks easy to see. All right?"

Billy said he understood, so leaving the horse again, they went back to the point where the gully ended, avoiding the sandy area created by rain runoff. Still with a wary eye on the sleeping camp of travelers, Cody took the pine branch and smoothed over the tracks they had left there.

"Now," he spoke softly, "here's the part where you have

to do a little work. I want you to hop back into that gully where you got up on your feet."

"Where you grabbed me, right?" Billy asked anxiously.

"That's right. Then I want you to take off running outta that gully and head straight up that valley between those two hills behind us. And just keep runnin' till I catch up with you on my horse. You understand?"

"Yes, sir," Billy said. "So they'll just see my tracks runnin' up that valley."

"That's right. You're gonna lead 'em up that valley. And don't worry, I'm gonna come get you. Now go to it!"

Cody waited while the boy did exactly as he'd been told and started running up the valley. Cody shook his head and smiled, amazed by the boy's lack of fear. When he could no longer see him, he went back to get his horse.

As he rode Storm out of the trees at the base of the hill, his mind was working on a new strategy in the completion of his rescue plan. Billy was a gift from a merciful God. The spunky attitude of the young lad made the rescue of his sister a possible thing. And if God, or Man Above, was still willing, maybe a single Blackfoot warrior would come in search of Billy. If that was the case, it would give Cody the opportunity to gain another horse for Billy and Joy to ride.

Riding beside the trail so as not to leave hoofprints heading in that direction, Cody caught up with the boy, reached down, and lifted him up onto Storm. "We've gotta put a little distance between us and that camp in order to set up an ambush, so we'll be leaving some tracks to follow."

They rode back over the same trail the Blackfoot had followed that day, passing many spots that looked suitable in the dark of night, but might be questionable in the light of day. If he picked a place too close to their camp, he and

Billy might not have time to get away before the warriors arrived.

Cody guided Storm to a spot where the trail was confined as it passed directly beneath a narrow ledge that extended out to almost the center of a gap. "This oughta do just fine," he said, moving off the trail and up the side of the hill, riding around the almost barren hill until reaching a clump of trees on the backside of it.

He lowered Billy to the ground, then he stepped down. "I think it'll be safe to build a small fire here. If you're hungry, I've got a little bit of that beef the Blackfoot smoked."

"That sure would be mighty good. They didn't give me no supper tonight. Said I didn't earn it."

"You can stay here with Storm and get a little sleep if you want to," Cody said as he cut off another chunk of the smoked beef, leaving just a little bit for later on. "I'm gonna go back and keep an eye on the trail."

"I'll watch the fire for ya," Billy said. "I don't think I can go to sleep, though."

"I don't expect to see anybody before daylight, but I'm gonna go sit on that ledge just in case somebody checks on you durin' the night. You know where I'll be." Cody took his rifle and his bow and walked back around the hill to the ledge—an ideal spot to ambush a rider on the trail below.

Only a few trees and a lot of bushes grew on the ledge, but they were enough for concealment while he watched the trail. Thinking it would be perfect if he could look up in one of the trees and see a raccoon looking back at him, then he smiled, remembering Amy Boyd's first taste of roasted raccoon. Cody let his mind wander for a moment, hoping she was doing well. Amy was not a beautiful woman, but she was pleasant looking and would make some man a good wife. Maybe she would marry a soldier, he thought, then reconsidered. "She'll most likely end up an old maid, takin' care of her daddy in his old age," he decided aloud, "because she won't forgive herself for what the Sioux did to her."

Calling his mind back to the business at hand, he took a position beside a fir tree and settled himself to last out the rest of the night alert. As there was no sign of anyone coming in search of the boy, he figured no one had checked on him yet.

Figuring it had been a couple of hours, Cody decided to walk back to check on the boy,. The fire was just about out and Billy was fast asleep. A large possum was eating the piece of smoked beef Billy had started. Cody had no taste for possum, otherwise there was breakfast ready to be skinned and gutted. Raccoons were all right when a rabbit wasn't available, but possums ate too many things that could mess with your insides. He put wood on the fire, then went back to his post on the ledge.

CHAPTER 19

"The boy is gone!" Blue Willow cried out when she went to the tree where Billy had been tied. "Iron Claw! The boy is gone!"

"How can he be gone?" Iron Claw demanded. "I tied him to that tree, myself. Have the ropes been cut?"

"No, the ropes aren't cut. He untied the knots."

"He could not untie his ropes," Iron Claw insisted. "Someone untied his ropes while we slept. Find him!"

"I don't think anyone untied him," Blue Willow said. "I think he untied himself. Look at the tracks from the tree to the gully. They were left by little feet."

Since the gully ran the entire length of one side of their encampment, they hurried along beside it to the end where it sloped off toward the creek. By that time, they had collected a small crowd that had gathered at the end of the gully.

"Look! He crawled into the gully. "See," Blue Willow cried triumphantly. "There are his tracks where he ran away."

"It's good that he's gone, I say," Iron Claw declared. "I was ready to kill him, anyway."

"I want him back," Blue Willow said. "I want to break his spirit and punish him for running away."

"Then you go get him," Iron Claw told her. "The boy is bad luck."

"Please go," she pleaded. "He could not have gone far. You could catch him quickly on your horse."

"I will go with you, Iron Claw," Many Scalps offered.

"I don't want to go after him. He is bad luck," Iron Claw insisted.

"Will you go get him, Many Scalps?" Blue Willow asked.

Many Scalps shook his head. "I would not offend Iron Claw, especially if he does not want the boy back."

"It makes no difference to me whether you go after him or not," Iron Claw said. "She is the one who wants the little coyote. Go if you want to. It is time to start our journey."

"I'll go get the little coyote, Blue Willow," Many Scalps told her. "My pony is fast. I will be back before the village is packed up and moving." He left at once to saddle his paint pony.

Blue Willow turned to Iron Claw. "You see, your brother is not too proud to go after a child who needs to pay for his disobedience."

A movement in the distance served to bring Cody's attention to focus again on the trail leading to the ledge. Not sure his tired eyes were not playing tricks on him, he stared at the distant end of the valley and soon the motion took shape. Seconds later, it became an Indian riding a paint horse at a gallop. The Blackfoot reaction to Billy's escape was what he had hoped for—only one rider coming for the boy. Knowing a rifle shot would be heard back in the camp, a distance of about two-and-a-half miles, Cody readied his bow.

A few seconds later, he recognized the horse and rider as the same who had ridden to check on their back trail. The rider reined the paint to a walk.

He must have galloped all the way from the camp, Cody thought, *but walking makes my bow shot easier.* He hid behind the tree until the horse walked under the ledge then moved quickly to the other edge to wait for the horse to pass under it. As soon as the paint cleared the ledge, Cody released the first arrow.

Many Scalps responded with a heavy grunt when the missile drove deep into his back. It was followed by a second grunt when the second arrow drove deeper. He made an attempt to draw his rifle from a buckskin saddle sling he carried but succeeded only in dropping the rifle before he fell from his horse.

As Cody backed off the ledge and hurried down to the base of the hill, the mortally wounded Many Scalps struggled in painful effort to reach his rifle. Cody ended the Blackfoot's suffering with a quick slash across his throat. He thought about taking the warrior's scalp but decided he didn't want it. He dragged the body to the side of the trail and rolled it into a weed patch where it could easily be seen from the trail. He made no attempt to pull his arrows out, thinking it wouldn't hurt to let Chief Bucking Horse think his warrior was killed by another Indian. With that thought in mind, Cody went back to the corpse and took the scalp, which he wrapped around a rock and threw into the middle of the weed patch.

Looking at the paint horse standing in the middle of the trail watching him somewhat nervously, he took his knife and cut half of Many Scalps' shirt off. With the piece of shirt draped across his shoulder, he walked slowly toward the confused paint and talked softly in the Crow tongue, thinking it would sound more normal than white man's English. The horse, still uncertain, nevertheless stood still.

Cody took hold of the bridle and stroked the paint's neck and face, rubbing the piece of shirt on him, letting him smell the shirt. He climbed into the Indian saddle and walked the horse up and down the trail for about twenty yards in each direction. Content the paint was satisfied under the new management, he rode him up the hill and circled around to Billy, who was just waking up.

Storm asked for an explanation, and the paint answered him.

Cody slid off the paint and said, "Good mornin'. I brought your horse around. Whaddaya think of him?"

"Where'd you get that?" Billy asked, astonished.

"I had it sent out from the Blackfoot camp, but right now, we need to get on our horses and leave this place. In a little while they're gonna come lookin' for your horse and the fellow who was ridin' him. How 'bout it? You ready to go?"

"I gotta pee," Billy said.

"Right," Cody said. "Well, you go ahead and do that. You can go right there on the fire if you want to. We gotta put it out, anyway."

While Billy took care of that, Cody took Storm's reins and led him over to the paint. "You two might as well get acquainted, since you're gonna be travelin' together. How you doin', Billy?"

"I didn't have enough to put the fire out," Billy answered.

"That's all right. We'll put out the rest with dirt."

That taken care of, Cody picked up Billy and put him on the paint. Since the horse offered no objection, Cody took the reins of both horses and led them back around the hill and down to the trail. "You ever ride a horse before, Billy?"

"No, sir. This is the first time I've ever set on a real horse. My pa let me set on the mule's back sometimes when he was leadin' 'em outta the barn."

"Well, this ain't a whole lot different as long as the horse is just walkin'. That Indian saddle doesn't give you a lot to hang on to, but it's better than bareback. You'll get used to it pretty quick." Still holding the paint's reins, Cody climbed up on Storm and started walking the horses in the direction the Blackfoot had come the day before.

After a few minutes, he looked back to make sure Billy was still on the horse. "How you doin'? You hangin' on all right?"

"Yes, sir," Billy answered. "Ain't we gonna try to get Joy back?"

"We sure are," Cody assured him. "I don't plan to leave your sister behind, but it'll take a little time to get another chance to get her. Here's what we've gotta do now. No doubt some warriors will be sent to find out what happened to the man who didn't come back after looking for you. What I'm countin' on is when they find him back there with two Crow arrows in his back, they'll think they've got some Crow trouble to worry about. Since there aren't many Blackfoot warriors left in that camp, they might decide it best to go back to protect their people. When that happens we'll get back to the business of trailin' 'em till we get a chance to snatch your sister away from 'em. All right?"

"All right," Billy answered. "What is your name?"

"Cody. Cody Hunter."

"Thanks for comin' to get me, Cody. I didn't think anybody would, and after them Indians stopped the soldiers they said nobody would. Shows how much they know."

"You're welcome." Cody was amazed by the youngster's courage to have made his escape down the gully. Even more impressed with the absence of any sign of fear, he decided to ask, "You wanna take the reins now?"

"Yes, sir," Billy answered without hesitation.

Cody reined Storm back to let the paint come up beside him and he handed the reins to the boy. He showed how he held the reins and Billy copied him. Cody nodded his approval and gave Storm a nudge with his heels. Immediately, the big dun started forward and the paint followed.

They rode for what Cody estimated to be about a mile before they came to the first stream of any size. He turned the dun into the middle of it and followed it to the north. Looking back occasionally, he was pleased to see Billy was coming along behind him, riding easily with the horse's motions. The boy and the paint had evidently accepted each other.

With the notion in mind he was at least parallel to the Blackfoot camp's intended route, Cody kept following the stream for as long as it continued to flow in a general northerly direction. He figured at some point, he would determine a likely cross-trail that would allow him to intercept the Blackfoot trail.

Another concern to deal with pretty soon, however, was hunting for food, left as he was with only a few days rations in his parfleche, and a hungry little mouth to feed.

"We have waited long enough for Many Scalps to return," Bucking Horse told Iron Claw. "The camp is packed up and ready to get underway. Many Scalps has spent too much time looking for the troublesome coyote. He should have returned to the camp by now. He will just have to catch up."

"He knew he only had a short time before the village was ready to travel," Iron Claw said. "I think he would have come back if he didn't catch up with the boy right away. I'm afraid he has run into some kind of trouble. Let the people get started on their way. I will take Two Toes and go find my brother."

Bucking Horse nodded his understanding of Iron Claw's concern. "Very well. Perhaps you will meet him already on his way back."

The two Blackfoot warriors rode away from the camp, following their backtrail of the day before as Many Scalps had. Iron Claw was especially angry to have to do so. The white boy had caused too much aggravation to be worth chasing after. Iron Claw, Many Scalps, and Two Toes should be riding out ahead, hunting for food. The people could not make it on the smoked beef alone. They needed fresh meat. Iron Claw found himself getting more and more irritated as they held their horses to an easy lope for over two miles with still no sign of Many Scalps.

"There!" Two Toes suddenly cried out, pointing to an object lying halfway into a weed patch beside the trail.

Iron Claw howled in despair, for he knew what it had to be. They pulled their horses to a stop beside the body and Iron Claw jumped off and ran to his brother, while Two Toes looked all around him cautiously before sliding off his horse to join him. Iron Claw angrily yanked at the two arrows, breaking them in the process and throwing them onto the ground. He turned Many Scalps faceup and saw the ragged scalp and the gaping slash across his throat.

Two Toes, still cautious for fear they, too, might be in an ambush, picked up one of the arrows and examined it. "These are Crow markings."

His declaration caused Iron Claw to howl again in furious anger with hatred for the Blackfoot's bitter enemies.

"We must get back to the camp," Two Toes said. "If there is a Crow war party lurking, our people are in danger. I am sorry about Many Scalps. He was a brave warrior. But we must go to our people now."

Iron Claw clenched his teeth together in a painful grimace as he tried to hear the truth in what Two Toes was saying. "You are right, but I will not leave Many Scalps here like this."

"I will help you," Two Toes said. "We can lay him across your horse's rump and take him back to the village."

That done, Iron Claw climbed on and Two Toes pushed the body up against Iron Claw's behind. Then they took the body back to the camp along with the disturbing news of their hated enemy in the area. The women wailed upon seeing the body of Many Scalps, none louder than Blue Willow, she who was the cause of his pursuit of the boy.

"We must bury Many Scalps," Iron Claw pleaded to Bucking Horse. "He must be buried deep in the ground. He cannot be left in a tree to be mutilated and disgraced if Crows are in these hills."

"Iron Claw is right," Bucking Horse said. "We must honor Many Scalps for his many brave deeds. He will be missed. We will bury him here before we leave this place."

Thinking he had walked the horses in the stream long enough, Cody led the paint out of the water and continued following it to the north. Looking up ahead, he saw a heavy line of trees weaving in and out of the hills that appeared to cross his path—a river or creek making its way through the hilly terrain. *That might be the cross path I was hoping to find.*

Up to that point he had not come across a likely path. When he reached that spot, he would rest the horses and let them graze. If his traveling companion was having any problems, he wasn't sharing them. He hadn't heard a peep out of Billy since they'd left the main trail.

Reaching the line of trees, they found it was a creek, not a river. But it was deep and wide. The stream they had followed emptied into it. Cody figured it to be an ideal spot to camp, since there was bound to be some form of critter to hunt. He picked a grassy knob on the south bank of the creek to let the horses graze and told Billy to help him collect wood for a fire. While picking up wood, Cody looked for deer sign, but he didn't see any. It was a little too late in the morning for deer to come to water, anyway.

"It looks like our dinner is goin' to be some of the army's bacon and hardtack." *And some more hard-luck coffee*, he thought.

"If I had my slingshot, we could have us a fat rabbit," Billy said.

"Is that right? You pretty good shot with a slingshot?"

"Yes, sir," he answered, "especially when they're as big as that one."

Cody froze. "Where?" he asked softly, afraid he was going to make it bolt.

"Over there." Billy pointed toward a small tree near the creek bank.

Cody saw a large rabbit sitting under a low-hanging limb. Not moving, it seemed to be watching them. It was no farther than ten yards away from them—dinner, just sitting there. He considered risking a shot with his pistol, not at all concerned he might miss. The hesitation to pull the weapon and kill the rabbit was due to his reluctance to trigger the sound of the firearm. His bow and small game arrows were five or six yards behind him on his saddle.

If his guess was anywhere near accurate and he and Billy were really on a parallel course with the Blackfoot camp, they would be about three-and-a-half miles apart. A shot might be heard at that distance, but would it be loud enough to make the Blackfeet decide to investigate it? There were two other possibilities, if his guess was off. One was they might be farther apart than he figured. The other was that they were much closer together, which would cause the Blackfeet to find the source of the shot. If the rabbit had been a fat deer, he would have risked the shot, but for a rabbit, maybe not.

"Stay real still," he said softly to Billy. "I'm gonna try to get to my bow without spookin' him. Maybe he won't scare, since I'll be movin' away from him."

Billy nodded slowly.

Moving like a turtle getting underway, Cody slowly backed away from the fire, one step at a time. The rabbit flicked its ears back and forth slightly several times, its legs quivering as if getting set to bolt, but it remained under the limb. Since he was moving away from it, Cody figured the rabbit probably thought it hadn't been detected. He continued his slow progress back to his horse, keeping his motions slow and deliberate. Untying his bow from the saddle, he strung it, notched the arrow on his bowstring then stepped out from behind his horse, drew it back and released the arrow.

"God A-mighty!" Billy blurted in surprise as the rabbit sprang into the air with the arrow all the way through its body, to fall flailing on the ground.

Cody hung his bow on his saddle as Billy clamped his hand over his mouth to stifle any more swear words from escaping.

"Whaddaya say we skin this fellow and cook him for dinner?" Cody proposed. "First, let's make him comfortable." He took his skinning knife and put the dying animal out of its misery. "Now, let's take him over by the creek and skin him and gut him. The quicker you skin him, the quicker the meat cools off." He realized he was acting like a teacher and he had not intended to. "You probably know how to skin and butcher a rabbit."

"I've seen my pa butcher one before, but I ain't never done one myself," Billy said.

"Well, if you're gonna have to hunt food to eat, you need to know how to fix it. You wanna try your hand at this one?"

Billy nodded excitedly, so Cody handed him his knife. "Let me work my arrow back outta him first."

Finished with that, he held the rabbit up and showed Billy where to make his first cut then handed the rabbit to him and coached him through the skinning. He showed him how to clean the guts out. While Billy was finishing up, Cody cut a green limb and trimmed it to roast the rabbit over the fire. He smiled when he remembered how excited he'd been when he skinned and butchered his first rabbit. Although unsure how old he was at the time, he was certain it was not with the threat of a Blackfoot war party hovering over him.

"I never saw nobody kill a rabbit with a bow and arrow before," Billy declared when they were eating the rabbit. "Where did you get your bow?"

"I made it," Cody said. "It's a handy weapon when you don't wanna make any noise, or if you're runnin' short of cartridges for your rifle."

"You made it? You musta known some Indians or something."

Cody had to chuckle at that. "Yep, I've known a few."

"I'd like to learn how to shoot a bow like you can," Billy said.

"It takes a lot of practice. I've been usin' a bow since I was about your age, I reckon. I'll tell you what, when we get your sister back from the Blackfoot, and get both of you somewhere safe, I'll help you make your bow and show you how to make your arrows."

"You promise?"

"I promise. These horses are ready to go, so we'd best get back to business." Cody was somewhat surprised he had allowed his mind to wander off in innocent conversation, especially when his actions in the days ahead could result in both of their deaths. Realizing he had a great deal of compassion, since he'd been orphaned as well at an age half that of Billy's, Cody imagined it was even harder for Billy. He had known his parents twice as long as Cody had known his. He shoved all those thoughts out of the way and returned his thinking to snatching Joy Lassiter out of the hands of the Blackfoot. He washed his knife and his army meat can in the stream, since the water was running faster than it was in the creek. They put out the fire and prepared to mount up.

"We're gonna change our direction now," Cody told Billy. "Instead of runnin' away from those Blackfoot, we're ready to run toward 'em. We're gonna follow this creek back toward the east." He didn't think it would help to tell him they would be following the creek on a wild hunch that it would intercept the trail the Blackfoot party was traveling. If his hunch was wrong, he might waste precious time trying to find them in that mass of rolling hills.

As he had halfway expected, a small game trail followed the creek, but it was on the other side, so they crossed over. When Storm climbed out of the belly-deep water onto the north bank, Cody looked behind him to make sure he hadn't lost Billy. The tough little trooper was lying forward on the paint's neck, with his feet and legs stretched out behind him on the horse's rump. Cody smiled. If he came off the horse, he'd just have to swim. If he didn't know how, it was time he learned.

When the paint came out of the water, Billy was still on his back, and judging from the expression on his face, enjoying the challenge. Starting down the game trail for a ride of close to three-and-a-half miles, if Cody's estimate was accurate, they should find themselves behind the Blackfoot villagers once more.

CHAPTER 20

Joy Lassiter stood tied to the same tree her brother had been tied to while her Blackfoot captors mourned the death of one of their warriors. They blamed Many Scalps' death on Billy, since the warrior had gone in search of Billy. Up to that point, Joy had experienced no abuse from the women whose job it was to confine her, other than to be led around by a rope around her neck and to sleep with her ankle tied to the ankle of one of the women. Her treatment had become somewhat more harsh since Billy's escape, especially from Iron Claw's wife, Blue Willow. For it was Blue Willow who had persuaded Many Scalps to go after Billy.

When Iron Claw and Two Toes brought Many Scalps' body back to the camp, Blue Willow had screamed, enraged at the young white girl, as if she, personally, was to blame. She had spat on her and slapped her face.

Joy thought the woman was going to kill her. Lone Dove had tried to calm Blue Willow down, but Joy could only guess at what she was saying since it had all been in their native tongue. Afraid her treatment was going to be little better than what Billy had suffered before he escaped, she didn't know whether to be glad he got away or to mourn, for no one in the camp knew what had actually happened to him.

From the tree where she was tied, she could see the mourners and the digging of the grave. She had always thought Indians were dressed in their finest garments and holding their weapons, then laid to rest in a tree. But these Indians were digging a deep grave to put Many Scalps in to guard against any predators digging him up. She wondered if they would put her in a hole in the ground when they had finished with her.

She was glad Billy had escaped. Things were not going well for him in captivity. She would just pray that he was all right.

When they had finally finished burying Many Scalps, the camp hurried to get underway again. Four warriors were left in the village to protect the women and children. It was why Bucking Horse was concerned they had been delayed for almost half a day. It was still a half day's travel to the valley of the trees where they would camp for two or more days, depending on how successful the hunting was. For that was where they must acquire enough food to take them past the hills of no trees. No grass, and very little water stood between them and their mountain home. When they were ready to start, Joy was relieved to see Lone Dove—not Blue Willow— coming to untie her.

Using the rope Joy had been tied to the tree with, Lone Dove tied the length of rope around Joy's neck again to lead her. "Come. We go now."

Still following the game trail beside the creek running between the tall hills, Cody was unaware he and Billy were riding up the valley of the trees, as the Blackfeet called it. His thoughts were concerned with whether or not the creek crossed the trail the Blackfoot camp was traveling on, as well as whether they were ahead of them or behind them. Even with those concerns dominating his mind, he couldn't help seeing the potential for hunting deer in the little valley. As a real *hunter* he saw sign everywhere. That was his last name, he liked to remind himself. Under different circumstances, he would have liked to camp by this creek. He could school Billy on the correct way to butcher a deer.

After they had ridden about two miles or more, Cody spotted what looked like a trail crossing the creek. It was a little closer to the stream than he had estimated the trail the Blackfeet were traveling on. Maybe it was another trail running parallel to the main one. But that didn't seem likely. He was anxious to find out.

At the crossing, he looked back down the trail to the south. It looked so much like the trail he had followed the Blackfoot camp on before he'd picked up Billy, Cody was reluctant to continue on along the creek. He'd thought for sure when he struck their trail, he would be behind them again.

He looked around again, realizing without a doubt the camp had not passed that point on the trail. No tracks except for an abundance of deer tracks, which indicated a favorite crossing for them. He looked at Billy, who was watching him and wondering.

"We musta got here before they did," Cody said. *They should have already passed this point,* he told himself. *Unless, they picked up the one that came looking for Billy and took him back and gave him a funeral. That might have accounted for their delay. If that is the explanation, they will be passing this point before long.*

He took another look back down the trail, halfway expecting to see a scout suddenly come into view.

"Billy, I don't know how much time we've got, but we've got to find us a spot to hide these horses, as well as ourselves. With all these trees, we oughta be able to handle that with no trouble a-tall." Cody took a minute to look at both sides of the creek and decided the side the game trail was on offered the best possibility.

Seeing as the forest grew well up the slope of the hill on that side, he figured he could hide the horses and pick a good spot to watch the camp when the Blackfoot stopped to water their horses. He told Billy what he was thinking and what they were going to do. "First, let's let the horses get a good drink of water before we take 'em up in the trees."

The spot he picked was in the trees, halfway up the hill where the slope leveled off a little before becoming steep again. Cody tied the horses, so they would not wander. Satisfied he could see everything he needed to from there, he went back down to the creek to take another look down the trail. For a long several minutes, there was nothing, then a single rider appeared at the far end. *A scout*, Cody thought, and he knew then it was the right trail.

The rider came on at a fast walk, then broke into a lope, evidently recognizing the creek just ahead. Cody retreated back into the trees and climbed up the hill where Billy was waiting.

Two Toes pulled his horse to a stop where the road dipped down to the creek and wheeled the buckskin around a couple of times while he looked all around him. Satisfied, he headed back the way he had just come.

"They'll show up here pretty soon," Cody told Billy. "Most likely, they'll stop for a while to water their horses. Then we'll see what they decide to do. It's still early in the afternoon. They might move on after the horses are watered and rested, but I expect they may decide to camp here tonight. Maybe let their men go huntin'. And if they do, we can't stay here. We'll have to ride back up the creek again. You ready for that?"

"Whatever you say," Billy replied. "Me and my horse are ready."

"Good. If we have to back away, we'll have to stay in the trees on the side of this hill till we get a good ways up the creek."

"Yes, sir. I understand," Billy said.

Cody nodded in reply, thinking the kid must be the oldest ten-year-old in the world. He seemed ready to take on anything that happened.

Almost half an hour had passed before the other Blackfoot riders arrived at the creek crossing with the walkers not far behind them. The warriors on their horses talked a few minutes then one of them, Bucking Horse, made the decision, and they crossed over the creek and went into camp on the other side. Some of the older women were carried across the creek on the backs of the horses, but most of the others waded across.

"They're fixin' to stay a while," Cody said.

"There's Joy!" Billy whispered suddenly when Lone Dove waded into the creek, leading his sister with the rope around her neck. "If I had a bow, I'd shoot that old bag pullin' her by the neck."

"I know how you feel, but we gotta be patient. It won't do Joy any good if we don't wait till we get the right chance and we all end up gettin' shot."

Cody continued to watch the Blackfoot people setting up their camp. He was especially interested in the warriors who were obviously discussing all the deer tracks they saw at the crossing. With no doubt in his mind they were talking about adding to their food supply, he imagined they were deciding to just set up around the crossing and wait for the deer to come. He hoped that was what they would decide to do, instead of heading out to hunt the creek.

If they chose the latter, he and Billy were going to have to retreat, probably all the way back to the stream they had followed to the creek. His question was answered in the next few minutes when the group of men broke up and went to take the decision to the rest of the people. Already fixing their camp, they picked up their packs and bundles again and moved everything to a new location about forty yards north of the creek.

"Good," Cody murmured. "That means they're gonna set up around that deer crossin'. It's gonna be inconvenient for the rest of the camp, but it will be worth it for the meat." And he and Billy could stay on the hillside where they were to keep an eye on them

"What are we gonna do about Joy?" Billy asked.

"We just might have to wait another day," Cody answered, and when he saw the disappointment in Billy's face, he explained why. "I came close to snatchin' Joy one mornin' when I first caught up with the camp." He went on to tell him how Joy had been brought away from the camp to answer nature's call, guarded by only the one woman leading her. "We'll see what happens in the mornin' when she has to pee. Depends on where they take her, but I won't be able to get very close because it looks like there's gonna be four warriors set up around that creek crossing, waitin' for deer to show up. There might be *five* guns if that chief goes huntin' with 'em. Our best bet is when they get on the move again, after the huntin'."

"We're gonna keep tryin' to save her, though. Ain't we?" Billy asked.

"Oh, we ain't gonna give up, even if we have to follow 'em to Canada," Cody assured him. "But now, it looks like they're gettin' ready to set their camp up again, so we might as well go back down the creek far enough to build us a fire. Sorry we don't have another rabbit, though. We'll just have to settle for that bacon and hardtack. Then we'll come back here and keep an eye on 'em, just in case they get careless with your sister."

They backed away from their lookout position, being careful not to break any limbs or leave obvious tracks for someone to happen upon. Then they untied the horses and led them back toward their camp where they had eaten their dinner. Since it was not that far back, Cody decided to go all the way to the stream. There, he would not be as concerned about someone spotting their fire.

When they had finished their bacon and hardtack, Cody shared his cup of hard-luck coffee with Billy, but he was only game for a couple of swallows of the bitter brew.

"Why do you drink that stuff?" the boy asked.

"I can't give you a good answer," Cody replied. "'Cause there ain't nothin' else to drink, I reckon."

"That stuff tastes like dirt," Billy insisted.

"I'll have to take your word for that," Cody said. "I never tried dirt."

They returned to their lookout position after tying the horses in the same place as before. It was just beginning to get dark and the Blackfoot camp was settling down for the night. When it became a little darker, Cody decided to move around the side of the hill to get him closer to the camp, since it had been moved away from the creek. Billy could stay there if he wanted to, since Cody doubted he would stay very long, not expecting to be able to see much. Billy said he would wait there for him.

Cody started to leave, then paused, thinking maybe he should say something that hadn't been brought up before. "You know, I oughta tell you, if something happens to me, you need to jump on that paint of yours and hightail it away from here. Get back on that main trail they've been traveling and follow it back to where it started."

"Just don't let nothin' happen to you, all right?" Billy said. "You promised you'd help me make my bow."

"That's right, I did. Well, I can't break a promise. I'll be back in a little bit." Cody disappeared into the trees.

Disappointed to find he could see even less inside the camp than he expected, he also saw no sign of Joy among the women going about the business of bedding down for the night. One thing that came to him as a surprise, however, was the appearance of the land beyond the camp. Even in the growing darkness, the rolling hills he saw beyond the creek looked barren of any trees at all. He couldn't tell if the hills were grass or stone. It appeared the dense forest stopped on the south slope of the hills beside the creek. No wonder the creek was rich with deer sign. Evidently, the Blackfoot camp had planned all along to stop there to hunt.

When no more than one or two souls were stirring in the camp, Cody went back to get Billy. He found him, fast asleep, sitting up against a tree.

Up before the first light of day the next morning, Cody pulled Billy out of a deep sleep. "Come on, boy, we've gotta get movin' or we'll miss the big deer hunt."

As soon as he was awake, Billy responded at once and followed Cody to the horses where he put his bridle on the paint just like Cody had taught him.

"We'll go back to our usual spot. I think the horses will be all right where we had 'em before. Oughta be out of the way of any stray shots." Cody didn't wait to be asked but grabbed the boy and set him on his horse. Then he jumped on Storm and they headed up the path toward the crossing.

They heard the first shots of the hunters as they were climbing the hill to their lookout point. In a few moments, the valley rang with the sound of gunfire as a large herd of deer came down from the hills on the opposite side of the creek. Every once in a while, Cody could hear the snap of an errant shot pass through the trees above him. *Not good*, he thought, and sent Billy back where the horses were tied. "You hunker down there low on the ground and wait till I come get you."

"What are you gonna do?" Billy asked anxiously. It was plain he didn't like the thought of bullets flying around.

"If the hunters are hittin' half of their shots they oughta be runnin' around like ants in a fryin' pan in that camp, trying to take care of all that meat," Cody told him. "They might be too busy to watch your sister, so I'm gonna move in closer to the camp. You just find you a place to stay hid till I get back."

Billy nodded rapidly and ran back along the hill to the horses. Cody ran around the hill toward the camp. Looking down through the trees, he could see the deer, scattered now and running for their lives. At least a dozen deer lay on the ground and the shooting was still constant. He moved down a little closer to camp. Some of the women were dragging the deer carcasses into the camp while others were hauling them up to hang from tree limbs to be skinned and gutted.

He spotted Joy in the middle of a half-dozen women who were butchering. He didn't see much chance of getting to her. Maybe it would have to be on another day. All he could do at the moment was wait and see.

The four warriors who had rifles were openly competing with each other to see who could kill the most deer.

Iron Claw, who had boasted he would kill more than any of the other three, had already knocked down four. But so had Two Toes. The shots were getting harder to make. The last of the herd had scattered into the hills. Finally, they spotted one lone deer, running toward the creek about fifty yards away. Two Toes was quickest as he raised his rifle and fired, but missed. Iron Claw shot then and the deer stumbled and almost fell but managed to stay on its feet.

"I hit him!" Iron Claw roared. "That is five for me!"

"He stumbled," Two Toes said, "but I did not see him go down. You did not kill him."

Iron Claw turned to Talks To Him. "You saw him stagger when I hit him."

"Yes, I saw him stagger, but I don't know if he went down."

"We are only counting deer that we kill," Two Toes said.

"I shot him," Iron Claw insisted. "He stumbled up the creek to die. We all know that." He looked at Talks To Him again. "He is dead by now."

"All I have to say is that he was not dead when I last saw him, and he was running down that path by the creek."

Angry that they would dispute his claim, Iron Claw snarled, "I will go up that path and find that dead deer and bring him out on my shoulders. Then who will you say killed the most deer?"

"I would think you would have been proud to have killed as many deer as I did," Two Toes teased.

"Ha!" Iron Claw snorted in disgust. Then he turned and walked straight to the point where they last saw the deer. His three fellow hunters laughed when he disappeared.

"You should be careful," Talks To Him said. "He is a very proud man. I think the deer was most likely hit, but I could not say for sure."

"I think he hit the deer, too," Two Toes said. "I want to see him carry it out of the forest on his shoulders."

They laughed at the thought but didn't doubt the possibility. Iron Claw was a powerful man.

Motivated by his pride and his need for recognition, Iron Claw stalked his trophy, his eyes scanning left and right as he walked the path beside the creek. *The deer would not have kept walking the path. I shot him. He would be looking for a place to hide, but could be anywhere in all these trees.*

And then Iron Claw's grimace turned to a wry smile when he saw blood on some leaves of a laurel bush. He pulled the limbs aside, saw more blood at his feet, and could see the probable path the wounded deer had taken up the hill into a fir thicket. Rushing up to the thicket Iron Claw thought he saw a flicker of movement, the last quivering moments of the deer's life. There! He saw a movement under the bottom bough.

"Ha!" he uttered triumphantly and pulled the bough aside, only to stagger backward a couple of steps when he saw him. "You!" he gasped in disbelief.

Billy could only cringe in mortal fear as he instinctively drew his feet and legs up in front of him in self-defense.

When Iron Claw realized it was not an illusion, it was really the little coyote he had come to despise, he could not contain his emotions. This hated little coyote who had caused the death of his brother and had escaped his vengeance was now presented to him to extract that vengeance one hair at a time. Forgotten was the dying deer, lying several feet away from the boy.

When the fearsome Blackfoot warrior just stood glaring at him, Billy started inching away from him, hoping to get far enough to jump to his feet and run. But he was stopped when Iron Claw shot his right hand out and clamped it around his ankle. The smile that broke out across the evil man's face conveyed a message of pain and terror to follow. Iron Claw dragged the terrified youngster out from under the branch and pulled him up close enough to feel the monster's breath upon his face.

He drew his skinning knife from his belt and held the blade up before the defenseless child's face and said, "You have caused me a great deal of trouble, little coyote. Now it is time to pay me for all that trouble."

Billy closed his eyes, knowing he would join his mother and father in death.

"Maybe you oughta pick on somebody your own size, Blackfoot coward." The voice came from behind him.

Iron Claw reacted quickly to turn and face the threat . . . but not quickly enough to evade the rifle butt that crushed the bones in the side of his face and knocked him sprawling on the ground.

Not certain if he was alive or dead, Billy opened his eyes to a vision of an angry Cody standing ready to fight as he hovered over the fallen Iron Claw.

Aware that his fate would be determined in the next seconds of his life, Iron Claw rolled over to his hands and knees, still holding the knife in his hand, waiting for the final shot from the rifle. When it didn't come, he pushed up to his feet and stared at Cody, seeing him clearly with only one eye, the other having filled with blood. "Who are you?"

"I am Crazy Wolf, Crow warrior. I have come for your scalp."

Even more enraged and with no other choice left to him, Iron Claw charged into him, thrusting savagely with the long skinning knife. Cody dodged deftly to the side and delivered another blow with his rifle butt, this one to the back of Iron Claw's head, slamming him facedown on the ground. On top of him before he could recover, Cody took the knife from Iron Claw's unresisting fingers and opened his throat. Then as he had just promised, he took his scalp.

That done, he sat for a few moments, still astraddle the Blackfoot's back while he waited for his anger to subside. He attributed his intense anger to having found Iron Claw preparing to kill the young boy and associating that with his memories of the Blackfoot slaughter of his father and his brothers.

He turned to meet the wide staring eyes of Billy Lassiter, still not recovered from witnessing the savage killing of the Blackfoot. Cody was at once afraid the scene would cause many nightmares to visit the young boy. He wished Billy had not seen it, but unfortunately, it happened the way it had. Finally, he asked, "Are you all right?"

Billy nodded in reply, then asked, "Why didn't you just shoot him?"

"I didn't want anyone to hear the shot. Come, we need to get away from this spot now before his friends come looking for him."

"There's a dead deer right behind me. Aren't we gonna take that?"

"No," Cody answered, somewhat relieved to see Billy was apparently not in shock over what he had just seen. "We don't have time to skin it and gut it, and by the time we do, the meat will already be spoiled. Right now, we need to get our horses and ourselves away from here and go farther up the hill toward their camp."

They untied their horses and Cody led the way a little higher up the side of the hill through the heavy growth of trees.

"Ain't we gittin' closer to their camp?" Billy asked.

"Yes, we are. I think right now is a good time to be

watchin' that camp, when they're all so busy trying to take care of all that meat before it spoils. I keep hopin' we'll get a chance to steal your sister back."

They walked a little farther before Billy spoke again. "You know what? I thought I was fixin' to die when he found me."

"Is that so?" Cody replied, not really wanting to keep Billy's mind on it.

"Yes, sir. I wonder why he came lookin' for me."

"Maybe he was lookin' for that deer. I don't think he had any idea you were hidin' in these woods."

"I knew you would come save me," Billy said, "but I wish you'da come sooner."

Cody nodded. "I wish I had, too."

CHAPTER 21

"Maybe Iron Claw can't find that deer," Two Toes said to Talks To Him, chuckling. "He's been gone a long time."

"Maybe so," Talks To Him replied. "Or maybe he found it, but he can't carry it on his shoulders like he said he would. I think we should send one of the women to help him carry it."

"He might be hiding in the trees watching us do all the work skinning these deer," Short Rope offered.

The three of them were quite entertained by Iron Claw's refusal to be beaten in any contest of shooting or fighting.

After a while, with still no appearance of the boastful warrior, it became a question of more concern.

Later still, with no sign of Iron Claw, Two Toes told Chief Bucking Horse of their concern and he was going to look for Iron Claw. "If there is some kind of trouble, I will fire two shots in the air, so that the village can be alert." He thought about getting his horse, but since Iron Claw had walked down the path by the creek, Two Toes decided not to bother with catching and saddling his horse. Most likely, he supposed, Iron Claw had climbed up higher on the hill and a horse just might be more trouble than going on foot. As Two Toes started walking toward the path by the creek, Short Rope suggested, "Maybe one of us should go with him."

"He will fire two shots if he needs help," Bucking Horse said. "We must hurry to butcher the meat."

The warriors went back to work on the carcasses to keep them from spoiling.

High up on the side of the hill where they had made their previous lookout positions, Cody led Billy and the horses to a new spot around the eastern side of the hill. "On this side of the hill, you can see more of their camp."

After they'd tied the horses, he explained they would be safer there until after the Indians found the Blackfoot warrior. "They are sure to be searching down that path by the creek, so right now, we're better off here, close by their camp."

They left the horses then and went a little farther around the side of the hill to the place where he had been watching until he'd decided to go back to check on Billy. *A most fortunate decision*, he thought to himself.

They watched the seemingly frantic efforts of the people in the camp below as they worked to skin and gut the deer as quickly as they could.

"Do you see your sister?" Cody asked, and Billy said that he did not.

Cody directed him. "There," he said, pointing. "See the tall woman at the edge of the camp, stripping the hide off the deer? That's Joy on the other side of the deer."

"Oh . . . I see her!"

No sooner had he said it when they heard two rifle shots in quick succession, sounding as if they had come from back down the creek. Everyone in the camp seemed to pause and look around at each other.

"They're still killin' deer!" Billy commented.

"That sounded more like two warnin' shots," Cody said. "I think they've found that fellow we left back there in the woods. Look at the camp." He pointed again.

The women were running around as if under attack. The two men with rifles picked up their weapons and talked briefly with the old chief then ran back to the creek, leaving the camp of mostly women in temporary confusion.

Cody saw it as an open invitation to make his move. Watching the woman working with Joy walk away from her to talk with some other women, he didn't hesitate. "Billy! It's time you show me you can ride that horse!" He picked him up and placed him on the paint. "We're gonna go get your sister while they're all stirred up down there. Do exactly what I tell you, all right?"

The boy nodded excitedly.

Cody pointed to the small Blackfoot horse herd north of the camp. "We're gonna ride down this hill and you're gonna ride straight to that herd of horses. I'm gonna swing by that camp and get Joy, then I'll be right behind you. Can you do that?"

"Yes, sir!" Billy exclaimed.

"Git goin' then! And don't fall off that horse!" Cody gave the paint a swat on the rump.

"No, sir!" Billy replied, and away he went.

Cody followed the paint down through the trees, hoping like hell the boy didn't come off that horse. They made it all the way down to the clearing and Billy headed the paint toward the horses as Cody swerved to run straight through the north side of the camp. Women and children scattered, screaming when they saw the big dun gelding charging right at them. Leaning all the way over to one side of the galloping horse, he headed for the confused girl too terrified to run. hoping she wouldn't run before he got there.

He could see the look of horror on the petrified young girl as he swept by her, plucking her off her feet with one arm wrapped around her.

Only then did she scream, trapped in his powerful arm with the ground of the valley racing by.

Behind them, he could hear the screaming and shouting of the stunned village, punctuated with a single shot from a pistol, possibly from old Bucking Horse.

Clear of the village, he tried to calm her. "Joy Lassiter, don't be afraid. Your brother's waiting for you up ahead." She didn't speak, but he felt some of the tension leave her body. "I'm gonna swing you over behind the saddle, all right?"

She nodded frantically, still unable to speak. "When I say three, okay?"

"Okay," she finally said.

"When I say three, just throw your leg over and I'll do the rest."

She nodded again.

"One, two, three." He swung her over behind him. "There's Billy. You see him?"

"Yes." She put her arms around Cody's waist.

"Good." Catching up to Billy, Cody told them, "I'm gonna make some noise to scare those horses." He held his .45 up for Billy to see. Then he yelled, "We're gonna stampede these horses. Give us a little more time to get away."

Billy nodded, then yelled, "Hey, Sis!"

She yelled back.

Two happy kids, Cody thought. *I hope I can keep them that way.* He raised his pistol in the air and fired a couple of shots.

The Indian ponies started moving down the valley at once. Cody kept behind them, firing his .45 and herding the horses. He couldn't help a feeling of deep satisfaction, knowing he had stolen the Blackfoot village's entire horse herd. No way he could keep them but he'd bought a sufficient amount of time for the kids' and his escape.

Cody gave thought to the kids. He was especially impressed by the way Billy and the paint had taken to each other, which surprised him. He hadn't been all that confident the boy could stay on the horse throughout the whole operation. Always thankful for small favors, Cody was doubly thankful for huge ones like the one just granted him.

While he was thanking the powers that be for their good fortune, he also realized the fat was not out of the fire yet. He had a good many problems to solve before delivering the two children someplace that wanted them.

His first realization came quickly. He was traveling in country he had never ridden before. It was strange-looking at the least. His previous glimpse of the terrain beyond the valley of the trees was at night and he hadn't been able to tell what the hills were made of. Riding between them in broad daylight, he still wasn't sure what covered them. Maybe it was grass, but it looked more like *dead* grass.

Right away, his plan was to head west for five or six miles, then head back south to strike the creek they'd just left. With two hungry kids and one hungry man to feed, he was sure he could find food for them back at that creek.

Riding at a slower pace, Joy finally asked, "Who are you?"

"My name's Cody Hunter, miss. I was riding with that patrol of cavalry that came after you and Billy."

"Why didn't the soldiers come after us?"

"Well, they had to take all those people the Blackfeet

lost back to Fort Ellis. The soldiers couldn't take care of 'em if they kept chasin' Buckin' Horse."

"You just came by yourself?"

"Yep, all by myself," Cody said. "I figured you and Billy were worth a little bother."

"Well, God bless you for coming," she said. "And thank you."

"You're welcome, but we've got a long way to go, and I don't have any supplies with me a-tall. I started out with some skimpy rations the army gave me to last for fifteen days. Most of that's gone already, and it really wasn't fit to eat, anyway. I can feed you, but we've got to get to some place where there's game to hunt, like that creek we just left. I'm hopin' you and Billy can be patient till we find something. What I wanna do right now is get shed of that bunch of Blackfeet you've been traveling with."

"I understand. We'll be patient. I'll tell Billy we have to tighten our belts."

"I've got to tell you," Cody thought to say, "your brother has been takin' all this trouble like a man. You see the way he's ridin' that horse? And when he got away from that camp, he said he wasn't leavin' without you."

She laughed. "I'd kiss him for sayin' that, but he gets mad when I try to kiss him."

"I'm not surprised," Cody said and chuckled. Something just occurred to him. "Can you ride a horse? Or were you like Billy and never on one before?"

"I've never ridden one either, but I'm willing to try."

"Before we leave this herd, we'll pick one out for you. You won't have to ride behind Billy on his paint."

They continued along the valley, even though Cody knew it was the trail the Blackfoot were following. At the present, his concern was to put plenty of distance between them and their horses. He alternated the pace, keeping the herd loping part of the time, then walking part of the time to be real sure when they stopped to rest their horses, nobody on foot was going to catch up to them.

To his surprise, they came to a small stream after a distance he figured close to ten miles. It was not a great deal more than a trickle of water, but he called for a stop to rest and water the horses, making sure Storm and the paint got into it before the herd drank it dry.

Brother and sister were glad to get their feet on the ground for a while and indulged in a big hug.

Joy got a little weepy. "I thought I would never see you again, that you might already be dead. But Cody told me you said you weren't gonna leave me with those people."

"Better walk upstream a little way and get yourselves a drink of water," Cody told them. "I don't have any idea when we'll reach the next water." He smiled at Billy. "Joy wants you to help pick out a horse for her."

"How's she gonna ride one?" Billy replied. "She ain't got no bridle or saddle."

"She'll ride bareback, just like you," Cody said. "I noticed you never put that Indian saddle back on the paint. As far as a bridle, I've got rope. I'll make her an Indian bridle or a hackamore."

Since the stream was running pretty close to east and west, he was thinking it might be a good place to bid the Blackfoot herd adieu. He had to pick some point to turn west, so it might as well be at the tiny stream. If his idea to cut back to the south again didn't present a likely passage, the Missouri River was west of them somewhere.

After their drink of water, Joy and Billy, along with Cody's help, looked over the horses. Since the Blackfeet men were the only ones riding horses, there weren't that many to consider.

"You see one you like?" Cody asked.

"I think that one is pretty," Joy said, pointing to a buckskin mare.

"Well, you picked one that's well suited to a woman. She's a mare. She oughta be gentle, although all mares ain't gentle. Just like all women ain't, I suppose. Why don't you give her a try?" Cody took his rope off Storm's saddle, made a lasso on one end, and went among the horses still sucking water from the stream.

The mare didn't move while he put the rope over her head and led her back to Joy. Handing the rope to her, he said, "Here, you can introduce yourself and see if you girls can get along." He stepped aside then to watch.

The initial meeting of the girl and the horse was much like the introduction of Billy to the paint. Whoever had been the previous owner must have employed a gentle touch when taking care of his horse, for the mare was of a similar nature. Needing to see no more, Cody took the lasso off the horse's neck and began fashioning a bridle for her right away while Joy continued to pet her new horse.

Cody put the bridle on, then picked up Joy and set her on the mare's back. The mare took two steps to the side in reaction to the sudden weight on her back, then calmly settled down again. It was enough to cause Joy to give Cody a look of concern.

He quickly assured her it was just the horse's surprise to feel the sudden weight on her back. "Wouldn't have been any different if a bird had landed on her back."

"It woulda had to be a mighty big bird," Billy remarked.

"You're lucky I can't reach you," Joy threatened.

Cody figured that to be a teasing remark from an earlier time. At the present, the girl didn't look much bigger than a bird. It served to remind him he had to find some food for all of them pretty soon.

He gave her the rope and showed her how to guide the horse. When she said she was ready, he stood back and told her to ride the horse around in a circle in one direction, then back in the opposite direction.

Cody continued the lesson. "You don't have to pull so hard on the reins when you want her to turn. Just a little tug and she'll know what you want."

In a short time, Joy was comfortable

Cody turned to Billy. "I reckon we're ready to say goodbye to the rest of these horses and get on to findin' our way back home. Let's see if this stream leads us anywhere we wanna go."

He lifted Billy onto the paint, and they started off following the stream toward the east. The rest of the Blackfoot horse herd remained at the stream. Cody figured some or all of them might follow for a while, but without any encouragement, would probably drop off to wander in some other direction. Whatever happened, it was going to create an unhappy situation for the Blackfoot camp, and likely a few more walking companions for the Blackfoot women.

Moving on, Cody had a measure of confidence the recent turn of events would rid them of any more threats from Bucking Horse and his people. They had been detained enough already in their quest to reach their destination in the Big Belt Mountains, and had suffered too many losses to risk more. To ensure that, Cody wanted to travel in the direction the Blackfeet had come from.

He turned in his saddle to look at his "troops" coming along behind him. *Not really a ready combat unit*, he thought. *I hope I'm right about Bucking Horse.*

They followed the stream for a couple of miles as it found its way through a series of treeless hills, the only sign of growth a border of low bushes and weeds hovering close to the shallow stream. After another mile or so, it took a definite turn to a more southerly direction, which served to encourage him. When the stream gradually began to turn even more to the south, he also noticed it was a little bit wider than when they first encountered it. Catching a glimpse of trees between two barren hills a couple of miles farther confirmed his plan worked out just as he had hoped. He was back where he'd hoped to be, near the creek in what the Blackfoot referred to as "the valley of the trees."

Behind him, he heard Billy yell his name.

Cody looked back at him. Billy was pointing excitedly at the trees in the gap between the two hills ahead. Cody grinned and nodded his head in return, certain the boy was probably thinking about fresh deer meat.

They rode between the two hills and followed the stream up to the game trail that ran along beside the creek, once again in the little valley where the hillsides were covered with trees. Not sure how far away they were from the spot where the stream emptied into the creek, Cody would have liked to camp where he and Billy had camped before. From there it would be a relatively straight line back to the main trail that had brought him into the hills in the first place. Because of its close proximity to the Blackfoot camp at the crossing of the creek, he rejected that plan. Since he had driven their horses away, the camp would most likely still be there, which meant the men would have to find the horses and bring them back to pack up the camp. The horses would need to carry all the food and packs.

Deer was the only game he was sure of in the little valley, but to hunt them, he would have to move farther up the creek, away from the Blackfoot camp—far enough so they might not hear his rifle. Figuring the deer might have been frightened away from their favorite crossing after the slaughter of that morning, anyway, he changed his mind. He didn't know this country at all, but he knew for sure the Missouri River was to the west, so there was a pretty good chance the creek would take them there. And when he struck the Missouri, he could turn south again and head for Three Forks. He turned Storm and followed the game trail along the creek, hoping the deer sign would be just as strong as it was behind them.

Feeling they had ridden far enough a rifle shot would not be heard at the Blackfoot camp, Cody paid more attention to the likelihood of deer. With particular interest in what appeared to be several little game trails coming down the hill on the other side of the creek, he stepped down from the saddle and looked around on the ground.

Billy and Joy sat on their horses wondering what he was doing, until Billy finally asked,

"Whatcha doin', Cody?"

"Lookin' for deer tracks. And I found some." Back in the saddle he said, "Now, let's go see if we can find a good place to make our camp."

It turned out that they were less than a quarter of a mile from a prime spot, so they didn't waste any time gathering firewood for a fire. They hoped they could cook something to eat but needed it for warmth as well. The nights were pretty chilly this time of year, especially when there were no blankets. The only form of comfort was Cody's bedroll, which he gave Billy and Joy to roll up in to keep warm.

He hobbled the paint and the buckskin mare to make sure they didn't wander far. It was unnecessary to hobble Storm. The dun wouldn't go very far away from Cody.

"Billy knows this already, but I'm afraid I didn't come after you two very well prepared. I know you're both about to starve, but I can't feed you till I kill something. It'll be a little while yet before the deer come out to eat. Before sundown, I'll go back to where I saw all the sign. Sometimes deer come out earlier, especially in a shady valley like this one. If I can get a deer, we'll have a big supper tonight, no matter how late it is, but it'll be a little while yet before they'll likely show. In the meantime, here's my parfleche. You're welcome to anything you find in there to chew on. There's some bacon and some jerky and might be some hardtack. I ain't hungry, myself," he lied. "I can just wait till I kill something. If I'm wrong about the place I picked to hunt, I'll find a better place."

Joy wanted to ask questions, but she was hesitant, since he had just rescued her from a captivity that would have likely been too hard for her to endure.

Billy thought he knew what she was thinking, and was eager to set her straight. "You're wonderin' how come Cody didn't bring no supplies or food to feed us, ain'tcha?"

"No such a thing!" she exclaimed "I never even—"

"He didn't bring no supplies because he didn't have any to bring. All he had was what the army gave him to feed hisself. Ain't that right, Cody?"

Cody laughed "That's a fact, and if I ever ride with an army patrol again, I'm takin' a packhorse. And I'll surely remember my little coffeepot."

Joy blushed red. "I wasn't even thinking about that, Billy Big Mouth. You're not as smart as you think you are. Cody knows I wasn't worrying about when I was gonna get to eat."

"Well, if we're lucky, maybe it won't be too long," Cody said. "It'll all depend on how anxious the deer are to eat."

* * *

When Cody decided it was late enough in the afternoon to go to his deer stand, Billy asked, "Are you gonna take your rifle or your bow, Cody?"

"I thought I'd take my rifle. I'm not worried about anybody hearin' a shot now, and my rifle gives me longer range."

"You want me to go with you?" Billy asked.

"Well, I'd enjoy havin' ya, but I think I'd feel better if you were here lookin' after your sister."

"Yes, sir. I guess I should stay here and take care of her."

Joy looked up and rolled her eyes impatiently, but she was glad she was not going to be left alone.

"If I've picked the right spot, I shouldn't be too long," Cody told them when he was ready to go. "I won't be very far from here. If you hear my rifle shot, you'll know I was lucky. If you hear me shoot more than one time real fast, take the hobbles off those horses and ride away from here, up that trail that way." He pointed west.

Two pairs of eyes stared wide in response.

"I don't expect any trouble, but I just thought I'd tell you what to do in case I did."

He jumped on Storm's back and rode him back to the path, then he headed back up the game trail to the spot where he planned to wait for the deer. He needed the horse to carry the deer he intended to shoot, and Storm would remain still and quiet while Cody was watching a deer.

At the stream where he had seen the game trails, he selected a stand of firs big enough to hide his horse and himself then talked to the dun gelding a few minutes to make sure he was calm. Satisfied, Cody cranked a cartridge into the chamber of his Henry rifle and settled down to wait. As he'd expected, he didn't have to wait long before a buck came down the game trail from the top of the hill. As he went down to the creek, Cody thought,

Walking proud. A big mule deer, he was followed by another buck, this one a young one.

Where are the ladies? Ah, here they come. Cody counted four, selected a young one, and laid the front sight of the Henry right behind her front leg. He squeezed the trigger and she went down on her knees. All the other deer bolted and she attempted to as well, but she staggered and fell when she tried to get to her feet.

Cody was out of the thicket and on the deer before she could try again. He ended her suffering with his knife. Wasting no time, he whistled for Storm and the horse came at once. He hefted the young doe up and laid her across Storm's back then jumped on behind the deer and rode back to their camp to an excited welcoming.

Billy got the lesson on the correct way to skin and gut a deer he had been promised, and in a short time, they were all chewing on freshly roasted venison while they went about the work of butchering the deer.

Joy was a little ahead of her brother in that department, since she had been under the harsh instructions of Blue Willow and Lone Dove. In fact, had it not been for her contribution of a skinning knife, Cody's knife would have been the only one available and the whole process would have had to be done by him alone. Joy had been skinning a deer with Lone Dove when Cody charged through the camp and had stuck the knife in her belt at the moment she was snatched. Certain he was another wild Indian come to steal her, she'd thought to pull it out of her belt and stab Cody with it. So terrified, however, when she found herself flying over the ground she was afraid to let go of his arm. Fortunately for them both, he said her name right away and that her brother was waiting for her before he swung her back up behind him.

After they were all sated with fresh roasted venison,

Cody turned his attention toward smoking a quantity of the uncooked meat. Since he had not come prepared to do what was required to feed the two children on the long trip back to Three Forks, he was required to improvise. Close to the creek, he chopped down a willow with his hand ax, thinking the green wood and boughs would make more smoke. Then he used his ax to chop a large branch to be propped over the fire to hang strips of deer meat. Doing that reminded him how unprepared he had been to rescue the two kids.

"How we gonna carry the smoked meat?" Billy wondered. "We ain't got no packs or packhorses."

"We're gonna carry it in the same thing she did," Cody answered and nodded toward the deer hide hanging to dry. "And we'll carry it on one of our horses—the horse with the lightest load."

Billy thought about that for a minute, then protested, "That ain't fair. She ain't that much bigger'n me."

"We'll stuff my parfleche as full as we can get it," Cody said, "but that won't handle but a little bit of the food we might need before we get back."

"Where are we going?" Joy asked. "Mama and Papa are dead."

That was a question Cody had avoided raising because he didn't have an answer. "I don't know," he confessed. "Have you got any kinfolks where you were livin' on the Gallatin River?"

She shook her head. "No. All our kinfolks are back in Missouri."

"I don't wanna go back to Missouri," Billy said.

Cody realized the problem he had taken on for himself when his thinking had gone no further than saving the two children from the Blackfoot Indians. For a brief second, he thought maybe they would have been better off living with the Indians. It had worked out pretty well for him. Remembering how the Blackfeet were treating them, he immediately rejected that notion. It was not the same as when Spotted Pony rescued him.

"I wanna stay with you, Cody," Billy said.

That statement really struck home, and Cody was hard put to answer it. "Well, I'm not gonna leave you two till I know you're in a safe place. We'll go back to Three Forks first and see if they know someone who would love to have two fine kids like yourselves. But you don't wanna stay with me. I don't have a home. I don't own anything but my horses and my weapons. I'm just a scout for the army. You wouldn't have any kind of life with me." He saw the disappointment in Billy's face and the lack of emotion in Joy's, she having expected nothing more. "I ain't gonna leave you till I think you'll be all right. I promise you that."

"I believe you, Cody," Joy said then. "You're a good man, and Billy and I owe our lives to you." She cut her eyes to her brother to make sure he'd heard it.

CHAPTER 22

It had not been quite the day Chief Bucking Horse and the Blackfeet had expected. Instead of everyone preparing the freshly killed deer meat for the continuation of their journey to the mountains, the men had walked ten miles to recover the horses. Even then, they did not recover all the horses. And to make matters worse, they lost one man and one additional horse after the men found the herd.

Talks To Him tried to explain that Two Toes had already been highly upset upon finding Iron Claw dead, brutally beaten, and scalped. When they found all the horses together except Two Toes' buckskin mare, it was more than he could bear, and he swore vengeance for Iron Claw. He would follow the tracks by the stream where they had found their horses, which led back in the direction of the big river.

"He said he would track this man who scalped Iron Claw and stole his mare. He would take Iron Claw's horse and track him down. He would not scalp him. He would leave his scalp and take his whole head instead."

Ordinarily, a man of the village who rode to avenge the death of a great warrior would be admired. But with all the recent hardships his village had suffered, Bucking Horse would have advised Two Toes that it was crucial at this point to see the people safely to their camp in the high mountains. Darkness had settled upon the little valley and still no sign of Two Toes. Bucking Horse had a bad feeling about the devil Two Toes sought to kill. He'd seen him when he loped through the camp and grabbed the girl. Bucking Horse had taken dead aim with his pistol, but the bullet went wide of the target.

The two white children had been bad luck and brought this devil man upon his people.

"Two Toes is a strong warrior," Talks To Him said. "He will be back soon."

Two Toes was closer than they imagined. Still following the tiny stream from the spot where they found their horses, he could no longer see the tracks in the dark, but there was no point in stopping. The stream was obviously the man's path. It would lead him to the man. When he led his horse through the last two hills before the creek, like Cody, he knew at once where he was.

"I knew it would lead back to this creek," he muttered to himself.

The question was, which way had the man gone when he struck the creek. Two Toes knew that if he went to the east, he would run into the Blackfoot camp, so he turned to the west and led Iron Claw's bay gelding along the game trail beside the creek. He didn't know how far he walked when he saw the first sign of smoke and sparks floating up in the trees ahead. His heart started pumping blood to his brain like the beat of a drum. *He had found him!*

Two Toes cautioned himself to be alert and careful as he continued along the path until he was close enough to see the fire through the trees. He tied the bay to a tree limb and continued on foot, leaving the path when he was about thirty yards from the fire, an easy shot with his rifle. Since there was plenty of cover in the trees, he moved closer to about ten yards. The man was smoking meat and he turned at that moment to almost face him squarely. Two Toes could not miss. He raised his rifle and took dead aim, but then he paused. He had never actually seen the man before. What if he was not the devil he was after?

What if he's not? He's a white man. Kill them all.

Then he smiled. The little girl was bringing the man a strip of roasted meat. He put the front sight on him again, felt a blow like a fist in his side, and let out a yelp of pain as he automatically squeezed the trigger, sending a shot to zip through the branch holding the strips of deer meat over the fire.

Cody reacted without taking time to think. He dived in front of the fire to knock Joy to the ground. "Stay down!" he commanded and plunged through the bushes between the trees to find Two Toes pulling at an arrow in his side and Billy about five yards away from him, holding his bow and apparently frozen in fear.

About to shoot the boy, Two Toes turned back to meet Cody when he heard him crashing through the bushes, but not in time to keep from being knocked over backward to land on his back. Like a great cat, Cody was immediately upon him. Two Toes screamed painfully when Cody's knife plunged deep, up under his ribs. Cody held him until he stopped struggling, then slit his throat to send him the rest of the way.

"Go take care of your sister," he told Billy, who was still frozen in shock. "Go on."

Billy finally came to and ran back to the fire. Cody got up from the body, walked around and grabbed it by the ankles, then dragged it a good distance away from their camp. He stripped it of a knife and ammunition, then yanked the small game arrow out of the warrior's side. He briefly looked around to see if the Indian had been alone but didn't expect to find anyone. They would certainly have already attacked him.

Sure the warrior tracked them from the little stream where they left the Indian horses. Cody went back on the game trail until he found the Blackfoot's horse. *Good. I can trade the horse for the supplies I need to get me back to my packhorse at Fort Ellis.*

He led the horse back to the other horses and hobbled it. Over in the bushes, he picked up the rifle Two Toes had dropped and brought it with the knife and cartridges. Still a little bit in shock, Joy and Billy sat on the ground, hugging each other as they watched him.

He placed the rifle and ammunition on the ground away from the fire, held the arrow up, and looked at Billy. "You need the big game arrows when you're gonna shoot a man."

"I was gonna surprise you with a possum or a coon," Billy said, thinking he was going to be in trouble for taking Cody's bow without asking permission. "I was gonna ask you, but you were busy with the deer."

"Well, I think I can let you get by with it this time," Cody told him, "especially since you saved my life with that shot."

"I did?" Billy replied, not really aware that he had.

"That Indian trailed us all the way from where we left their horses this mornin'. He came to shoot me, and if you hadn't shot him with that arrow, I expect I'd already be dead. And you'd be eatin' fresh meat with him instead of me."

"Then you ain't mad at me?" Billy asked.

"No, I'm not, but I would prefer you ask whenever you're thinkin' about borrowin' any weapons."

"Are you sure there aren't any more Indians running around out there?" Joy asked.

"I'm pretty sure they're not," Cody answered. 'Course I was wrong about that one Billy shot, so I don't know if you oughta believe me or not." He smiled. "Did I hurt you when I knocked you down?"

"No." She shook her head. She paused for a few moments, then she went ahead and said what she was thinking. "Doggone it, Cody, don't you go getting yourself killed. Billy and I can't make it if something happens to you."

"Believe me, I'll do my best not to get killed," he assured her. "So, tomorrow mornin', we're gonna ride this creek as long as it keeps goin' west. I'm hopin' it'll take us to the Missouri River, and we'll be out of this hilly country."

They continued smoking a good quantity of the meat late into the evening. Billy had already passed out by the time Cody told Joy she needed to get some sleep. She would have a full day tomorrow. She crawled into the bedroll beside Billy, no longer worried about the possibility of another attack on their camp. Cody finished cutting up a portion of the brisket he was working on, then stoked up the fire before wrapping Storm's saddle blanket around himself and joining the kids in sleep.

It was difficult for Billy and Joy to understand why they had such a hard time trying to wrap up all the meat they had smoked in the deer hide.

"It was all inside her skin when she was running around

in the woods," Joy argued. "And that was before we ate so much of it."

"Maybe it just swells up when you stick it over the fire," Billy suggested. "Whaddayou think, Cody?"

"I think the deer just knows where to tuck it in all the nooks and crannies of her body," Cody said.

He had used up all the rope he could spare as well as some deer sinew to hold the bundle together. He used the rope he'd hobbled the horses with to tie the bundle onto Iron Claw's bay. And with his parfleche packed full, they set out on the next leg of their journey with Cody hoping they would not encounter a situation where they were called upon to run for it. In that event, he was confident they would lose all their food supply, except for that in the parfleche.

Luck seemed to be with them, however, at least as far as the morning was concerned. The path they followed continued to weave its way in and out of the many little valleys but always leading in a generally west direction. They stopped to rest the horses after about three hours on the trail. Cody estimated they had ridden about ten miles. He figured the horses could have gone on for a while yet before absolutely needing a rest, but his two traveling companions appeared to need a stop. Afraid they didn't get enough sleep the night before, they stopped for dinner and he built a fire so they could have a hot meal.

He had kept a small quantity of uncooked venison to eat freshly cooked today, and that was what they'd had for breakfast. There was still some uncooked meat left that he figured would be all right to eat, but he didn't want to take a chance on making the kids sick. He asked Joy to sniff the meat to see if she thought it was all right to eat.

"I can't tell," she said, and sniffed it again. "It's kinda got a little odd smell, but it doesn't seem real bad."

Cody took it from her and smelled it again. It was fine as far as he was concerned. He had eaten plenty that had smelled worse. He looked at her, then looked at Billy. They were like two little puppies looking up at him with trusting eyes.

He took the piece of meat from her. "Maybe it needs washin'," he said and threw it into the creek.

They both stared up at him, astonished.

"We got plenty of smoked meat to eat." Cody figured they had a long way to go before he got the two of them settled permanently somewhere. No sense in taking any chance of making them sick on meat that's turned.

"I swear, sometimes you do some crazy things, Cody," Billy said.

"I reckon," Cody replied.

The problem he had with "his children" came to mind more often in the last couple of days. He was at a total loss when it came to what to do with them. When Joy had told him they had no relatives in Montana, it stopped him cold. He hadn't given that any thought, not that it would have kept him from trying to save two children kidnapped by Indians, sworn enemies of the Crow Nation as well. But it was his nature, he guessed, that he didn't care for things to be complicated. He'd gone into this venture hoping to save the two children and return them to a loving family of aunts and uncles. So now, what to do?

All he could think of was to first go to Three Forks and talk to Ernest Blanchard. He hadn't asked Joy or Billy how long they had lived on the farm before the attack by Bucking Horse's warriors. Possibly they had been there long enough to become friendly with other farmers and ranchers. Maybe one of them would welcome the two orphans into their homes. *Well, that's the plan, so we'll go see Mr. and Mrs. Blanchard*, he told himself. *Somebody oughta want two bright young children.*

Two hours after leaving their stop for dinner, they suddenly came out of the hills to see the river ahead of them, perhaps half a mile away. And where the creek joined it there were a couple of log buildings. As they drew closer, Cody thought it appeared to be a trading post with a barn next to it. Two horses were tied to a hitching post in front of one of the buildings.

I just hope they've got some coffee and a coffeepot for sale, he thought. He had a little bit of money with him, although most of what he had saved from his scout pay was in his packs in the army stable at Fort Ellis. He hoped he hadn't been wrong when he'd thought his money would be safe in an army stable where somebody was on duty all the time.

But he had things to trade, if the owner of the trading post was willing.

When they pulled up to the building, he saw a small sign nailed to a porch post that read BLACK'S STORE. He stepped down, then helped Joy off the mare while Billy slid off the paint. Cody tied their horses and Iron Claw's bay to the rail and dropped Storm's reins to the ground. Both of the kids ran up the steps and into the store before him.

When he walked in the door, they were standing just inside, staring at the two men behind the counter, who were staring at them in return. Cody was alert at once. Something didn't look right. If he had to guess, he would say the older man with the balding gray hair, wearing a long apron was Mr. Black. The younger fellow, standing close to him, wearing a high-crown black hat and a leather vest, half his face covered with black stubble, looked to be irritated at seeing the two children.

"Are you Mr. Black?" Cody asked.

"I'm Mr. Black," the older man answered, then flinched slightly, as if something had poked him in the side.

"Sorry, mister," the other man said. "The store ain't open today. You'll have to come back tomorrow."

"Oh, well, that's all right," Cody said. "We didn't come to buy much, anyway. I just came in to tell you we were gonna go down to the river on the other side of your barn to cook us a little dinner, if that's all right with you."

"Yeah," the man in the black hat said. "Why don't you just do that?"

Seeing a jar filled with peppermint candy on the counter, Cody said, "I just came in the store 'cause I promised the young'uns I'd buy 'em a peppermint stick."

"That's a good idea," Black Hat said. "Just step up to the counter and get you a couple. No charge. They're on the house."

"I declare, that's mighty neighborly of you." Cody stepped up to the counter and while he opened the lid on the jar, he caught a glimpse of an older gray-haired woman watching him through a window behind the counter. She had a definitely worried look on her face. He pulled two peppermint sticks out of the jar and replaced the lid. "Thank you again. Billy and Joy are gonna enjoy these." He handed one to each of them and forcefully spun them around. "Come on, kids, they're busy in here."

Outside, Cody wasted no time lifting both of them onto their horses.

"Cody," Billy complained, although already sucking the peppermint stick. "We just ate dinner a little while ago. I thought you needed to trade for some stuff."

"I do, but I'll do it later. Come on. We're gonna get down by the river on the other side of that barn."

"Something's not right in there," Joy said, a little more perceptive than her brother.

"That's a fact," Cody said, "and that's why I want you two away from here." He put the kids on their horses, climbed up into the saddle, and turned Storm toward the far side of the barn.

They rode beyond the barn to a grassy spot in the trees close to the river where Cody jumped off his horse and tied all the horses to some tree limbs, so they wouldn't wander. "You two stay right here with the horses."

"What are you gonna do?" Joy demanded.

"Never mind what I'm gonna do. You two stay right here till I get back."

Inside the store, Zach Spitz yelled toward the window between the two rooms, "He's gone, Ned. I believe he's smarter than he looked. He didn't waste no time gittin' hisself and his young'uns outta here."

"Tell that old buzzard to get busy and get that strong box outta the floor," Ned Fletcher yelled back, "or I'm fixin' to cut another mouth under his old lady's chin."

"He's gittin' to it now," Zach replied. "He's got so damn many boards nailed over it. I don't know what he'd do if the place was to catch on fire." He prodded the old man again with his pistol to speed him up.

With his rifle in hand, Cody ran along the riverbank, keeping the barn between him and the store until he got almost directly behind the store. There was no cover of any kind. He was going to have to cross an open expanse of yard about twenty yards wide to get to the back of the store. He just had to trust to luck that Black Hat's partner was not watching the back.

Holding his rifle ready to fire if he'd guessed wrong and was met with gunfire, he sprinted across the open yard to gain the cover of the back steps. *So far, so good*, he thought.

With no way of knowing if he was too late or not, he took only a couple of moments to look over the back of the store. It appeared the living quarters were on one side of the building and the door directly over the steps probably led into the room behind the front counter where he had seen the woman standing.

His rifle already set to fire with a cartridge in the chamber, he walked carefully up the five steps to a small porch, his moccasins making no sound on the rough lumber. He went to the door and paused while he tried the rough handle to see if it was locked. The handle would not turn. He was going to have to find another way into the back of the store. Then he realized it probably wasn't a modern door lock, considering the rugged log structure of the building. He tested the door with a small amount of force against the handle and it moved a fraction of an inch. He knew then the door was locked by placing a heavy board across it on the inside. And since it moved slightly with a little effort, he knew the board was off. He pushed it a fraction more and confirmed it.

Counting heavily on surprise to be his advantage, he gradually pushed the door open, but only enough to allow him to peek into the room while he still used the door for cover. He had guessed right. It was a storeroom of sorts with an open passage window in the wall behind the counter. As he'd suspected, the rider of the second horse tied at the hitching rail was standing beside the pass-through window, one hand holding the woman's arm up behind her back, the other one holding a pistol jammed up against her back. Obviously unaware of the slight movement of the back door, his attention was captivated by his partner's progress in finding Black's cash reserves.

Cody pushed the door open wide and stood ready to fire, although still undetected by the man holding the woman. "Hey," Cody said calmly and put a bullet in Ned's chest when he whirled around to shoot. Behind the counter, his partner, Zach, made the mistake of springing to the window when he heard the shot, only to be rewarded for his foolishness with Cody's second shot to his forehead.

The woman screamed and slid down the wall to sit, dazed by the sudden violence.

"Ruth!" Clyde Black yelled as he stepped over Zach's body and ran into the storeroom, startled when he saw Cody standing there.

"She ain't been hurt," Cody said. "I think I just scared her awful bad."

Clyde reached down to help his wife up, but she said, "Just let me set here for a minute till my heart drops back outta my throat."

Clyde turned to Cody then. "Mister, I don't know what angels look like, but I suspect I'm lookin' at one right now. When you and your young'uns was in here a few minutes ago, I didn't blame you when you got yourself away from here. It was pretty doggone obvious what was goin' on, weren't it?"

Cody started to answer, but Ruth spoke first. "Clyde, help me up from here. I think my legs will hold me up now."

Clyde and Cody both jumped to assist her up. "Thank you, sirs," she said, then turned to address Cody. "When you said, 'hey,' and I looked around and saw you, I thought you were another one of them. I forgot I already saw you through the window when you came into the store. But he started to shoot you. I didn't know what was gonna happen then."

Clyde just stood there staring at Cody and shaking his head. "I just can't tell you how grateful I am for what you did," he said. "Blamed if you didn't take care of our problem in about two ticks on the clock. What I can't understand is why you did it. Most men I know woulda been damn glad to get away from here, and wouldn'ta thought two seconds about comin' back to help us."

Cody was surprised he would wonder. "It was pretty plain what was goin' on," he replied, "but I had to get those children outta here before I could try to help you. And I expect I'd better go get 'em now. They'll be worried about those gunshots they heard. But first, I expect you'd appreciate it if I pulled these two outta here."

"Well, I can sure help you do that," Clyde said. "We can put 'em out behind the store for right now, just so your young'uns won't see 'em and give 'em nightmares."

"Good idea," Cody said, "although they've seen enough already till they've most likely got nightmares aplenty. I need to see about buyin' a few things from you, anyway. I got caught without my packhorse and we've been havin' to make do for a spell."

He and Clyde carried the two bodies out and dropped them behind the house and Cody told him he would take them off into the woods somewhere to feed the buzzards when he got back. "You might wanna see if they've got anything worth keepin'."

When he came back with Billy and Joy, Cody found Ruth Black mopping up some blood spots on the floor. Seeing the children, she put her mop aside. "You want another peppermint stick while your daddy's gettin' some things?"

"Cody's not our daddy," Joy replied. "Our mama and daddy were killed when the Blackfoot Indians raided our farm and burned our house down. The Indians carried us off with them, but Cody came and got us."

"My stars!" Clyde exclaimed when he heard that. He looked at Cody and asked, "Is that a fact?"

"Pretty much so, I reckon," Cody answered. "That's the reason I'm needin' to get some things from you. I wasn't prepared to go after 'em at the time I had to go. I ain't got the things I usually have with me."

"Well, you just call off the things you need and I'll see if I've got 'em," Clyde said.

"I don't reckon you'd happen to have a packsaddle, would you?"

"As a matter of fact, I do have a packsaddle and a saddle blanket to go with it," Clyde said. "I traded a fellow a barrel of flour and a barrel of salt port for it when he didn't have any money. I never thought I'd ever get a chance to sell that packsaddle."

"How much you want for it?" Cody asked. "It would sure make it a lot easier for me to tote everything I've got to tote. 'Course I'm gonna need some sacks, too."

"Let's just wait till you call out everything and then I'll make you a price for the whole thing, all right?"

"I ain't sure I've got enough money for everything I need," Cody said. "But to start with, I want that coffeepot I'm looking at right there on that shelf. Have you got a coffee grinder?"

Clyde said he did, so Cody said he'd take twenty pounds of ground coffee. He went on to complete a list of the things he thought he could get by with at least until he was able to return to Fort Ellis. "I don't know if you do much tradin', but I thought I might have to trade you one of my horses to get what I needed. If you're interested, it's the one carryin' the big load of smoked deer meat. I've also got a couple of rifles."

"Where are you takin' those young'uns when you leave here?" Clyde asked.

"I'm headin' to Three Forks next, since their farm was nearby. I'm hopin' there's some folks around that knew their folks and might be glad to give 'em a home. If we don't find anybody there, I'll go on to Fort Ellis and I don't know what I'll do after that. Learn to be a daddy, I reckon. They're two good kids. I can't just turn 'em out."

Clyde bit his lower lip and shook his head slowly. Then he asked frankly, "How much money have you got on you?"

Cody took his pouch out of his shirt, took his money out, and counted it on the counter. "Don't forget, I owe you for two peppermint sticks. There it is, thirty-nine dollars and some change."

"I'll take thirty dollars and one of the rifles you told me about," Clyde said.

"That don't sound like a good deal for you," Cody said, having expected to be deciding which items he was going to do without.

"That's my price," Clyde insisted. "Take it or leave it."

"That's awful doggone kind of you, Mr. Black. I appreciate it."

"I owe you a helluva lot more than that."

While that was going on, Ruth was in the kitchen fixing Billy and Joy a cup of tea to eat with a jelly biscuit.

CHAPTER 23

A good part of the day had been used up by the time Cody loaded two bodies onto Billy's paint and led the horse about half a mile down the river to leave them in a little clearing. *That would surely seem attractive to a buzzard,* he thought as he took a last look at the bodies. It would most likely be the most noble purpose those two individuals could claim as a good reason for their birth. He jumped onto the paint's back and rode him back to Black's Store where Joy was waiting to tell him they were expected to stay for supper.

"Ah, we couldn't put you folks out any more than we already have," Cody immediately protested.

"Nonsense," Clyde declared as he walked out to join them in the back yard . "You've got to fit your new pack-saddle on that horse and pack your supplies in those bags. And the poor horse is already tired just from standin' around with that load of meat on his back. You know you ain't gonna start out for Three Forks tonight, so you might as well camp right here in our back yard. Your horses will be handy to the river and the two youngsters can sleep in the house with their new blankets if they want to."

Cody didn't want to intrude upon these people any

more than the outrageously cheap price he was quoted for all that he had bought. But he saw the two upturned faces of Joy and Billy, pleading like two hound dogs at a deer skinning. "Thank you for the invitation. I reckon we'll stay. You were right about that poor bay standin' under that load of meat all afternoon. I need to take that offa him, and I might as well leave you some smoked venison. Lord knows, we've got plenty of it."

"I was wonderin' if I was gonna have to come right out and ask you for a sample of that meat," Clyde joked.

One thing was bothering Cody, so he decided to go ahead and ask. "This thing that happened today with those two outlaws, does something like that happen very often?" With no one there but the older couple, they seemed extremely vulnerable to a whole passel of outlaws who would take advantage.

"I could see why you would ask," Clyde said. "I'm not usually as careless as I was with those two today. I let 'em slip up on me and I didn't have my shotgun under the counter where I usually keep it. I cleaned the blame thing last night and forgot to put it back. It wouldn'ta happened most other days when my two boys are here. Jesse and Robert took the wagon down to Three Forks to pick up a load of merchandise off a paddleboat on the Yellowstone. It woulda been a different story if they'd been here. I send both of 'em to pick up the goods 'cause I always figured that was when we oughta worry about outlaws—when we're haulin' 'em back in the wagon. These two today musta known my boys were gone."

"When are you expectin' 'em back?" Cody asked.

"Any day now," Clyde said. "Kinda thought they'd be back today. I expect they'll show up tomorrow sometime."

"You want me to wait around a little while in the mornin'?" Cody asked, feeling responsible for the old couple, just like he did with the kids. *I gotta learn to keep my nose out of everybody else's business,* he told himself.

"I don't think that's necessary. I've got my shotgun back under the counter where it's supposed to be. And like I said, my boys will be back tomorrow. You'll most likely meet 'em on the trail to Three Forks. Tell 'em I said to quit lollygagging and get on home with them goods. Besides, you got business to take care of. Find them young'uns a home. I sure wish you luck with that. They seem like bright little young'uns."

Clyde's explanation gave Cody a little more peace of mind about leaving the old couple. He didn't insist on delaying his departure in the morning, and they enjoyed a supper of beans and ham and fresh baked biscuits. Ruth said there was plenty because she had fixed enough to feed her sons, if they showed up by suppertime. But they still had not arrived by bedtime.

Cody thanked Clyde and Ruth for their hospitality and told them he planned to leave before breakfast. They protested, but Cody insisted he and the kids had already been too much trouble. They would wait till time to rest the horses to fix some breakfast, now that he had supplies.

The next morning they were only a little later than Cody had planned to get away, since Joy and Billy had accepted Clyde's invitation to sleep inside the house. That, in turn, resulted in getting Ruth out of bed and starting a pot of coffee while Cody was saddling the horses. Faced with a fresh, hot cup of coffee, Cody could only yield. According to Clyde, the distance to Three Forks was only twenty-five miles, which meant they had plenty of time to get there.

They had not been on the trail but about four miles

when they met a heavily loaded wagon with two men in the seat and a canvas tarp covering the load.

Coming up even with them, Cody pulled Storm to a stop. "Mornin'," he offered. "You headin' to Black's Store?"

Jesse pulled the wagon to a halt. "That's right. You folks just come from there?"

"We camped there last night and met your folks. They're nice people. Your pa said he thought you'd be back today." Cody chuckled then. "He said if we met you on the trail to tell you and your brother to quit lollygagging and bring them goods home."

"That sounds like somethin' he'd say," Robert said. "He's a tough ol' bird. He don't need us a-tall. Does he Jesse?"

"Reckon not."

"Reckon not," Cody echoed. "Well, good day to ya."

Cody, Joy, and Billy continued following the Missouri River and stopped to rest the horses and fix something to eat when still about ten miles from the town of Three Forks. Cody built a fire so they could warm up some of their smoked deer meat, but primarily because he was anxious to try out his new coffeepot. He filled it with water from the river and measured out the coffee grounds.

When he placed the pot on the fire, Joy asked, "Shouldn't you wash that pot out before you make coffee in it?"

"What for?" Cody asked.

"'Cause it's brand new, and it's been sitting on that shelf behind Mr. Black's counter for who knows how long, collecting dust and bugs and mice, and anything else that's been crawling around on that shelf."

"When the coffee comes to a boil, it'll take care of all that stuff," Cody said. "Besides, that gives it flavor."

She made a show of impatience but brought out her new cup after Cody pulled the pot out of the flame to let it

settle a moment before he filled the cups. She sipped away
at the hot coffee while she chewed on a strip of smoked
venison without realizing she was no longer eating hurriedly, or fearful someone might spot the smoke from
their fire. When breakfast was finished, she took the pot
and the cups down by the river to wash them, and they
continued on to Three Forks.

Ernest Blanchard looked up from the front counter to
look through the open door of the store when his eye
caught the motions of someone approaching outside.
He stared at them for a moment then called out, "Janet!
Come look here!"

In a moment, his wife walked over to join him. "What
is it?"

He said nothing but motioned toward the door with his
head. She looked for only a moment before she realized.
"Oh, my sweet Jesus! It's the Lassiter children! Who's that
with—?" She started, then recognized him. "It's that
young scout that was here before!" She ran to the door to
meet them, her arms open wide to receive them.

As soon as the children saw her, they ran to her and
collided in a happy reunion.

Cody paused in the doorway to watch. In his mind, it
was a perfect picture of two lost children returning home
to their parents. *Trouble is*, he thought, *she's not their
parent*. It cast a sad pale over the reunion.

Blanchard came around from behind the counter to
join the welcoming. Since they remained locked in Janet's
embrace, he patted each of the kids on the shoulder and
walked over to the door, extending his hand toward
Cody. "Come in," he invited. "I'm sorry but I can't recall
your name."

"Cody Hunter," he said, shaking Blanchard's hand. "I don't know that Lieutenant McCall ever gave you my name."

"Well, Mr. Hunter, I can't tell you what a happy sight it is to see those two children back safe and sound. Is the rest of the patrol here? Lieutenant McCall?"

"No, sir. It's just me. Lieutenant McCall and the patrol had to escort some of the captured people back to Fort Ellis quite a few days ago."

"Did you ever get it figured out if they were Blackfoot or Mormon?" Blanchard asked with a chuckle.

Cody obviously didn't know what he was talking about.

Blanchard tried to remind him. "You know, that other scout with you . . . he kept sayin' they were Flathead, and you said you didn't know if they were Mormon . . ."

Cody finally remembered his remark and nodded. "They were Blackfoot."

That caused Blanchard to chuckle again. "Well, come on into the store. What can I do for you? How do you happen to have the children, anyway?"

"I went and got 'em," Cody said simply.

"The Indians were willing to sell 'em to ya?"

"Well, no, not really. I just took 'em."

Blanchard, confused by Cody's simple answers was about to ask another question but was interrupted by his wife.

"Ernest, maybe you'd do better listening to these two. They've been talking a mile a minute about how Cody came to take them back from the Blackfeet. They've had an incredible journey to get back to Three Forks. Joy, tell Mr. Blanchard what you just told me."

Joy took them back through the whole adventure, with Billy making clarifying remarks where he thought they were needed. Cody was amazed they remembered every detail. Ernest was just plain amazed.

When Joy's story brought them to where they all were now standing, he asked, "So Lieutenant McCall doesn't know you rescued Billy and Joy?"

Cody said that was a fact, and Blanchard asked, "So what are you going to do with them?"

"Yeah, Cody," Billy piped up. "Whaddaya gonna do with us?"

"Well, if there's a slave market here in Three Forks, I figure I'll put you up for sale," Cody teased. "I might get as much as fifty cents for a ten-year-old who shot a Blackfoot warrior with a bow."

Janet wisely thought Cody would talk more frankly about what he planned to do with Joy and Billy, if it was not in their presence. "Come on, you two," she said to them. "I'll bet you haven't had a slice of apple pie in a pretty good while. If you'll follow me to the kitchen, I think I know where one is." She didn't have to repeat it, and they clamored off to the kitchen behind her.

Cody got serious then. "I'll be honest with you, Mr. Blanchard, I didn't know what I was gonna do with them. I just knew I couldn't let 'em get carried off to a Blackfoot village. I'll tell you the truth, if I was a family man, I'd keep 'em and raise 'em as my own. But I've got no home for them. I'm just an army scout, blowing with the wind. Since they lived near here, I stopped by here on the chance you might know some friends of their parents who might like to take on two fine youngsters. That was all I could think of at first.

"But if that don't work out, I reckon I'll take 'em on to Fort Ellis. Maybe something there, but it'll have to be somebody who'll love those kids. They're worth it. If Bozeman doesn't work out, I think I'll ride back to

Fort Keogh. I know a young lady there who was captured by Sioux Indians and she's a mighty fine woman. I think she might take 'em to raise."

Blanchard could see the young scout had genuine compassion for the two orphans. "You do have a serious problem on your hands. Let me talk to Janet. She talks more to the women here in town and she might have some idea who could help you. You're gonna be in town tonight, ain'tcha?"

"Yes, sir. We'll be here tonight and longer if Mrs. Blanchard needs time to talk to some of her friends."

"Let me interrupt you for a second," Blanchard said. "It's Ernest and Janet. You don't have to call us Mister or Missus."

Cody nodded. "All right, Ernest. Like I said, we'll stay here tonight. I need to find a place to camp 'cause I need to take care of my horses."

"Why don't you camp behind the store? There's an open field of grass and good water in the stream that runs across it. I don't believe you'll find a better spot close to town."

"I reckon not," Cody said. "That's mighty friendly. I 'preciate it."

"Why don't you go ahead and set up your camp and take care of your horses. When you've finished, you can join us at the house and we'll see if we can rustle up some supper. You don't need the kids for that, do ya?"

"No, although Billy is mighty picky about takin' care of his horse. He's a might particular about that paint. Joy ain't that particular about her horse, that buckskin mare. But I think they'll trust me to take care of 'em."

"Good. You do whatever you have to do. The kids won't be no bother. I think Janet is havin' a bigger time than they are. Just come on in when you're ready." Ernest walked Cody out the front door of the store and watched while he got on his horse and led the other horses around the side of the building. Walking back through the store, he told his clerk he was going to the house and to yell if he needed him.

At the house, he found Janet sitting at the kitchen table with Billy and Joy.

She got up and went to meet him. "Honey, I need to talk to you."

"I had a feelin' you did," he replied, directing her to the parlor.

"Where did Cody go?" she asked.

"He went to take care of his horses and set up his camp," Ernest answered. "He's gonna camp behind the store tonight. He'll be back here for supper."

She laughed at that. "Billy said he wants to give us some smoked deer meat for supper. He and Joy helped smoke it. I told him if he did, I'd throw it in the pot with some beans and rice." She paused to meet Ernest's eyes, the smile frozen on her face. "Ernest, they're delightful children. Frank and Carolyn did a wonderful job with those two."

"I expect they'd be proud of them, if they could see them right now." He knew what was going through her mind.

Thousands of thoughts of failure and never sure. Is it her failure or his? It didn't matter. It was *their* failure he had told her, and it was God's plan for them. And then the one time they were successful, she'd carried the baby for five months before she lost it. Ever since, she was convinced she was the failure.

"I know what you're thinkin', and I'm thinkin' the same thing. You remember when I told you I thought it was God's plan for us not to have children? I think maybe it was because he wanted us to be here to take care of these two orphans. Maybe Frank and Carolyn mighta had somethin' to do with this chance meetin' with Cody Hunter."

"You mean it, Ernest? You feel the same as I do about those two?"

He nodded, smiling.

"I think we should say a little prayer for Cody Hunter. When you hear those two talk about what he did to steal them from the Indians, you have to think something inspired him to do it." Janet fairly beamed with happiness, then a thought occurred. "If they'll have me."

"Let's go find out," Ernest suggested.

They walked back into the kitchen and Ernest sat down while Janet got a cup of coffee for him. She sat down with them and looked around at the gathering. "This looks like a perfect little family setting, doesn't it?"

Billy and Joy beamed back at her. "Do you know where Cody is gonna take you when you leave here?"

"No, ma'am," Joy answered, "but he won't leave us till he finds us a home."

"You don't think you could just stay with him?" Janet asked, eager to hear what the two of them were actually hoping for.

"That would be all right, I guess," Joy answered. "But we can't stay with Cody. He's gotta go back to scout for the soldiers. He'll find us a home before he leaves us, though," she repeated.

"How about right here?" Janet asked.

Her question was followed by a few seconds of total silence as Joy and Billy looked at each other in shocked surprise.

"You mean it?" Joy asked while Billy just continued to stare with eyes and mouth wide open. It was obvious they had not expected to be welcome anywhere.

Ernest reached over and took Janet's hand. "We mean it. We need two children to complete our family, and you and Billy are the two we've been looking for. So whaddaya say?"

"Yes!" Joy exclaimed.

Billy, still speechless, just nodded his head up and down vigorously, his eyes and mouth still wide open.

"All right, then," Ernest said. "You have to make it official with a hug."

Both children gleefully attacked him in his chair, almost causing it to topple over. Janet joined the celebration.

When Ernest could get his breath again, he said, "It's official now. Your new names are Joy Lassiter Blanchard and Billy Lassiter Blanchard. And you have to call me, Papa."

"And I'm your mama," Janet said, with tears welling up in her eyes.

Walking into a family preparing for supper, Cody paused at the kitchen door.

Seeing him, Janet yelled, "Come on in, Cody. Ernest is at the store. He'll be back in a minute. You can grab a chair or go sit in the parlor if you'd rather. Supper's gonna be ready in a few minutes, soon as the biscuits are done. Joy, honey, take a look at those biscuits, please. Billy, we're gonna need a little more wood for the stove."

He went out the back door to fetch it.

"It looks like I might just be in the way here," Cody said. "I'll go wait in the parlor."

Janet said that would be fine. It wouldn't be long before supper was ready.

"Yes, ma'am." He wasn't there but a few minutes when he had visitors. "Supper ready?" he asked Billy and Joy.

"Yes, sir," Billy answered.

"But we have something to tell you first," Joy said. "We're staying here . . . if that's all right with you."

Cody was amazed. "Did they ask you to stay?" He wanted to make sure.

Both nodded rapidly.

"Well, I'll be. 'Course it's all right with me . . . if you want to."

"We want to, but we're gonna miss you," Billy said.

Joy nodded in agreement.

"I'm gonna miss you, too," Cody replied, "but I believe you're doin' the right thing. The Blanchards are real fine people. I'm happy for you."

Ernest walked in the front door then. "What are you folks doin' in the parlor? Supper oughta be about ready."

"It is." Cody said, "They just came in to get me."

"They give you the news?"

"Yep, just now. Couldn'ta been a better piece of news for me right now." He winked at Joy, who was watching his reaction intensely.

As Billy and Joy ran on down the hall to the kitchen, Ernest took advantage of their absence to check on something with Cody. "I wanted to ask you what you intended to do with those horses. Billy and Joy think they own two of those horses you've got out there."

"They do," Cody answered right away. "The paint and the buckskin. Are they gonna cause some trouble for you? Because I can—"

"No, no trouble," Ernest was quick to interrupt him. "I've been thinkin' about using that piece of ground you're camped on. I own it, but I keep my horse at the stable down the street. Now that we'll have three horses, I'm thinkin' about buildin' a small barn back there and fence that whole pasture in. Whaddaya think? I might even buy a milk cow."

"Sounds to me like it was a good idea to stop here first," Cody said. "I think you and Janet went about this business of havin' children the smart way. Wait till you see what kind of kids you want and skip all that diaper changin' and colic and mess you get with babies."

"I have to admit, I hadn't thought about it like that," Ernest said with a laugh.

They enjoyed a nice supper, prepared by the new mother of two, with help mostly from her twelve-year-old daughter. Afterward, while the two men remained at the table finishing the coffee, Janet took the kids upstairs to select a bedroom from three available.

Planning to head out for Fort Ellis in the morning, Cody said goodnight to the Blanchard family with a handshake from Ernest and hugs from Janet and the two kids.

When Janet stepped outside the back door the next morning to see if Cody was ready for breakfast, only two horses were in the pasture, the paint and the buckskin. A short piece of rope with a bow and a quiver of small game arrows was tied around the paint's neck.

CHAPTER 24

"Well, I'll be damned," Ira McCall exclaimed. "I wondered if I'd ever see you again." He got up from his desk to meet Cody in the doorway. "I shoulda known you'd show up sometime. I swear, I was thinkin' about you this morning, wonderin' if you ever caught sight of those two children the Blackfeet kidnapped. I felt bad about givin' up on those kids, but I didn't see any way I could continue to follow ol' Buckin' Horse when I had the captives to take care of."

"I reckon not," Cody said.

"Did you follow them long enough to find out where they were going?"

"No, not all the way," Cody answered, "but they were sure headed toward the Big Belt Mountains."

"Too bad you didn't follow them all the way to their camp up in the mountains. Maybe the army could send the whole D Troop up there to escort that village to the reservation and hopefully save those two children. But I understand that woulda been stickin' your neck out maybe a little bit too far." He chuckled and added, "Hank Fry says you're most likely already dead."

"Hate to disappoint Hank," Cody said. "You can tell

him he don't have to worry about Billy and Joy Lassiter
anymore. They're livin' with Ernest and Janet Blanchard
in Three Forks now."

"You rescued those two children?" McCall exclaimed
excitedly.

"That's what I went up there to do."

"That's wonderful news! I declare, job well done!"
McCall could hardly believe it. "Well, what about it,
Crazy Wolf? You ready to get back to work scoutin' for
Troop D of the Second Cavalry?"

"I reckon not," Cody said. "I just came back to pick
up my packhorse. My Crow father told me I had completed my life circle as a Crow warrior, and I should start
my life circle as a white man now. I reckon that's what
I'm gonna do. I'm thinking to head up to Mullan Pass
where I was a five-year-old white boy and start out again
from there."

The idea to begin his new life where it was interrupted
as a child was not simply a spur of the moment thought
when he was saying farewell to Lieutenant McCall. The
more he thought about it, the more he believed it to be the
appropriate place to begin his circle of life as a white man.
He would visit the place where his white father and
brothers were slain. Old Spotted Pony would most likely
believe Cody could make strong medicine there for the
rest of his journey.

Leading two packhorses, he left Fort Ellis on a trip that
would take him over three and a half days before he reached
the Mullan Pass. Although he passed through Three Forks,
he didn't think it wise to stop, and took a more northerly
route to stop at Black's Store for more coffee.

"Well, I declare," Clyde Black uttered to himself. "Ruth! Come lookee here."

"What is it, Clyde? I'm busy peelin' potatoes."

"It's Cody Hunter and he ain't got the children with him."

In three seconds, she was standing beside her husband. "He musta found 'em a home right quick."

Clyde chuckled. "I reckon so. There ain't nothin' slow about that feller."

Cody walked in the door.

"Howdy, Cody," Clyde called out. "Didn't expect to see you so soon."

"Mr. Black, Miz Black," Cody returned the greeting respectfully. "I'm headin' up toward the high mountains and thought I'd stop, get a little more coffee from you. This time, though, I expect to pay your regular price for it."

"Whatever you say," Clyde said with another chuckle. "What happened with the young'uns? I didn't think they'd ever let you outta their sight."

"We had a real fine piece of luck in Three Forks right after we left here. You know Ernest and Janet Blanchard at the general store there?"

Clyde said he sure did, and Cody went on to tell them of the adoption of Billy and Joy and how happy everybody was as a result of it.

"That sure is good news," Ruth said. "I understand you met our two sons on the road." She had to chuckle, thinking about their reaction when they found out what Cody had done when he was at the store.

"Yes, ma'am," Cody replied. "They seemed like two fine young men. Are they back here now?"

"Yeah," Clyde answered for her. "They're down in the barn, puttin' a new floor in the loft. Jesse like to fell through it the other day. That ain't all they been doin', though, is it, Mother?"

"I should say not," Ruth replied.

"Just day before yesterday, we had another one of them attempted robberies," Clyde continued. "It was two of 'em again, but just one of 'em came into the store while the other'n stayed outside and held the horses. He was a big son of a gun, tall as you, but about twice as wide, I expect. Had one of them Derby hats stuck on the back of his head. I reckon they didn't expect much trouble outta me, but Robert and Jesse was on 'em like a chicken on a June bug. Jesse come walkin' outta the storeroom with his twelve-gauge, double-barrel leveled at this big ol' ape of a feller and asked him how lucky he felt. Didn't he, Mother?"

She nodded.

"That ape never said another word. He stuck his pistol back into his holster, turned around, and walked outside again where Robert was coverin' his skinny little partner with his shotgun. They found out this business has guards. We've had some word that a couple of outlaws was hittin' some of the little places all along the river, so you'd best be careful."

"'Preciate the warnin'," Cody said. "I will be."

"I want you to meet the boys," Clyde said. "Ruth, call 'em up to the store, hon."

Jesse and Robert were very interested to meet Cody again after hearing their parents' account of his first visit to the store. Cody was glad to see the boys seemed to be conscientious sons who wanted to be there to take care of their parents. They visited for a while until Cody said he needed to get back on his way. He graciously turned down an invitation to supper and finally took his leave.

After leaving Black's Store, he began to look for a possible place to cross to the other side of the river. His

path to Helena would leave the Missouri before very much
farther and he hoped to find a place to cross that would not
be too much of a strain for his two packhorses. Riding
about six miles north of Black's, he came to a section of
the river that looked as if it had been designed as a horse
crossing. The banks on both sides were not too steep and
an island was in the middle. Taking a closer look, he discovered hoofprints from shod horses entering the water.
Satisfied he would not likely find a better crossing, he
checked his packs and saddles, and committed Storm to
the water. Heading for the island, the water level soon
came up above his knees as Storm began to swim. He
looked behind him at his packhorses and couldn't help
thinking of Amy Boyd crossing the Yellowstone. His
packhorses had a similar look in their eyes, but their
hooves caught the bottom again as they neared the island.
It occurred to him every once in a while something would
make him think about Amy, and he always hoped she
had found peace and happiness at Fort Keogh.

Once again on dry land, he walked the horses over to
the other side of the little island and dismounted to check
them once more before committing them to the water
again. His main concern was the load of smoked venison
Iron Claw's bay was carrying. He was not as worried about
the food supplies he carried on Bloody Axe's horse, for
it had been wrapped to protect it from the elements.
Climbing back on Storm, he headed for the west bank.

Once across, he decided it a good crossing, but thought
he might as well find a spot to camp. That didn't take long,
for he found a good spot with remains of old campfires in
a pocket of cottonwood trees next to a grassy clearing that
extended almost to the bank of the river, evidence others
had chosen it, as well. He relieved his horses of their
burdens. He gathered enough wood to keep it going all

night. Once he got his coffee working and some of the smoked venison that hadn't taken a bath in the Missouri, he pulled his moccasins off and set them close to the fire to dry. Then he made himself comfortable, using his packs as a backrest.

"Reckon what he's totin' on them two packhorses?" Mule Simon asked his partner.

"How the hell do I know?" Ebb Batson replied. "It don't have to be a helluva lot to beat what that last poor devil we welcomed to this side of the river yesterday had, does it? He weren't hardly worth the bother"—he paused—"except for my new fancy boots. Too bad your feet are too dad-blamed big to get in 'em," he gloated. "From here, he looks like a pretty good-sized feller. Maybe you can wear them wet moccasins he's got dryin' by the fire."

"He must have somethin' worth havin' in them packs," Mule muttered, paying no attention to Ebb's rambling remarks. "That big'un wrapped up in deer hide must be all meat 'cause that's where he got his supper."

Ebb cast a disparaging glance at his big, slow-witted partner and remarked, "We'll split it down the middle. You take everything on that packhorse, and I'll take everything on the other'n."

"I'll be damned," Mule responded. "You think I'm dumb."

"You are dumb, Mule. That's why you're ridin' with me. So you don't have to do no thinkin'. Now that he looks like he's got hisself all comfortable, let's sashay on down there kinda neighborlike and say howdy."

I was wondering when they were going to make their move, Cody thought when the two riders suddenly appeared from a tree-covered ridge paralleling the river. He'd been aware of their presence soon after he'd settled down by his fire. Storm had announced their presence, but he had not been able to determine their location until then.

He reached over and pulled his rifle across his lap, cranked a cartridge into the chamber, and moved a little closer to the tree he had stacked his packs against, just in case. Then he waited while they rode slowly toward him. He remembered Clyde Black's description of the two would-be robbers who were routed by his two sons—a skinny little fellow and one he described as a big ol' ape. The fact that the big one was wearing a Derby hat left little doubt in his mind these were the same two who visited Clyde.

"Whaddaya say, neighbor?" Ebb called out. "We got a camp 'bout a quarter of a mile from here. Thought we'd come over and say Howdy."

"Is that a fact? That's mighty friendly of you. How'd you know I was here?" They were close enough to see them clearly, and Cody noted the heavyset one immediately looked to the scrawny one for an answer to the question.

Ebb didn't disappoint. "My horse heard your horse whinny. We was doin' some huntin' on the other side of the ridge."

Cody recognized their visit for what it was, a scouting mission to get an idea of the potential reward. "What were you huntin'? Just anybody makin' that river crossin'? People like me? Have you been doin' better at that than you did at Black's Store?"

He'd rather get it on right then, instead of lying around waiting for them to come sneaking into his camp that night. "I'll save you some trouble. I'm carryin' a sizable load of smoked deer meat on one packhorse, and about thirty or forty dollars' worth of other supplies on the other one, plus some weapons. I've got a little bit of cash money on me and some in my saddlebags, and I'm ridin' three fine horses. Now, my question to you is, is all that worth losing your life for? Because that's the price you'll pay."

Both men were stunned and looked as if having been struck by lightning. Neither knew what to do in response. Still sitting on their horses, they were staring at a man who seemed completely without regard for his life.

Finally thinking to call his bluff, Ebb said, "That's mighty big talk for a man settin' there lookin' at two guns to his one."

"I'm holdin' a Henry rifle with a cartridge already in the chamber, cocked and ready to fire at the first touch of my finger. I'm lookin' at two saddle tramps sittin' in the saddle, handguns in their holsters. You get my first shot"— he pointed at Ebb with the barrel of the rifle—"because I know I can crank another cartridge in and cock it before your slow-witted friend can even get his gun out of his holster. All I need to get this thing started is for one hand to make a motion toward one of those handguns. So, who wants to start the killin'? How 'bout you, big man?"

"Ebb's the fastest with a six-gun," Mule blurted.

"That's what I figured," Cody said.

"He's tryin' to trick us into a shootout, Mule," Ebb said. "Must be a professional gunfighter. And we just came for a friendly visit. Well, Mr. Gunfighter, we'll just take our leave. We sure didn't come to shoot nobody. Right, Mule?"

Mule nodded his understanding of Ebb's intent and held his horse where it stood.

Ebb said, "So long," and wheeled his horse around to leave.

Instead of wheeling halfway and galloping off, the horse made a complete circle, coming back to face Cody again. Ebb's pistol was in his hand.

Anticipating some form of trickery, Cody was ready and calmly put a bullet in Ebb's chest, cranked in another cartridge and stopped Mule before he could level his six-gun to fire.

He removed the bodies from his campsite and saddles and bridles when the horses calmed down. In the morning, he would let them make the decision to follow him or stay. He really didn't want the horses, but if they chose to go with him, maybe he might get a chance to sell them. He thought about going back to tell Clyde Black he need not worry about seeing Ebb and Mule again but didn't want to go back across the river.

On his way again, Cody continued to avoid the several little settlements along the Missouri River, enjoying the emptiness of a world with just him and his two horses. He avoided Helena as well, passing to the west of it on his way to the Mullan Pass.

To make sure he remembered the place where the attack on the three wagons had taken place, he backtracked until finding a game trail and followed it to the point where it came out—the place where the Blackfeet had struck. The killing place.

Memories swirled. He'd been walking beside the Frasier's wagon with Bobby Frasier when the boulder had crushed their wagon wheel. An arrow had pierced his back, and he'd crawled under a bush to hide. Looking at the place after so many years, he hoped he could tell which bush, but the bushes and trees were all grown up. He couldn't see where he had hidden with the wolf.

Out of the corner of his eye he caught something that seemed out of place. He turned to focus on it and discovered a piece of stone that looked like a grave marker sticking out of the ground. He went at once to examine it. Obviously it had been there a long time, for it was covered with dust. Evidently it was a memorial for someone having died there.

He took his bandanna and wiped the face of the stone to read the inscription.

In loving memory of
Our Mother and Father, Robert and Rose Frasier
Our brothers, Tim and Bobby
And their friend, Cody Hunter

He could not breathe for a moment when it struck him! Cody read it over again. It was not his father and brothers Spotted Pony had found! It was Mr. and Mrs. Frasier and two of their four children! His father and Morgan and Holt were alive!

Visit our website at
KensingtonBooks.com
to sign up for our newsletters, read
more from your favorite authors, see
books by series, view reading group
guides, and more!

Become a Part of Our
Between the Chapters Book Club
Community and Join the Conversation

Submit your book review for a chance to win exclusive
Between the Chapters swag you can't get anywhere else!
https://www.kensingtonbooks.com/pages/review/